PRAISE

"Patel has written a touching tale of one young woman's reckoning with her family's generational legacy, staying true to her roots and traditions while at the same time forging a path for herself. Full of warmth and humor, this book is recommended for all fiction collections."
—*Booklist*

"Full of softly beautiful descriptions and remarkably rendered characters, Patel's sophomore novel grapples with familial pressures and legacies. It's a sensual read, full of details pertaining not only to scents, as might be expected, but also to foods and visual descriptors."
—BookRiot.com

"A thoroughly entertaining rendition of one woman's search for belonging."
—*Kirkus Reviews*

"Full of lively characters who will win readers' hearts and keep them thinking long after the book is finished, this book is a genuine, charming debut. Long-buried secrets and a journey of self-discovery will keep the pages turning."
—*Booklist*

"[A]n inherently fascinating and impressively scripted novel . . ."
—*Midwest Book Review*

"Namrata Patel's debut is a delightful exploration of identity, community, and growth. I was drawn into Meena Dave's captivating journey from the first pages and was rooting for her until the end. This poignant and witty story is perfect for book clubs!"
—Saumya Dave, author of *Well-Behaved Indian Women*

YOUR NEXT LIFE IS NOW

OTHER TITLES BY NAMRATA PATEL

The Curious Secrets of Yesterday

Scent of a Garden

The Candid Life of Meena Dave

Your Next Life Is Now

A Novel

NAMRATA PATEL

LAKE UNION
PUBLISHING

This is a work of fiction. Names, characters, organizations, places, events, and incidents are either products of the author's imagination or are used fictitiously. Otherwise, any resemblance to actual persons, living or dead, is purely coincidental.

Text copyright © 2025 by Namrata Patel
All rights reserved.

No part of this book may be reproduced, or stored in a retrieval system, or transmitted in any form or by any means, electronic, mechanical, photocopying, recording, or otherwise, without express written permission of the publisher.

Published by Lake Union Publishing, Seattle

www.apub.com

Amazon, the Amazon logo, and Lake Union Publishing are trademarks of Amazon.com, Inc., or its affiliates.

EU product safety contact:
Amazon Media EU S. à r.l.
38, avenue John F. Kennedy, L-1855 Luxembourg
amazonpublishing-gpsr@amazon.com

ISBN-13: 9781662529207 (paperback)
ISBN-13: 9781662529191 (digital)

Cover design and illustration by Kimberly Glyder

Printed in the United States of America

To Ramdas Amin, who lived to learn

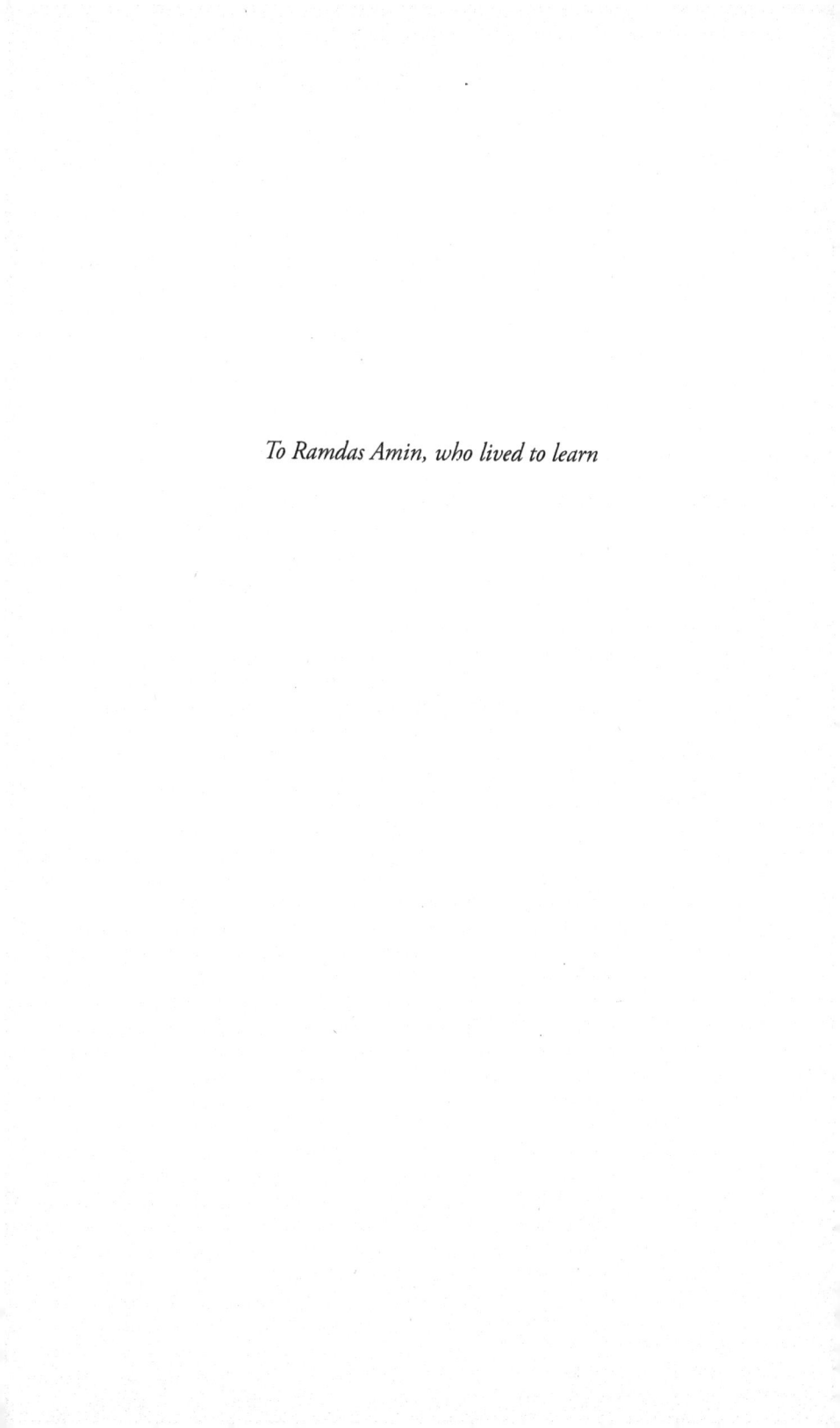

AUTHOR'S NOTE

I wanted to examine the effect of culture on personal choice. For Indian Americans who came of age between the 1970s and 1990s, being Indian in America was a vastly different experience. In the 1970s, they lived in a sacrificial generation, in constant tension between tradition and adaptation. During this time, parents and grandparents held on tightly to the traditions they did not want to lose. There was a constant negotiation of the East-West cultural demarcation line. This was at the height of the myth of the model minority. It was examined in books such as *Desis in the House* and *The Karma of Brown Folk*.

Individuals had to learn how to carve out their own lives amid the tension. In their early twenties, they had to make decisions that would commit them to a specific path, not knowing if there would ever be an off-ramp.

As with most things, it was women who were most affected, and they were the ones who wanted their daughters to have more freedom, more choice, and fewer burdens. In *Your Next Life Is Now*, Tara and Nikki come of age at different times and in distinct ways: Tara is the mother who decides that, despite her age, there could be more life for her. And Nikki, who has only known her mother, Tara, within the lens of a mom, now sees a woman taking ownership of her next life steps.

This novel is about how two women navigate their present circumstances while reckoning with past decisions. I hope you are drawn to their story and come to understand them in the context of their generational and diasporic upbringing.

CHAPTER ONE

The only moment you can't relive is this one.
—From the newsletter *Your Next Life Is Now* (*YNLIN*)

Jamaica Plain, Massachusetts, present

It is the genius of the universe that the biggest questions in life are answered with the smallest words. Yes or no. There are no qualifiers. No in-betweens. A simple response that comes from the soul. Are you fulfilled? Do you believe in God? Will you marry me?

"Yes." Nikki Parekh stared into Jay Mehta's dark-brown eyes.

She surprised herself with the quick response. Too soon. Too casual. Too spontaneous. A decision like this needed more thought. They hadn't even taken a compatibility quiz. Nikki still did not keep the bathroom door open when he was in her apartment. Yet, she was at home in his arms. His hold was strong enough for her to feel safe, but not so tight that she couldn't set herself free.

"Yes?" he asked, for confirmation.

She laughed. "Are you shocked?"

He nodded. Then touched his forehead to hers. "Speechless."

She leaned away, stepped out of his arms. "You did ask."

"I did."

Nikki turned back to the vanity mirror mounted on the wall of her bedroom. Her chaotic thoughts crawled around her brain, made her short of breath. She wasn't built for impulsive acts. Nikki had modeled her entire life around intentionality. It was her brand, her mantra, her way of being . . . up until she saw Jay's smile, the one that had made her approach him at a Halloween party last October. Six months! Their relationship was still in the "getting to know each other" phase. But her soul had already spoken.

Jay moved to stand behind her, his warmth against her back. This was his superpower, the way he touched her, held her. He'd become her comfort, even though she'd always prided herself on being a self-soother. Nikki leaned against him, making it easier for Jay to rest his chin on her shoulder. Gently he brushed his lips against her jaw. This. He'd become an addiction she never wanted to break.

His hands gripped her waist, a gentle pressure requesting she turn around, chest to chest. He loved to look into her eyes, which was unnerving. His own eyes showed every emotion—desire, joy, love—with an openness she'd never experienced.

She knew the texture of his smooth skin, slightly rougher than hers. Nikki wasn't someone who needed physical contact. Yet from the first time he'd held her hand in his, she'd begun to crave his warmth, the feel of his palm against hers, the slight pressure of his grip that made Nikki remember she didn't have to walk alone. Through the mirror, Nikki saw a version of herself that she liked. Since Jay, she was softer, sexier, slightly demure—words she would never put in her bio. With great effort, she removed herself from his hold.

"I'll call a Lyft." Nikki left her bedroom to grab her phone from the kitchen island.

"We have time." His bare feet made no sound on the hardwood floor. Jay hated socks because he said his toes were jealous of the freedom his fingers enjoyed. He wore them only when the weather or the occasion required.

"Traffic." Nikki kept her eyes on the phone screen, swiping to search for the app even though she couldn't recognize a single icon. *She'd said yes.*

"We have time," he repeated. Then Jay tugged the phone out of her hand and placed it face down on the counter.

"Evening rush. You know it takes forty-five minutes to drive three miles within Boston." Each word came out rapidly, as if she were running to catch the T before the doors closed in her face.

Jay took her arm, brought her closer, face-to-face, and Nikki inhaled. His aftershave still lingered from this morning—wood, smoke, and a hint of pine. His hold helped to slow her heart. He was attractive in a conventional way with angular cheeks, a prominent jaw, and thick eyebrows below his wide forehead. His lashes were the envy of every woman and framed the deep brown eyes that held no secrets.

"What's going on in that busy brain?" Jay asked. "Talk to me."

She leaned her head on his chest. "Did we just?"

He lifted her chin with his finger. "Remember when we went skiing up in Stowe a few months ago?"

"You insisted you could hang with me down Upper Goat," she said. "After one lesson."

"You were so worried," he said. "And I'm still in one piece."

Nikki laughed. "How's that wrenched shoulder?"

"A souvenir," he said. "Sometimes you have to take a risk."

Except this was marriage. A lifetime. She backed out of his arms. Jay leaned his body against the edge of the granite kitchen countertop. He was comfortable with silence, let it permeate the space between them. It was the lawyer in him. Nikki, having grown up with a mother who wielded it as a weapon, rolled back her shoulders to let him see that she could stand in it.

And yet he was right. She was Nikki Parekh, a life coach with a quarter of a million subscribers to her weekly newsletter. She often wrote about being open, accepting opportunities, doing things in spite of fear.

"I love you," he said.

The first time he'd said those words was eight weeks into their relationship. They'd gone ice skating at the Frog Pond in Boston Common. He'd twirled her around, pulled her close, and whispered them in her ear. She'd been paralyzed. He wasn't the first man to say them to Nikki, but he was the only one she'd believed. Still, it had taken her another two months to say them back to him. He'd been patient, never pushed. He would joke that the least she could do was say thank you, as a nod to sitcoms. "I love you too."

He gave her a wide grin. "We could skip dinner. Celebrate here." He grabbed her at the waist and pulled her in for a kiss.

She sank into him, became lost in his taste. After a few minutes they both retracted to catch their breath. She grabbed her dark curly hair and put it up in a bun. "Should we call and cancel? Or . . . was this dinner to celebrate?"

He shrugged.

"Why now? I mean, why tonight?" What she really wanted to say was *Did you mean to propose like this?*

"It feels right." He didn't waffle or hesitate. They were so different.

"Feels," Nikki said, and made air quotes. "I see."

"Air quotes? Really?"

Nikki dropped her hands. "Sorry. It's just that this isn't something you blurt out. We've never even talked about it."

"Marriage. Come on, you can say it, it's not a bad word."

She rolled her eyes. "Don't tease. I'm trying to have a serious conversation."

He nodded. "Look, the moment I saw you at that Halloween party, dressed in a white T-shirt that said 'Costume,' I knew you were the one."

She smiled at the memory. Jay had worn a top hat, a fake bushy white mustache, and a tailcoat, under which was a white shirt that was marked with a bloodstain from a protruding fake knife. The blue ribbon on his lapel said, "Kill all monopolies."

"Research shows that men marry the person they're with when they feel ready for marriage," Nikki said. "It has nothing to do with whether that person is the right choice."

He laughed. "Do you know that women who say yes to a marriage proposal usually throw themselves into their partner's arms and then spend the next hour texting all their friends?"

She wanted to bang her head against the wall. "You are exasperating."

"Rest of your life, babe." He spread his arms to his sides.

"No more joking. Why did you blurt it out like that? We were on our way to dinner. It's a Thursday night."

He nodded. "The flowers, ring, and all that feels too clichéd for us. It's more natural this way. I was listening to you talk about your day, switching from work Nikki to evening-out Nikki. I watched you struggle with the clasp of your necklace without asking for help. Then it hit me, this is how I want to end every day for the rest of my life."

She melted. He was right. She'd already said yes and she didn't want to take it back. He'd shown her how to be more spontaneous, less risk averse. "I still expect a ring."

He wrapped his arms around her waist. "Oh, just you wait. My mother's got an emerald that will look stunning on these long bony fingers."

She looked at her hands. "You sure that's a compliment?"

"I mean lithe and lovely," he clarified.

"Wait, your mom? You told her about this?"

He shook his head. "No. I told you this wasn't the plan. We have this tradition, goes back to our ancestors on my mother's side. They were kings or something in Rajasthan before the colonizers. The eldest child of each generation is gifted this emerald ring. It's a way to welcome you into our family and that you will now be a part of this legacy."

"I see."

"If you don't like it," he said, "we'll put it in a safe-deposit box, and you can pick something else."

"No, I mean, it's a nice tradition," she said. "I hope I'm worthy."

He brushed her lips with his. "Stop worrying. My mom likes you."

Nikki scoffed. She'd met his parents three times, and his mother had not been impressed by Nikki. "She barely talks to me. And she definitely does not approve of what I do."

"Well, it's a good thing you're not marrying her," he said.

She raised her brow. "I'm sorry, did you forget that we're Desi?"

He nodded. "Fine, you'll win her over or she'll have to deal. Stop worrying. Have faith in us. Marry me."

Again, her soul answered. "Yes." This time she was steadier. The obstacles were in her head. She came from generations of people who'd married without knowing their spouses. Her parents were the perfect example. They'd met once before agreeing to an arrangement, and they'd been together for thirty-five years. She and Jay had more. She knew his nature and his character, and most importantly, she loved him, and he loved her. They would be fine. Nikki took Jay by the hand and led him back to the bedroom. They'd order takeout, but first they would commemorate this moment in their own way.

CHAPTER TWO

Comfort zones are designed to keep you in the same place. Move out of yours!
—*YNLIN*

Nikki lifted Jay's arm from her waist, quietly left the bed, and wrapped herself in her silk robe to sneak out of her bedroom. Once she closed the door behind her, she quietly hopped on her toes and let out a soft squeak. She was getting married. Then she stopped and repeated the sentence in her head. What was she doing? Marriage wasn't in her life plan. Relationships, long-term partnerships, those were what she'd envisioned. Not marriage.

She paced back and forth in the living room she'd lovingly decorated herself. She'd invested in the white chesterfield sofa, the suede high-backed chairs in burnt orange, and the coffee table she'd restored from an antique shop. The art on her walls, the curated crystal vases, piece by piece, she'd surrounded herself with things she loved. Was there space for Jay and his college dorm aesthetic? He owned exactly two sets of sheets, and she'd bought him another towel because he had only one.

She'd said yes. This was big. Huge. Nikki reached for her phone, put in her earbuds, and prayed her older sister would answer.

It was after midnight. Heena was likely asleep, but Nikki let it ring.

"What? Is someone dead?" her sister's groggy voice answered.

"I did a thing and I'm not sure how I got to this place." Nikki spoke at a normal volume and then whispered the last word. Her two-bed, two-bath condo wasn't big, and only a wall separated her from Jay, whom she did not want to wake.

"Are you in jail? I'll be right there so I can get copies of your mug shot."

Nikki let out a heavy sigh, grabbed her soft yellow blanket from the sofa, and wrapped it around her before going out on the back porch. "Be serious."

"What time is it?" Heena mumbled.

"Can you just listen to me?" Nikki begged.

"Fine. Let me go to another room," Heena said. "Caleb is sleeping. The twins are finally down after we lost the battle and let them crawl into our bed."

Nikki heard sounds of her sister moving about.

"Ready."

"Okay," Nikki said. "So I did a—"

"Thing. Yeah, I heard you the first time." Heena cut her off. "What? Did you use the wrong-colored pen in your notebook and mess up your perfect planner?"

Nikki sighed. "Why do I surround myself with sarcastic people?"

"You need us to take that serious stick out of your butt," Heena said. "Now get to it or I'm hanging up and going back to sleep."

"I said yes," she blurted out. "Jay proposed and I said yes."

There was silence. Nikki paced not because her bare feet were stinging from the frozen porch wood but because her heart was beating so fast, she could handle it only by walking back and forth.

"Oh . . . congratulations?" Heena said.

"Why are you saying it like a question?" Nikki almost started crying.

"I mean, yay!"

Nikki heard the false cheeriness in her sister's tone. "Mom's going to freak out."

"Don't. This isn't her moment, it's yours," Heena said. "Are you happy?"

"Yes." Another short word to answer a big question. "I'm worried, though. It's too soon. You and Caleb were together for eight years before you got engaged."

"I met him at our freshman class orientation in college," Heena said. "I was eighteen. You're thirty-two."

"I never thought I wanted this," Nikki said. "My track record isn't great. The longest relationship I had was with Hugh, and that was only fourteen months." And he'd left her via a text message. Moving to Moldavia. Sorry.

"Is he still coaching soccer in eastern Europe?"

"I don't know," Nikki said. "That's not the point."

"Then what is?" Heena asked.

"Jay jumps in while I need a plan," Nikki said. "What if in two months he decides to join the marines?"

"He's antiestablishment," Heena said. "I don't think you need to worry about him voluntarily going into the military. How did he ask?"

Nikki almost threw her phone over the railing. She was on the second floor so it would shatter and then she would add another problem to the one she already had. "OMG, can you not be you for a minute?"

"Jay loves you," Heena said. "He told Caleb it was the 'at first sight' kind for him."

Nikki clutched the blanket tight around her. "He believes in that, and I don't. We're not compatible."

"Right. Because if it can't be proven, it can't be true."

"Well, love is one thing, but marriage?"

"We're arguing about the wrong thing," Heena said.

"I know."

"This isn't a you problem, it's about Mom. For once, live your own life, not one she wants for you." Heena hung up.

Her sister didn't understand. Heena had won all her battles against Tara. For Nikki, it was different. Nikki had always felt responsible for her mother's sadness.

She went back into the warmth of her living room. Her parents had been the first guests after she'd closed on the condo. Tara had been so happy all day as they unpacked and organized. Her mom talked about how proud she was that Nikki was an independent, self-made person. They had always been there for her major milestones, from college graduation to the day she'd told them she would be leaving her job in project management to start her own business. She never wanted to disappoint them.

She curled up on the couch and lay on her side, cocooned in her blanket. She was going to be a bride. She'd dressed up as a princess only once in her life. It had been Tara's least favorite costume. From then on, Nikki had never wanted a prince. And now she had to find a way to tell her mother that she was on the verge of a happily ever after.

CHAPTER THREE

Obstacles test your strength. Don't avoid. Don't back away.
—*YNLIN*

Newton, Massachusetts, present

Nikki loved the three-story colonial on a quiet dead-end street. It was the house she'd grown up in and where she'd become the person she was now. Here, among the neat furniture, dust-free surfaces, and minimal decor, Nikki had learned to be independent, fight for what she wanted, and know that she could always count on herself. Not directly from her parents but from their absence.

Nikki stopped at the threshold of her mother's sitting room. This was where Tara spent most of her time. Heena referred to it as their mom's vault. Everything that mattered to Tara was in this room, and no one entered unless invited. The bookshelves, antique secretary desk, and high-backed reading chairs were more tended to by Tara than any other room in their home. As a child, Nikki had run freely around, everywhere except across this threshold. If the door was closed, Nikki and Heena assumed it was locked.

"Mom?" Nikki stepped through the open door.

Tara jerked her head up. "Nikita?"

Hesitantly, Nikki entered, not knowing if she would be welcomed in or if Tara would usher them both out to another part of the house. She was relieved when Tara stayed at the desk, seated in the green leather library chair.

"What's that?" Nikki pointed to the necklace in her mom's hand.

Tara held up the gold chain. "Something from a long time ago. I found it in an old jewelry box."

"Can I see?"

Tara held it out. "It's old. Glass and metal. Not much value."

It was a thin chain with a crystal pendant. Nikki traced the charm. "A boat. I know you like the beach but didn't know you were a fan of sailing."

"It was from another life," Tara said.

"Before Dad?"

"Yes." Tara took the necklace back from Nikki. "What are you doing here? It's the middle of the day."

The most frustrating part of dealing with her mom was that Tara only answered questions she wanted to answer; everything else she avoided by changing the topic. Which was likely why Tara didn't have a social group or a best friend. Tara preferred her own company, unlike Devon, Nikki's father. He was a boisterous extrovert. They were very different from one another. *Like Jay and me.* It gave Nikki comfort to know that while her parents' marriage wasn't full of affection, they'd been companions for three and a half decades.

Nikki moved toward the tall windows. "The benefit of working for myself. I control my schedule."

"Which means you have to do more, not wander around in the middle of the day," Tara said.

Nikki let the jab go. Her mom knew that Nikki planned her time meticulously. "I came to talk to you. It's important."

Tara pushed back from the desk and faced Nikki. Her mom was tall and lean, with great posture and an angelic face. Tara's tan skin had only faint lines, and Nikki knew her mom didn't do Botox or fillers.

It was genetic. In her late fifties, Tara could easily pass for someone in her forties. Her mother was beautiful, serene, untouchable. Her father always said that he'd known he would marry Tara when he'd been shown a photo of her before their first meeting. He'd said it as a way of complimenting Tara, but her mother never showed any reaction to this comment.

Tara placed the necklace in a small silk pouch and slid it into the center drawer of her desk. "Go ahead. Tell me why you're here."

Nikki took a fortifying breath, squatted, and rested her hands on Tara's knees. "It's good news. I promise." Though Nikki remembered Heena's engagement announcement. She hadn't been there, but Heena had shared how upset Tara had been. The difference was that Heena never catered to Tara's reactions. Her sister either ignored them or went to battle. Nikki always took a softer approach to Tara. Ever since she was a little girl, Nikki had known that Tara was unhappy. Once, after taking Psychology 101 at BU, Nikki asked if her mother would be open to therapy. Tara became so upset that she gave Nikki the silent treatment for weeks. Nikki never brought it up again.

Nikki had run through various ways to break the news of her and Jay's engagement in a way that would ease Tara into it.

Tara frowned. "You seem nervous. Is it something with your business?"

"No."

"Nikita, this isn't like you," Tara said. "Why do you look worried?"

Because you won't be happy for me, which will make me question whether I'm doing the right thing. Nikki took a deep breath, rose, and decided to be direct. "Jay proposed."

Silence. Zero reaction. "I said yes," Nikki added. Not wanting to look at Tara, Nikki went to the window to stare out into the yard.

"Is this what you want?"

Nikki blinked her eyes clear as she registered the disappointment in Tara's voice. When she'd gotten her MBA diploma, her mom had given Nikki a huge bouquet of flowers and a cheesecake. "Yes. I know it's been only six months, and you and Dad don't know Jay very well. He's a great person. He's funny and smart. He comes from a good family. He's a better cook than I am."

"You don't have to recite his résumé."

Nikki couldn't stop herself from babbling. "I know you want me to focus on my career, not be dependent on anyone. And I won't. I'll still pursue my passions. I won't—" She stopped herself. She'd said what she wanted to say, no more overexplaining.

Tara rose and stood next to Nikki as they stared out the window. "This is your choice."

The guilt of not meeting her mom's expectations sat heavy in Nikki's stomach. Nikki looked outward to the trees that framed the edge of their backyard, which were beginning to bloom. The days were getting warmer. It had been a mild winter, but Nikki was happy for it to come to an end. "It will work out," Nikki whispered. "You and Dad did. I mean, you only went on one date, and you've been going strong for thirty-five years."

"That's what you learned from us?" Tara asked.

Nikki had to counter the sadness in her mother's voice. "I saw you and Dad give Heena and me a good home. I watched you two work together. Dad taught us what it means to have a good work ethic. You gave us the tools to avoid becoming gender stereotypes. I know you're both proud of me. All I want is for you to be okay with this. I promise this isn't going to take me off my path. I'm not going to turn my back on everything I've accomplished to be—"

"Like me," Tara finished the sentence.

"No," Nikki rushed to assure her mom. "That's not what I meant."

"Do you love him?"

"Yes, I do," Nikki said, but the question surprised her. Love wasn't something her family openly discussed. It was expressed through actions. Her parents showed them in big and small ways with teaching, discipline, and celebrating her and Heena's achievements. They didn't need to say the words. Nikki had never heard her parents say them to each other, though her father was more demonstrative and affectionate.

Tara stared at her hands. "Peptides."

"What about them?"

"Peptides carry chemical messages of our emotions, and they change the cellular makeup in our body and brain," Tara continued. "When you experience the right love, it physically changes you."

Nikki didn't know where this was going. "Okay."

Tara continued. "The shift isn't measured by time. It doesn't matter how long you've known someone. It's the level of change. There are people you feel deeply for, romantic or otherwise, and you become slightly altered. Sometimes, if you're lucky, a person comes along, and you experience them biologically. The way you feel is more than you've ever thought possible, and your entire composition is altered. It's a kind of love that marks you so fundamentally that you can't remember who you were before that person came into your life."

Nikki glanced over at her mom. Tara's face had softened, and she looked far away. "That's beautiful. Jay tells everyone that the first time we met, he took my hand, and that was it. He was all in."

"And for you?" Tara asked.

Nikki half smiled. "You raised me to be practical, pragmatic. I needed more evidence. I had to grow into it."

"Sometimes you can spend decades with a person and not be affected at the cellular level," Tara added.

Nikki didn't know what her mother meant. "In my case, it was only a few months."

"Nikita, you're capable of choosing what's best for you. There isn't anything for me to say when it comes to your decisions. Actions are yours, so are the consequences." Tara went back to her desk.

Sometimes Nikki wondered what it would be like to have a mother she could share her worries with, who would stroke her hair as Nikki lay on her lap when she was sad. Nikki knew she wouldn't get the approval she'd come here for. Still, she couldn't stop yearning for it.

"A heart is divided into two parts." Tara grabbed a textbook. "The left and right must work together, but they have different responsibilities. One side receives. The other releases."

"Yes, I got an A in biology. It doesn't mean I know what you're talking about." Nikki couldn't help the bite in her voice. Nikki and Heena had grown up with Tara's passion for science, and most of her topic changes involved some concept, formula, or theory. The built-in bookshelves were evidence of all that Tara had spent decades absorbing.

"It's something to think about," Tara said.

"You're saying duality."

Tara sat in the chair. "The heart doesn't function properly if only one side is working well. If it receives deoxygenated blood, it must process it and reoxygenate it. I've been thinking about this lately. I've concluded that you can't receive love if you don't have any to give and vice versa."

"Are you talking about me?" Nikki asked.

Tara opened the book on her desk.

"What does it mean if that is the case between two people?"

"You exist," Tara said. "But you don't live."

Nikki rubbed her sternum. She disagreed with the idea that a single moment could make her become someone different. She remembered the way Jay had cupped her face, looked directly into the depths of her eyes, and uttered those three words. In that moment, she'd been afraid, relieved, happy, sad, and frozen. Not from the cold but from her inability to say it back. Maybe her mom was implying that Nikki wasn't ready. That she couldn't love Jay in that forever way. "I love Jay." She said it more for herself than for Tara.

Tara focused on the text in front of her.

Nikki realized that she was being dismissed and walked out of the room not knowing if Tara was even aware of her daughter's departure, much less her disappointment.

CHAPTER FOUR

Life is built on single decisions. Choose wisely.
—*YNLIN*

Boston, Massachusetts, present

A week later, Jay had organized a Sunday dinner for both sets of parents. With Nikki's hand in his, they wove around other diners and black-and-white-clad waitstaff. She wondered when she'd started following Jay instead of leading. She waved off the intrusive thought. Tonight was to be a celebratory meal that would mark this new phase of their relationship. She'd calmed her nerves with a long yoga-meditation session in the morning, gotten her nails done in the afternoon, and was wearing her black stilettos, which matched her fitted cap-sleeved shift dress.

This past week, Jay had gone a little over the top to show how excited he was about their engagement. He'd left a coffee mug with a sticky note on the counter. "Coffee in thermos. Chia pudding (gross) in fridge. Love in my heart." He'd sent her six roses, one stem for each month he'd loved her. He'd taken her for pho at her favorite place. She'd tried to match his enthusiasm but couldn't shake the uneasiness after her conversation with Tara. Her mother's indifference shouldn't bother her, yet for some reason, Nikki would have preferred anger or a plea to change her mind. Instead, she silently repeated what Heena had said to her over text when Nikki had shared their mother's lack of enthusiasm over the engagement: "Don't let her yuck your yum."

Nikki grabbed Jay's arm with her other hand. "Are you sure they don't already know?"

He glanced at her. "I haven't said a word to my parents. If your mom spilled to your dad, then hopefully they'll pretend."

"I don't think she said anything." Otherwise her phone would have blown up with messages from her father. "I'm sorry I told my mom ahead of time. I needed to give her a heads-up." To warn her and shield her.

He shrugged, squeezed her hand, let go. They walked toward the round table where both sets of parents sat. The restaurant, Ostra, was one of her favorites in Boston. It was an occasion place with high-end seafood. Each of the few times she and Jay had come here, she'd gotten the same thing, the melt-in-your-mouth salt-baked branzino. Jay would tease her to try something different, but Nikki preferred ordering something she knew she liked.

"Great, you're all here." Jay greeted everyone and helped Nikki into her chair.

"Jayesh." Bijal, Jay's mother, greeted them. "You didn't tell me Nikki's mother was at Newton High School at the same time as me. We graduated together."

Jay glanced between the two women. "I didn't know."

That was good. Maybe Bijal auntie could bring Tara out of her shell.

"I knew her, but we weren't in the same friend group," Bijal added. "I was in theater and played soccer. If I remember, Tara, you didn't have many friends."

"I was in science club," Nikki's mother replied.

"I hated chemistry and physics and all that," Bijal said. "It's why I went to college for communications."

Nikki glanced at her mother, who was scanning the menu. Nikki was embarrassed that Tara couldn't bother with small talk. "Jay mentioned that you were also in an a capella group in college, Bijal auntie. Do you still sing?"

Bijal nodded. "A little."

Nikki grabbed Jay's hand. Squeezed.

He flipped his palm and clasped their fingers together. "I hope everyone is hungry."

"Nice choice, Jay," his father, Kirit, said. "You know it's going to be expensive when they give you actual leather-bound menus instead of making you click on a code for their website."

"Only the best for tonight, Dad."

"Are you paying?" Kirit asked.

Jay laughed. "Let's see if you let me."

Nikki's father, Devon, nudged her. "What's going on?"

"It's a celebration. Be patient." Nikki reached for her menu. "Should we order first?"

"Want to share the salt-baked branzino?" Jay leaned over, his sweet breath on her cheek.

She smiled. "Jay knows it's what I always get."

"And a French 75."

When the server returned, they placed their orders of tuna tartare and chilled shrimp to start, along with their entrées of the branzino, paella, and steak. As they all chatted, Nikki let Jay's warm voice vibrate through her, and she wished it were just the two of them instead of a table for six. But this wasn't a date. She watched as their dads made small talk with each other while Bijal auntie spoke to Jay. Nikki had met Jay's parents three times before tonight. His father was friendly and welcoming. His mother was tougher to read. Nikki didn't know how she would feel about the news. She was grateful when their drinks arrived.

"Bijal auntie, that is a great jumpsuit," Nikki said.

Bijal sat up taller at the compliment. "Ann Taylor."

"I don't know who she is, but that woman takes up two-thirds of our closet." Jay's father laughed loudly at his own joke.

Nikki's father joined him with a hearty laugh. "I'm lucky. Tara has a very simple style. My wallet is happy, too, because she doesn't like to shop."

Nikki winced. She'd grown up watching her father speak about Tara as if she weren't there. Nikki knew it was to make up for Tara's lack of participation in conversation, but this seemed too boisterous and over the top.

To her left, Nikki felt her mom go still. "Mom has always been minimalist. I think she knew about the capsule wardrobe before it became a thing. Right, Mom?" Nikki tried to include Tara and nudge her to speak for herself. Her mother merely nodded and sipped from her wineglass.

"I wish I could be simple," Bijal said. "I love to shop. Bags, shoes, clothes, jewelry. It's my vice."

"Tara prefers her books," Devon added. "She spends most of my money on science journals and textbooks."

Nikki was embarrassed. She'd often heard her father refer to it as his money because Tara had never worked outside of the home. But tonight, there was a sharpness and an emphasis on that phrase by Devon. "My mom is passionate about physics and astronomy," Nikki said.

"Oh, where did you study, Tara?" Bijal asked.

"Boston University," Tara replied.

"Not MIT?" Kirit said.

"I was accepted into their graduate program," Tara explained.

Devon cut her off with a laugh. "She chose marriage instead. I guess she likes me more than she likes quarks, protons, and all that stuff."

Tara said nothing more.

"Speaking of." Jay took hold of Nikki's hand.

She took a big sip of her French 75. This should be a happy occasion. Instead she was worried about how it would make Tara feel.

"Nikki and I are getting married."

The table erupted as both dads jumped up with congratulations. The men stood up and did the one-arm man hug, then cheered with their glasses of whiskey. Tara stayed seated with barely a smile on her face. Bijal was harder to read. His mother squeezed Jay's arm in affection and raised her glass of cabernet toward Nikki but stayed seated. No hugs for Nikki from anyone, simply pats on the shoulders from both dads.

"Blessings to the happy couple." Devon raised his glass. "To a prosperous life together. And to our expanding family."

"Agreed," Kirit added. "It's wonderful. We are proud to welcome you."

"Jay, beta," Devon said. "I know it's all modern now, but in our day, our parents had to approve the match."

"I understand, Devon uncle," Jay said. "But you raised an independent daughter who prefers to make her own decisions."

"That's her mother's influence," Devon said. "Still, tradition is important."

"And evolves," Nikki said.

"This generation, yaar, they speak freely," Kirit said to Devon. "We thought we were rebels and modern, but we were never as brave as our children. They date, live together before marriage—it's very American. Our time has gone by. We accept it, and we will pay for the big wedding."

"Not necessarily," Jay said. "I'm thinking a sunset, on a beach in Belize with immediate family."

This was news to Nikki. "We haven't discussed the details yet. Let's enjoy tonight."

"Nikita is right," Bijal said. "This is a big step. Let them give it more time."

"Beej, you and I went on four dates before we decided to marry. When you know, you know. Right, beta?" Kirit thumped Jay's back.

"Tara and I decided after one meeting," Devon added. "No regrets."

"None?" Tara asked.

The table went quiet. Nikki looked at her mother.

"It's not believable, is it?" Tara said. "Thirty-five years of marriage, there have to be some moments of pause."

"Well, of course," Kirit said. "But once you choose to spend your life together and raise children, it's a lifelong commitment. The annoyances are minor things that you let go."

Tara looked away. Luckily, their food arrived so it seemed more natural to pause their conversation.

Nikki didn't know what was going on with her mother, but she was finally too emotionally exhausted to care. For now, she wanted to enjoy the evening and win over Jay's parents.

"We should get a bottle of champagne," Kirit said. "To celebrate."

The mood lightened as Jay ordered. Once the champagne was poured and a toast was made, they settled into their meals. The branzino was perfect in its simplicity, deboned and served in a bowl with a generous amount of olive oil. Any other night, Nikki would savor the soft texture, the clean flavor, and the hint of lemon. She would feed Jay a bite as they talked about going to Italy someday. Tonight, she could barely swallow as she looked over to see if Tara was enjoying her meal or was still in a mood. At least the dads seemed to be getting along, and Nikki chatted with Bijal and Jay.

"Kids," Kirit said, "I think a summer or fall wedding would be fantastic. The best weather too."

"I like the idea of someplace like Maui in the fall," Jay said.

"Don't be ridiculous," Kirit said. "You can do your beach wedding, but we will have one here too. You're our only child. I'm not missing out on all the ceremonies."

Nikki appreciated Jay's father. "A wedding with everyone would be nice." She'd loved Heena's Chinese-Indian-American extravaganza. It had been fun to see how everyone came together. Nikki had made the most of it, believing she wouldn't get married. Now she was starting to imagine.

"Seriously?" Jay asked Nikki. "Don't tell me you have a secret binder with cutouts of wedding dresses, flowers, and all that."

She winked at him. "Just a vision board."

"Am I on it?" Jay asked.

"Right now, it's Theo James," Nikki said. "I'll swap him out for you."

He laughed and kissed her shoulder. "I should have never made you watch *Divergent*."

"Jay, you know that our families have a standing in our community," Bijal said. "Your grandfather started one of the biggest cultural organizations in this country. Your father is right, it's our responsibility to show that we fully welcome Nikki. A destination wedding might signal that we do not approve of your match."

"They should decide what's best for them," Tara interjected.

"Nonsense. Heena had a large wedding. So will Nikki," Devon cut in. "First, we start with the engagement party."

Jay groaned. "I'll agree to a wedding, but that's it. We don't need to have all the traditional stuff."

"Nonnegotiable," Kirit said. "You'll have to get on board."

"No one cares, Dad."

"Weddings are for families," Devon said. "It's not just about the couple, but two prominent families coming together."

Nikki glanced over at her mother. Tara's hand had a tight grip on her empty wineglass. Nikki turned away and hoped their server would come take their dessert order. This evening had taken a turn and it wasn't enjoyable as the parents argued over the details and talked over her and Jay. She'd expected that there would be time for all this at a later date.

"Nikki, I'm not sure if you know," Bijal said. "We have a family ring that will be presented to you at your engagement party. It's an heirloom and precious. It's not for daily wear but a symbol of being accepted into our prominent family, descended from a Rajasthani king."

Nikki nodded. "Jay mentioned it."

"I see," Bijal said.

There was something in her tone that gave Nikki pause. "I promise to take good care of it."

"You will have to or Bijal will kill you," Kirit said. "It's worth a lot of money, and to my wife, it's priceless. You will have the responsibility to pass it on to your son's wife."

"Or daughter," Bijal added.

Nikki looked at Jay. One thing they'd bonded over was that neither of them wanted children. She realized Jay hadn't been open about this with his parents. Nikki, on the other hand, had been vocal since she'd reached puberty. Devon believed she would change her mind, and Tara was happy with Nikki's choice. Heena had given their dad the grandkids he'd wanted, and while Tara wasn't a warm and involved grandmother, her mom did enjoy spending time with the twins. This was clearly not the time to get into this discussion. She'd leave it to Jay. "The ring feels like it's very important to your family. Maybe we can get something simple."

"If you wish," Bijal said.

"Nikki is the most organized and responsible person I know. She'll take good care of it. The party, though, maybe we do something small," Jay said. "At our house with a few friends."

"Nonsense," Kirit said, then added, "Devon, I agree about traditions, but we don't expect a dowry."

"We will do it modern style, with dry fruit, nuts, and small gifts," Devon countered. "To honor the symbolism."

Jay took Nikki's hand and stroked her knuckles. "I'm a big fan of cashews and almonds. So maybe some boxes of that, along with chocolate."

"We can place the announcement in the *Boston Globe*," Kirit added.

"Nikki is an influencer, with a known company. Do you know they featured her in *Boston* magazine?" Devon said. "It will be good publicity for your business."

"Let's talk about this later. Who's ready for dessert?" Jay saw the server and made eye contact for them to come over.

She would pay for it tomorrow, but Nikki ordered her third cocktail to get through the rest of the evening. She rested her head on Jay's shoulder as the conversation continued between the dads and Bijal auntie. Kirit and Devon opened their phones and discussed possible days and times for the parents to discuss details, then moved on to the number of guests from each side, which would help with location.

Tara seemed lost in her own world, as usual. Nikki imagined her mother doing formulas or calculations. Maybe Tara was pondering a theory. Regardless, weddings weren't her mom's thing. Nikki remembered how uninvolved Tara had been during Heena's planning, and there was no reason to think she'd act any differently now. She lifted her head and leaned toward Tara. "I hope you can be happy for me."

Tara looked at Nikki. "Are you happy?"

Nikki nodded.

"Then follow your own path," Tara said.

Nikki blinked back tears. The sadness in Tara's voice wrapped around Nikki's heart.

CHAPTER FIVE

Andover, Massachusetts, 1989

The orange Formica table was bare between them. The thick ceramic coffee mug warmed Tara Rajput's cold hands. Her stomach was too jumpy for the dark, bitter liquid she'd never acquired a taste for. But the stranger across from her had suggested coffee, and Tara had thought the right response was to simply agree. It was what was expected of her, and her behavior would be a reflection on her parents.

"What do you like to do for fun?" Devon Parekh was the first match her parents had approved of enough for them to meet.

Tara forced herself to calm her aggressive knee shaking. "Music. Travel. Movies. Reading." All the things listed on her biodata, which her parents had sent around to everyone they knew in the greater New England area a month before her graduation from Boston University with a bachelor's degree. Devon was the son of an old college friend of her father from the Chh Gam caste from Gujarat, one that preferred to marry within their community. More importantly, Devon had a similar educational background and healthy financial prospects. All of which made Devon an ideal husband for Tara.

Earlier, as the two families met at the Rajput home, Tara, silent and terrified, observed the eagerness in both sets of parents. They spoke about the importance of perpetuating culture and tradition. Tara had been instructed to serve chai that she'd prepared for this occasion, a ritual to show Tara's ability to care for her future family. That she knew to serve the men first showed her submissive nature, highlighted further by her speaking only when spoken to. She hated that her parents spoke for her, praised her as their dutiful daughter. Tara's mother mentioned Tara's cooking skills but did not talk about Tara's opportunities in the field of science. Even an acknowledgment of her first place in a high school physics competition would have been nice. Instead, it was her flavorful dal that merited praise.

Devon's father spoke of Devon's ability to become the head of the family by talking about Devon's GPA and his doctor of dentistry degree. Tara had silently noted that her GPA was higher. Devon had financial viability and no debt. He was also praised for his achievements in baseball, his devotion to his family, and his wide social circle.

Tara tuned out as the parents spoke on behalf of their children. She had shut down her feelings and preferred to be numb as she sat on the edge of her chair, her back straight, the sash of her salwar loose around her shoulders.

Tara had known this was what was expected of her. She was not remarkable or unique, and she would follow in the footsteps of other Desi girls who had gone from their parents' houses to their husbands'. It was the only path for someone like Tara who had never opposed her parents in anything. As long as he agreed to the one thing she wanted, she could survive this. Over and over again, her mother had instilled in her the notion of "marriage first, life next." She could do whatever she wanted once she was married into a good family.

If Devon was supportive of Tara's ambition, then Tara would settle. And Devon wasn't repulsive. In fact, he was attractive and age appropriate. He was taller than her, seemed to have a sense of style, was friendly, and had an education. Having no experience with relationships, Tara wasn't picky.

Once the chai had been drunk, Devon and Tara were released to get to know each other over coffee. The irony of never having been allowed to date but then being turned over to a stranger was not lost on her. Yet she got into the light-blue Oldsmobile Omega and let herself be driven to this diner.

"I like all those things, too, especially music. I'm really into basement bhangra right now. It's so cool how they mix hip-hop and Bollywood songs. Anything I can dance to, you know?"

She nodded, though she didn't know. Tara liked pop, Duran Duran, U2, and the Cure. When she worked, she preferred Mozart, Vivaldi, and Bach. At parties she would rather watch others than be in the middle of it all. She never watched Bollywood movies or really much television. But that couldn't be mentioned on matrimonial résumés, which were crafted by well-meaning parents to show that their children were assimilated but not fully Americanized. If she had been allowed to write her own biodata, she would have said she preferred being by herself over being in a group, that she needed only one friend, and that she had only two passions—astronomy and physics. But that wouldn't make her compatible. Eligible boys would think her too smart or too ambitious. She was both but could never show that side of her.

"After marriage." That was what her mom had said. She could be whoever, do whatever she wanted, once she was settled in her own family. Tara understood this to mean that she'd be given over to her husband's family, and her parents would continue on with their lives without her. It saddened her to think so, but that's how it had been for her mother, Kamla, who had left her family behind in India after marriage.

"It's cool that you majored in physics. You must be really smart." Devon added more sugar to his coffee. "Like me. I took a few science classes, but dental school doesn't have it on the curriculum. I was able to graduate faster than if I'd gone to med school, so I can make money sooner than later. And I don't have to pay back hundreds of thousands of dollars in loans."

To Tara, one thing didn't have anything to do with the other, but in their short conversation, she had learned that Devon could bring most topics back to himself. "That's nice." Because what else could she say? Money mattered. Her parents had immigrated to the US and had carved out a life here. They didn't have a lot of wealth, and it was important for them that Tara married well.

"Do you plan to work after college?"

This was her opening. "Actually, I got into a graduate program at MIT."

"That's great," he said.

Tara exhaled. He seemed open to the idea. "It's something I'm looking forward to."

"Cool," he said.

"You wouldn't mind? I mean, if we got married." Tara hedged her answer, not knowing what Devon wished for in a potential wife. She knew that if she didn't mold herself into a suitable candidate, it would be a loss of face for her parents. Though Tara knew that she would marry only someone who would agree to her getting her master's and eventually her PhD. After that she would find a job in academia.

"I mean it's cool, and it would be hard to get a job right now anyway. It's a tough market," he said. "I'm glad I got my DDS right after my bachelor's. I just got a job with a big practice here in Andover. I'm super stoked. They're investing in new technology that's going to revolutionize orthodontics. Better than braces. Clear molds that slide over your teeth and straighten them out."

As he spoke about teeth, Tara dreamed about the program she would join. She knew the curriculum and had read papers published by her future professors. Her head was full of space and calculations. She envisioned herself in a little rowboat somewhere remote, the sky bright overhead. Without light pollution, Tara could see constellations and spend time pondering the distance, the speed of light, and what it would be like to be in a spaceship that floated among them. Even though *SpaceCamp* was one of her favorite movies, she preferred studying the sky from Earth. The universe was crowded, full of fascinating materials, from gases to debris. The prospect of infinity was compelling, as was the idea of time. Her present, this reality, was her conscious timeline, but perhaps there were others where she would be free to design her life for herself without conforming to what others needed her to be.

"What do you think?"

Tara snapped her attention back to Devon. "Sounds great."

He smiled wide. Tara felt a glimmer of attraction as his face relaxed.

"Cool," Devon said. "So we're on the same page. Awesome."

And that's how Tara learned she'd agreed to marry Devon Parekh.

CHAPTER SIX

Communication, not love, is the main ingredient for great relationships.
—*YNLIN*

Jamaica Plain, Massachusetts, present

Nikki was at her kitchen counter working on her newsletter, *Your Next Life Is Now*. Each edition offered curated ideas for her subscribers, the goal of which was to help people live in the present, to not delay or put off what could be enjoyed in the moment. The title came from her maternal grandmother, a stern woman whom Nikki had never seen smile. When Nikki was young, Kamla ba would stop Nikki from doing what she wanted with the phrase, "You can do that in your next life." The idea being that the circumstances of this life need to be lived as prescribed. Nikki's takeaway was that she had to live hers based on what the elders decided. If Nikki wanted ice cream in the middle of the day, Ba would say, "You can do that in your next life. In this one you must eat an apple."

It had become such an irritating phrase that when Nikki decided to start her own business, she had chosen to rebut it. Her content focused on action in the present moment. Her philosophy was that the idea of a perfect moment, a perfect time, a perfect life, was futile because it meant you kept moving the goalposts toward increased expectation and satisfaction. Instead, she proposed, enjoy the abundance when it was in front of you. It was more than just saying yes to everything, it was about noticing opportunities and grabbing them if they aligned with the current version of who you were.

"Babe, pass that bowl of tomatoes, please?"

She glanced at Jay. "Oh, here." Nikki pushed the bowl toward him.

"Ask yourself, Nikki Parekh, are you in the present?" He added them to the skillet.

The sizzle startled her, and she rolled back her tense shoulders. "Ha. Ha. You know it's not about every second being devoid of planning or discipline. It's awareness of the big things."

"Like marriage proposals."

She closed her laptop and smiled as she watched him. "An excellent example."

Jay was comfortable among the accoutrements spread out around him—the bowls holding remnants of chopped garlic, the boiling pot of water on the stove next to the skillet, and the various spices in jars and bowls. This room had been used more since Jay had come into her life than in the three years she'd lived here before him. She couldn't remember the last time she'd survived solely on cheese and crackers or takeout for three consecutive days.

He grinned as he popped a tomato in his mouth.

She blew him an air-kiss. For the last two weeks, she'd tried hard to enjoy her time with Jay. She'd excitedly shared the news with friends. She'd started a digital collage with ideas for dresses, color palettes, and cakes. Unfortunately, the weight of her mother's indifference was hard to ignore. She'd meditated on how to not be so needy when it came to Tara. But a lifetime of prioritizing Tara's feelings was hard to let go. She knew there was no such thing as a perfect mother, but still Nikki couldn't help wishing Tara could become one.

"I'm having some regret, though," he said.

"About proposing?" Nikki asked.

"I should have planned it," he said. "Caleb asked your sister by covering their bed in rose petals, with a ring box in the middle."

Nikki laughed. "And Heena complains that eight years later she's still finding red petals every time they flip their mattress."

"I've been thinking about it," he said. "A redo, maybe at the Frog Pond. Or I can carve the question into pumpkins and line them up."

Nikki went to him, wrapped her arms around his waist from behind. "It happened the way it was meant to. I'm not bothered. I promise."

He turned his head and she kissed his cheek before going back to her seat on the other side of the counter.

"We should get them a new mattress for Christmas," he said.

"I think that's something they would probably want to pick out for themselves," Nikki said. "Besides, you know I already have a list of gift ideas that I jot down whenever someone mentions something they like." This was life now. Everyday mundanity. And it was good. There was security in knowing the future, spending holidays together, traveling, and growing alongside one another. It was too bad that fairy tales ended at the beginning. Then she got a spark for her next newsletter.

"Are you checking me out?" Jay asked, noticing her spacey look.

"Not when you wear hats indoors. At least it's not on backward."

"You love it." Jay kept his eyes on the skillet. "I'll get you another one. Pink?"

She threw an onion skin at him. It floated less than a foot away from her and back onto the countertop. Jay strained the pasta and added it to the pan of sautéed vegetables.

"Jay, can we talk?" There was something that she'd been worrying over that wasn't about Tara. It was regarding his mother.

His back tensed ever so slightly as he stopped stirring. He wiped his hand with a towel he'd had on his shoulder. "Isn't that what we're doing?"

"Does your mother like me?" Nikki asked. "I get this weird feeling."

"That's just her," he said. "She gives off this snobby, judgy vibe. But she's not like that once you get to know her."

He hadn't answered the question. That was his tell. Jay was a public defender. If a question was about something he didn't want to address directly, he answered around it.

"I sent her a few dates and links for engagement venues and options," Nikki said, "and she hasn't responded."

He kept his back to her. "She's been busy. The nonprofit she's on the board of is having a fundraising event. And your mom? Has she replied with dates and location?"

"Not yet." A second nonreply. This time she let it go because she couldn't pick at this thread when Tara had yet to reach out to Jay and congratulate him.

"And it begins," Jay murmured. "This is why I wanted beach and Belize. Your mom, mine. Family drama. I just want it to be about us."

"It is," Nikki assured him. "But we're lucky to have our families, Jay. It's important and right to have them involved. Same with our friends. I've been to countless weddings and celebrations. So have you. It's about being surrounded by people who are happy for us."

"Maybe you should tell your mother." He turned off the burner, then grabbed a beer from the fridge. "Look, I'm never going to understand Tara auntie. She doesn't make it easy for me to get to know her. I can't even tell if she likes me, and most people do. It's fine. As long as you're in, I'm in."

"I'm in." Nikki went around the counter again, put her hand on his shoulder.

He bent over, brushed his lips against her. "You want her to be happy for us."

I want her to be happy. Period. Had her mother ever experienced joy? Yes, Tara had smiled when Nikki reached professional milestones, but she hadn't seen her mother laugh at the small things. Tara's face was perpetually void of emotion. Nikki looked at Jay. His joy came easily. Even now, he was irritated, but if she winked at him for no reason, a wide grin would naturally appear on his face.

"Maybe both of our moms would be okay with something small." It would be a way to appease them.

"That ship has sailed, babe," Jay said. "Kirit Mehta has posted on Facebook, made a guest list, and called his tailor." He put his arm around her shoulders. "Let's eat. Forget about all this for tonight."

"Except the problem will still be there tomorrow."

He moved away from her. Took off his cap and ran his hand through his hair before placing it back on his head.

"Avoiding it isn't going to make it go away," Nikki added.

Jay tilted his head. Stayed silent.

Nikki chewed on her lip. "You're in lawyer mode. Using silence to get me to babble until I say something incriminating."

He shook his head. "Fine. You want to chat? Let's do it. You're so wrapped up in how your mom feels about *our* engagement that you won't let yourself be happy. This is a *good* thing, babe."

"That's not fair. She's my mother," Nikki said. "And aren't you giving in to your dad?"

"There's a difference," he said.

She turned away from him and stared at the sliding doors that led to her porch. "We're both trying to make our parents happy."

He went to her, rubbed her arms. Pulled her in for a hug. "All I'm asking is that you think about us. You and me. I don't care if Tara auntie helps plan the party or even if she shows up to our wedding. I don't want us to get sucked into their chaos. Can we just have dinner, watch TV, have sex, and go to bed?"

She wriggled out of his arms. "I'll try."

Jay's voice was soft. "Nikki, I'm not avoiding anything. I just want to . . . there are times when I am so overwhelmed by you that I'm speechless. That's going to be for the rest of my life. For me, you come first. Always. It's okay that we're different. You need to dissect and overthink. You worry about other people and how they're feeling, their opinions. Fine. In between that, I want moments like this, where I'm first."

It wasn't an unreasonable request. She nodded and wrapped her arms around herself. She understood what he needed, but it still made her feel alone.

CHAPTER SEVEN

Boston, Massachusetts, 1989

Tara never thought about loneliness. She had always been surrounded by people, especially during these last four years at Boston University. From the dorm to shared apartments near campus, Tara was always among a sea of people. And she had Mayuri, her freshman year assigned roommate who was now her best friend. Most importantly, though, she had space.

She'd been six when her father told her that her name meant star in Gujarati, and she'd decided that she was made to be in the sky, floating in the universe instead of grounded on Earth. She'd grown out of saying so aloud, but the longing remained. She imagined what it would be like to be up there, to be made of gas and dust. Her existence would be measured in millions of years instead of months, seasons, and decades.

In a few days, she would walk across the stage with a dual bachelor's degree in physics and astronomy. On this last day, as classes were officially over, she had carved out time just for her and the stars.

The patch of grass under her was cool enough to make the seat of her jeans feel damp, but the slope was comfortable. This spot on the Esplanade had been hers for four years. Directly behind Tara the Coit Observatory cast its shadow. In front, her view of the Charles River.

Across the glimmering water, her future. Tara paused. It wouldn't be as seamless as crossing the Mass Ave Bridge to reach MIT. She had agreed to wear the shackles of marriage on her ankles to go there. Tara didn't know what that would mean, but she'd seen examples of arranged marriages all around her. As long as she and Devon were compatible in the core things like mutual respect and helped each other in their individual pursuits, it could be a good relationship. Her parents would be happy. The aunties would find other innocent unmarried girls to nag. While Tara didn't know if she liked Devon in a romantic sense, it wasn't important. Her father had taught her to make practical decisions devoid of emotion.

"Beautiful."

Tara looked up at the deep voice. He was tall, or maybe it was because he stood next to her and faced the river. He had short dark hair that ruffled in the breeze. From his profile, he was cute in a boyish way. Though his T-shirt was loose, she could see the broadness of his back, the muscular arms, and the sexiest butt she'd seen to date. She blushed and grinned. Mayuri would be proud if Tara had uttered that last thought aloud, but then again, her friend was more flirtatious and daring. And today wasn't about boys, she reminded herself.

There were a lot of people, students, professionals, families, at this time of evening. Some strolled and others jogged along the river. A few read or hung out in groups. It wasn't unusual for someone to stop and say hello or hang out with random people.

He turned. "I didn't mean to interrupt, but the sunset from here is stunning. I love how the colors look like they touch the surface of the water."

"Studio 54," Tara said. "It makes me think of disco and glitter."

He smiled and took a seat next to her. "Club rat?"

She shook her head. "Farthest from it. Not even the famous ones in New York City."

He curled his legs in and rested his arms on his knees. "It's not my scene either. I went once this past New Year's Eve, and I know it's something I'll never do again."

Tara noticed how relaxed he was. Content. She could feel his energy calm her, give her a sense of peace. It was illogical, yet undeniable. Not knowing how to continue the conversation, she matched his posture and kept her gaze on the river. She'd miss this view. Especially once night settled in and she could look up and recognize the constellations, their placement changing slowly as the Earth rotated. It would be different from the other side of the river.

"I'm Ben." He didn't turn to reach out for a handshake, as if he couldn't bear to look away from what was in front of them.

"Tara."

As they sat in silence, time passed, and the bright pinks of the setting sun began to darken to purple before they faded into the coming night. The sliver of the crescent moon appeared.

"Waxing crescent," Tara said. "My favorite."

Ben looked at her. "Why?"

She shrugged. "It starts to grow from here, becomes brighter. I like beginnings more than endings."

He leaned back, his hands on the ground steadying him. "I never thought about it like that. I think I'm always chasing the end. What's that phase?"

"It depends." Tara wrapped her arms around her knees. "What are you trying to reach?"

"The horizon."

Tara pondered. "The unreachable."

"Because the Earth is round."

Tara laughed. "I'm a scientist, and yes, it is."

He laughed with his whole face. His teeth white against his full lips. Something in her heart stirred for the first time. She leaned into it, allowed it space to move, shift. She knew what attraction was. This was more. It was layered and textured, but she couldn't recognize a pattern. High entropy. Her atoms were in chaos.

"I grew up in Maine," Ben said. "And no matter the weather, being inside is a form of torture. I always wanted to be out on the ocean. Spend my life sailing."

"Pirate or lobsterman?"

He laughed. "Neither. Just me on my boat without any land in sight for days. Heading toward the thin line where the sky meets the sea."

"I can't imagine it," she said. "I'm not a strong swimmer."

"Life jackets."

She tapped her chin. "Interesting. Are they shark proof?"

He looked over and stared at her. "You're not a dreamer."

"I like to understand all the variables," she said. "I'm not brave."

"How do you know?" he asked. "To me, it's situational. Like if you're scared of thunderstorms, going out and standing in the street during one would be a mark of bravery."

She thought about it for a full minute. "I like to define it as consistent choices to not do things that frighten me."

He looked at her for a while as he shifted from his hands to his elbows, causing him to relax farther back. "What's the last thing you've done that was risky at best?"

"Talking to you. Sitting here with you."

He nodded.

"You're staring," she said.

"I'm thinking." His voice was deep and steady. No sign of nerves or irritation. "What variables would you have taken into account before talking with me?"

She shrugged. "Statistics."

He sighed and sat up. "Man is the most dangerous animal for women. My father burned that into my brain from a very young age to make sure I understood my responsibility. All I can say is that I'm not going to do anything to hurt you. Though, it's up to you whether you can trust me or not."

Threats came in different forms, and not always straightforward ones like an attack. Sometimes a threat could be as mild as a paper cut that became infected and destroyed your heart. "I believe you. Besides, there are a lot of people around."

"That's the spirit."

It was the way he rolled with it, the way he made her feel as he sat next to her . . . for the first time in the whole of her twenty-one years, Tara did something without thinking it through. "Are you hungry?"

He reclined back to the grass, lounging on his side. "Always."

Tara reached for her backpack, unzipped it, and began taking things out. She handed him a blanket. "I'm spending the night with the stars. And if you want, you can stay." She glanced over at him. "No pressure."

He rose to his feet and unfolded the blanket for both of them to sit on, then sat next to her as Tara emptied her backpack between them.

"Turkey sandwich, BLT, cookies, chips, soda, a thermos, and carrots. I'm impressed."

She handed him a wad of napkins. "I'm spending down my meal card."

"I don't get the carrots," he said. "It's like one of these things is not like the other."

Tara handed him half the turkey sub. "I don't like fruit or veggies, but I'm a grown-up, so I feel like I need to have a carrot if I want a cookie."

He paused before taking a bite. "Variables. Even on a picnic."

She was glad it was dark enough that he couldn't see her blush. For the first time, she felt understood. "What about you?"

"Oh, I don't need to earn a cookie." He took one from the pack of Oreos and popped it in his mouth. "And I don't wait until the end to have dessert." He grabbed another and held it out to her. "Try it. It goes great with turkey."

She took it from him, their fingers brushed, and Tara's attraction turned to desire. She ate a bite and he watched her chew. "I didn't think this combination would work, but . . ."

He reached over and wiped a crumb from the side of her mouth. "But?"

She couldn't speak. It was the first time in her life that she'd wanted a kiss. This wasn't the drunk sloppiness of a frat party. It was more. Real in a way that she'd never imagined.

He broke the connection and turned toward the water.

Disappointment warred with practicality. She couldn't act on this. Could she? She glanced over at MIT. If she wanted to go there, to continue her education, to have a career, she had to follow through on the arrangement.

Tara finished her half of the sandwich and put the wrapper in a plastic bag for the trash. She no longer wanted Oreos. They ate in silence, and he thanked her for sharing her supplies.

After their meal, Tara put things away in her backpack and lay on her back. Ben beside her. His hands on his stomach.

"Which one is your favorite?"

Tara gave him a puzzled look.

"Which star?" he asked.

She looked up. "Hmm . . . I can't pick one. It's not like a movie or a book. They all have something special."

"Which one, when you see it, makes you dream?"

She scanned the sky. Her brain lit up. There was so much information, she didn't know how to distill it for him. How much did he already know? If she went too technical, it would bore him. What if he fell asleep? She felt his hand rest on hers. Her mind quieted. She breathed. "Dhruva. It means effort and determination. In the West, we know it as the North Star. In Hindu mythology, Dhruva was a young Indian prince, very disciplined. For most of his life, he was ignored by his father, a king, and he was mocked by his stepmother. Dhruva didn't let that affect him. He had this unshakable faith in himself. Ultimately, the way he led his life, without envy or malice, was noticed by the god Vishnu, who gave him a special place in the sky. The brightest star, one that other stars spun around. Still Dhruva stays humble."

Ben took her hand and stroked her knuckles with his thumb. "That's beautiful. Do you see yourself in him?"

She turned her palm and clasped his hand. "No. Not even close. I doubt everything. It's the scientist in me. Dreams. Faith. Wishes. They're too intangible."

Tara felt the vibration of his laugh in their clasped hands. They were close enough for her to lean her head against his shoulder, and she surprised herself by doing what she wanted. He was warm next to her. His T-shirt smelled like fresh laundry. His silky skin made her want to disappear into him.

"What do you like about being on the sea?"

He was quiet for a long time. Tara thought he might have drifted off to sleep.

"When I'm on land," Ben said, "I forget that I exist. It's strange, but the monotony, the ability to walk without thinking about the earth beneath me, makes it feel like I'm going through the motions. On sea, I have to stabilize myself as the water moves the boat with waves and ripples. I have to be intentional when I move. I have to be conscious of the spin of our planet, gravity. I'm forced to recognize that everything changes from second to second because we're never in the same place."

"It's still true for land," she said. "We've been here for hours, but the sky above has changed with Earth's rotation."

He pointed to the path visible above their feet. "Those people sitting on the bench. They don't recognize it. To them, it's a fixed position."

"You don't always have to be conscious of it to know," Tara said.

"I want to remember everything," he said. "I don't want a life that keeps me from noticing or spend forty hours a week in a cubicle or have the same commute every day. Being here, existing, it's a gift. The sea keeps me aware of it."

She'd never known anyone like him. He was fascinating and soulful. As if he'd awakened her to something more than the life that had been mapped out for her.

"I used to pretend I was a star." Tara pointed up. "Not Dhruva, but a dimmer one in its vicinity. I could spend thousands of years observing and noticing, trace outlines of continents, see the creation of a galaxy or the end of a distant sun. The only pressure would be the kind that kept me alive. It would release slowly until I turned into space dust again."

"Alone," he said. "You want to be alone."

Tears welled and she cleared her throat. "It's the only time I know who I am."

"I get that." He squeezed her hand. "I'm the only person I like to be with."

She curled over on her side toward him. They stayed like that throughout the night as they drifted in and out of sleep. One occasionally waking the other up with a question or an observation. She found Dhruva in the night sky and asked him to help her become more determined. Become brave in the face of expectations and carve her own path.

As the sun rose, they both shifted. On their sides, they faced each other.

"Good morning," Ben said.

"Good morning."

He reached up and brushed back her long black hair and tucked it behind her ear. "You're beautiful."

Her heart melted. She felt it dissolve. No one had ever said those words to her. Not that she could recall. "So are you."

He cupped her face, then leaned over and brushed his lips against hers. They stayed like that, lips against each other's, for what felt like forever and a millisecond. When he released her, they both sat up.

"I have coffee." She didn't want this to end. She couldn't bear to have him walk away, even though she knew they couldn't be here forever.

He accepted a few sips from the cup of her thermos. "Whenever I see a variable, I will think of you, Tara."

"Rajput." She wanted him to know her whole name.

"Tara Rajput. I'm Ben Anand." He took her hand in his.

The nerves that hadn't been present showed up with a vengeance. "Are you, I mean, um. Can I find you in the student directory? For BU."

He kissed her knuckles. "U of Maine. I'm starting my master's-to-PhD in oceanography there. I'm here visiting a buddy of mine for a couple of days."

"Oh." She didn't know how to ask for his number.

He pointed to her backpack. "Do you have a pen and paper in there?"

Excitedly she pulled out her small notebook and handed it over. She watched as he wrote his number. But he didn't ask for hers.

He stood and pulled her up. "Can I help you pack?"

She shook her head.

Ben took both her hands in his. "A night I will never forget." He leaned over and brushed her lips again. "Don't forget to dream, Tara Rajput."

"Invent a shark-proof life vest, Ben Anand."

He winked. His dimples deepened in his cheeks. And then, with a wave, he walked away.

Watching him disappear down the footpath of the Esplanade, Tara understood love for the first time. She wanted to spend a lifetime with Ben, except she'd agreed to marry Devon. In the span of a minute, she went from love to heartbreak. She glanced up, Dhruva no longer visible. Would she be brave for the first time in her life?

CHAPTER EIGHT

Siblings are both your biggest fans, and your worst enemies.
—*YNLIN*

Jamaica Plain, Massachusetts, present

"What took you so long?" Nikki pulled Heena into her apartment. "Why don't you have anything with you?"

"Stop frisking me."

Nikki grabbed the boho bag from Heena and dug inside. "Wallet. Baby wipes." She rummaged around. "There's nothing here for what I need."

Heena tapped the side of her forehead. "You said you wanted my advice."

"Help," Nikki said. "I need H-E-L-P."

Heena sat on the couch, her long ribbon skirt floating around her as she curled her legs toward her body. Older by two years, she couldn't be more different from Nikki. Physically they resembled each other, but their likes and dislikes, the ways they approached life, how they navigated the world, were completely different.

"I thought you'd come here with balloons or a cake or I don't know, stuff." Nikki paced on the other side of the coffee table.

"Are you throwing a birthday party for a six-year-old?"

Nikki sat and put her face in her hands. "I can't believe I asked *you*. Caleb's the romantic one, you don't know anything about how to do this."

"Neither do you," Heena said.

Nikki threw a pillow at her sister. All she wanted to do was show Jay that she would prioritize him by planning a magical evening. She'd reflected after the night he'd cooked for her a few days ago. He'd been right, she'd been too worried about their families. It was important to nurture their relationship as a newly engaged couple. The problem was that she didn't know how to set the scene. Jay did the flowers-and-chocolates thing. Nikki wanted to plan something different, a night where he felt special.

"Did you two have a fight?"

"No, we don't do that," Nikki said.

"That's unfortunate," Heena said. "A loud, roaring argument is great, better if one of you throws a glass or something."

Nikki glared at her sister. "How did we grow up in the same house? Mom and Dad never fought. Neither did we."

"No, because you usually go all 'let's talk about this' with your Oprah voice. So instead, I wrote a lot of mean things having to do with you in my journal," Heena said. "A lot."

"I don't see the point in yelling. It's not constructive. And that's not what happened anyway. Jay got frustrated over stuff with the engagement party and our parents. I want to make sure we're back on track."

"Well, you lit candles," Heena said. "That's a good start."

"They're scented," Nikki mumbled into her hands.

"Good for you!" Heena reached over and tugged her hands away from her face. "You can do this. You live in the world. We're hardwired for romance. And honestly, Jay's so used to carrying that burden in your relationship, all you need to do is wear something sexy and he'll help you get through the rest."

"Are you saying I'm not a good girlfriend to him?" She knew there was an imbalance. He did so much for her, so often. Nikki remembered the important parts, like getting him a thoughtful present for Christmas. She'd even tried baking banana bread for him once because she'd heard him say it was one of his favorite foods. It came out burnt and undercooked at the same time, but he had appreciated the effort.

"Whatever you do works for him," Heena said. "He asked you to marry him. Maybe Jay's love language is to take care of you."

Nikki stared at her sister. "What's mine?"

Heena shrugged her shoulders.

"Seriously?" Nikki said.

"Look." Heena leaned forward. "You've always dated men that were like you. Independent, career obsessed, and preferred separate lives. You were comfortable in relationships like that. Remember when Hugh was sick, and you sent him soup from a meal service? And when you sprained your knee skiing, he sent you soup from the same place? You were compatible. Jay is different. He would stay with you, carry you to the bathroom and stuff. That probably scares you because you're not used to it."

"Do you do those things for Caleb?"

Heena laughed. "He cleans the house, and I let him."

Nikki put her face in her hands.

Heena tugged them away. "Every couple is different. Caleb and I have our own way. We met so young that we grew up together. We love fiercely and we fight unfairly. You and Jay are still learning how to be a couple."

"What if we don't?" Nikki knew this was fear talking. Still, she was worried.

"Then you'll break up and find someone new," Heena said.

Nikki winced. Even the idea of it made her physically sick. "That's not an option."

"Then light more scented candles," Heena said. "Did you know that the most stubborn animal on earth is a donkey, according to this book we're reading to the kids? You're worse. Stop being so fixated on wanting everything to be okay. Focus on what needs to be said."

Nikki looked up. "You're quoting my newsletter back to me."

"You forced me to subscribe." Heena held Nikki's hands in hers and stared at her. "Tell me what you plan to say to him. I know you rehearsed it."

"'I promise to not worry and enjoy the time we spend together.'"

"Well, it's no 'She walks in beauty, like the night.'" Heena let go and paced the living room. "Wait, that's why you're doing all this?"

"I told you. I made him sad," Nikki mumbled.

Heena stared at her in shock. "So?"

"You don't understand," Nikki said. "I hurt his feelings."

"And he'll get over it. He's an adult. Jeez, Nikki. Mom really did a number on you."

"This isn't about her." Nikki heard the defensiveness in her own voice. "All I want to do is give Jay a special night."

Heena went to the kitchen and filled a glass of water. "Wear his favorite color. Tell him you love him and sit on his lap. He'll be fine."

"That's all?"

"Men are not that complicated." Heena tapped her finger to her chin. "What do you wear that makes his eyes pop out of his head?"

Nikki frowned, then understood. "Pencil skirts. Glasses."

"Huh." Heena sipped her glass of water. "I wouldn't have guessed he has a librarian-teacher thing."

"What? Stop. I'm not talking about this with you." Nikki went to her bedroom to look through her closet. Jay liked blue, and she had a dress that he loved.

"Caleb has a thing for togas. He's really into the Roman Empire. At first, I thought we might have to do couples therapy, but then I realized it works for me too," Heena called out from the living room.

"I don't want to know that," Nikki yelled as she changed her clothes.

"That's how the twins were conceived," Heena added.

"Lalalalala. I can't hear you." Nikki walked back to the living room as she put her hair up in a bun with little tendrils pulled out around her face. "What do you think?"

"Damn. He's going to swallow his tongue and forget his name," Heena said. "The spaghetti straps really show off your shoulders. Pilates?"

"Four days a week," Nikki said.

"Lipstick?"

Nikki shook her head. "He hates it. And gloss. Not even lip balm. I moisturize my lips when he's not around."

"See? Your love language is suffering through chapped lips," Heena said.

Nikki thought about it for a minute. "I also keep my nails longer than I like because he likes to fall asleep while I scratch his arm."

Heena clasped her hands over her heart. "You're so romantic. The sacrifice! I can't handle it."

"I hate you."

Then she heard a knock on the door, then the lock turned. The door opened and Jay came in.

CHAPTER NINE

Be daring. Make the first move.
—*YNLIN*

Nikki stared. His tie was undone, as were the top two buttons on his shirt. His suit jacket hung on his arm. She grinned when his eyes widened, and she saw a bobble of his Adam's apple. She could feel the heat from his gaze.

"I can feel the temperature change," Heena said. "You might want to turn on the AC."

It was Jay who broke their eye contact. "Heena."

"Love you, future brother-in-law." Heena gave a side hug to Nikki, then a full one to Jay before seeing herself out and closing the front door.

Jay dropped the spare key on the table under the coat hooks. She'd given it to him as a gift on Valentine's Day, a sign of trust that he could come and go as he pleased. Still, he always knocked before entering unless he knew she wasn't home. "Going somewhere? Or did I forget plans?"

Nikki shook her head.

He pointed to her sapphire-blue silk dress. It was fitted to show every curve and just short enough to highlight her long lean legs. "Oh, um. No. Heena told me that . . . never mind. How was your day? Are you hungry?"

Jay furrowed his brow, then looked around. "Did we teleport to the 1950s?"

Nikki closed her eyes and prayed for patience. "Is everyone sarcastic now? You and Heena act like I'm not a considerate person."

"Sorry. It's just that you're dressed like that and offering dinner." He rubbed the back of his neck.

For the first time since she'd met Jay, he was hesitant, unsure with her. Nikki led Jay to the sofa, draped his jacket around the back of the counter stool, and sat next to him. She stared at the base of his bare throat. He loved it when she kissed him there. She leaned closer. He shifted away, then gave her a puzzled look.

She cleared her throat. Her stomach acid gurgled, and she placed her hand on her belly for calm. "I'm so sorry about the other night. You wanted to have a nice meal together and I focused on, well, you know."

"You've been worrying over that?" His voice was more gravelly than usual. "It wasn't a big deal."

"I hurt your feelings," she said.

He rolled his neck. "Babe, it's been a long day. I know you want to talk it out, but honestly, it's not a thing for me. Now, can we just reheat leftovers and crash?"

She wanted to show him that she was there for him. "Rough case?"

"I'm working on keeping a thirteen-year-old out of juvie," he said.

She rubbed his palm with her thumbs, traced the lines that defined his life. His heart was so big, and she knew anything involving kids weighed on him. There was exhaustion in his face, the slouch of his shoulders. "Is there anything I can do to help?"

His first smile made her legs tremble. "That dress is a good start."

She laughed. He leaned back, rested his head against the back of the sofa, and put his arm around her. Nikki rested her cheek against his chest. The steady beat of his heart released the tension she'd been carrying for the past week. She toyed with the button on his shirt. "There's cold pasta in the fridge. How do I reheat it?"

He kissed the top of her head. "Steam. Reheat with steam."

"Uh-huh," Nikki said. "Tell me more."

Jay tipped her chin up and stared into her eyes. "Or I can show you." He lowered his lips to hers, and Nikki sank into the kiss.

Nikki stopped thinking and gave in to all her feelings for this man. She stroked his sinewy muscles through his shirt. He wrapped his arms around her, brought her closer. She could feel the fast beat of his heart. She cupped his face; the silky scruff at his jaw scratched her palms. She'd never wanted someone as much as she wanted him. Nikki wrapped her arms around his neck and deepened the kiss. She concentrated on Jay's soft skin, the hard ridges of small muscles. Nikki shifted to straddle him, but the hem was too restrictive, so she sat sideways on his lap. She loved the feel of him, the taste. He was warm and Nikki didn't realize how cold she'd been without him.

"Nikita." His voice was full of need.

She leaned back. "You always say my full name when you're aroused."

He brushed her hair away from her face. "I can't pick you up to carry you to bed."

She frowned.

"You keep the coffee table too close to the sofa, I can't move my legs." He shifted her from his lap. "Plus, I don't want to knock over the lit candle."

Nikki stood and blew it out. "It's so I can stretch my legs out, rest my feet." She tried to straighten her dress. The fabric around her thighs was too tight and short.

"Need help?" He didn't hide his laughter.

"You try wearing a silk minidress."

"Deal." He picked her up and carried her toward the bedroom. "Let's take it off first?"

As he lay her down on the bed, she grabbed his face with both hands and brought his mouth to hers.

"Brain off?" He kissed her jaw, then her neck.

"What?" She unbuttoned the third, then the fourth button of his shirt, tugged the bottom out from his slacks, and reached to undo his belt. Her body needed him.

"Perfect."

And that's when the buzzer rang.

He groaned.

Nikki touched her forehead to his. "Likely a delivery person for the building. I'll ring them in and come right back."

She ran to the buzzer, pushed it, then rushed back to the bedroom, throwing herself into his arms. He hugged her and rolled on top of her as she threw the extra pillows off the bed. Then there was a knock, followed by her mother's voice.

"Nikki?" her mom called out from the hall.

Jay let her go, groaned again, and lay face down.

"What is she doing here?" Nikki asked him.

"I have the same information you have," he said with his face buried in the mattress. "Go. See if she's okay."

Frustrated at the interruption, Nikki wrapped herself in her silk robe and went to see why her mom had suddenly shown up.

CHAPTER TEN

Andover, Massachusetts, 1989

Gravity, while useful to keep humans from flying off the face of the earth, was sometimes inconvenient. Mostly because Tara had to carry fifty extra pounds on her small frame thanks to a heavy red sari with gold threading. A giant fake bun on her head held together with a hundred sharp pins that bored into her skull. A gold-and-diamond set that sat like a shackle around her neck, matching earrings that felt as if they weighed a pound each, not to mention the ankle bracelets that were more like cuffs that turned her into a human rattle every time she walked. She was a gilded bird being gifted to the first man who'd asked. The jewelry would go to her in-laws as part of the dowry, a dated tradition that parents of sons clung to with tight fists.

"Stay still." Mayuri secured the big gold bracelets on Tara's wrists. They covered the whole of the tops of her hands, their rings attached to each finger. Pancha sakra, the traditional jewelry for a bride.

"You try carrying thousands of dollars of silk and gold and then tell me what to do." It was better to take out her irritation on Mayuri instead of where it really belonged. On her mother. The woman had been a nightmare these past six months as she planned every detail of the wedding. If Tara attempted to offer an opinion, like that Mayuri should be a bridesmaid, it was rejected outright with "Indian weddings don't have things like that." There was nothing about today that was for Tara. Not even the man who would be waiting for her at the mandap.

He had the wrong name.

Tara had spent the last five and a half months dreaming about Ben. She'd created elaborate fantasies of their love and life. All the while knowing that she would never see him again. It had been one night, two kisses, and a memory that was imprinted on her heart. She tried hard to be the version of herself from before they'd met but knew that he had changed her forever. Her life would now hold a longing for him, and she would live knowing she would never again have the kind of love she'd felt, even for one night. She'd dialed the first six of the seven digits of his phone number countless times, never having the courage to push that last number. What would she say?

Run away with me.

Except he wouldn't and Tara couldn't. She'd settled for the life she had, not the one she dreamed about. She would keep only the memories she would revisit over and over again. Eventually she would forget. Stop imposing his face over Devon's.

Ben would be her secret never to be told. Not even Mayuri knew that she'd fallen in love in the span of one night. That's how long they'd been in each other's company. She didn't want to share Ben with anyone. That night would stop being perfect. If she told her best friend, Mayuri would view this wedding as Tara giving up, and Tara didn't want to disappoint the only person who pushed her to reach for more. Her whole life, she'd been told that her parents would decide whom she married. If she'd been born with courage, she might have tried to run away. She knew of girls who'd done as much in similar circumstances.

"Okay, you look, umm, well, like a proper Indian bride."

In the mirror, Tara didn't recognize herself beneath the heavy makeup and the nose ring with a chain that hooked into the top of her ear. It was just as well. Because the person facing her was the one marrying Devon. Tara would save her heart for Ben. Devon would get this mirage for a wife.

"Before your mom and the aunties barge in here to come get you," Mayuri said, "I want to give you your wedding gift."

Mayuri was dressed in a pale-pink sari and delicate gold accessories that showed off her beautiful dark skin and thick, sharp eyebrows. She was the kind of beautiful Tara had always admired: unapologetic and confident.

"You didn't have to get me anything," Tara said. "Being here today is enough."

"I did, it's my duty as best friend." Mayuri took Tara's hands in hers. "My gift is parked by the back entrance of this hall."

Tara's brow rose, and she felt every touch of the gold strung across her forehead. "You got me a car? I already have one."

"More like a getaway vehicle," Mayuri said. "Say the word and I'll find us a way to sneak out of here."

"What are you talking about?"

"You don't want to do this," Mayuri said. "I know you. And this is too big for your ridiculous 'go along to get along' approach to life."

Tara shook her head. "This is what's expected. And I can't." Even though the idea of running away made her quiet heart race. "My parents have spent so much money. And there are people here from all over the world. I can't do this to them. It would cause a scandal. Embarrassment for them. Our whole family, really. And you know how proud my mom is of who we are and where we come from. Why would you even say something like this? Are you joking?" Tara wasn't brave. She was ashamed to know this about herself, so she could never admit it. But it was true.

Mayuri put her hands on Tara's shoulders. "I'm serious. I have never seen a less happy bride. You didn't want anything do with the menu, the decorations, the mandap design, or your clothes. And I know you don't care about Devon. You've never even told me if you think he's attractive."

Tara shrugged Mayuri off. "He is. My mom would never marry me off to someone who didn't look handsome next to me. She is too proud for that. And being the center of attention isn't my thing." Never had been, not since she'd auditioned for a lead role in the school production of *Oklahoma!* while she was a freshman in high school. Her singing was so off-key that even the music teacher laughed. She immediately signed up for backstage work, and only for the sake of an extracurricular for college applications. Tara had learned that she belonged behind the curtain, in the shadows, where she could watch others do the amazing things that came so naturally to them.

"Do you even like your husband-to-be?" Mayuri asked. "All you've said about him is that he comes from a good family and is going to be a dentist. Which, meh, not the sexiest of professions."

"He's nice." At least in the generic sense. They'd been alone a handful of times, and while he wasn't Ben, Devon wasn't repulsive. He was smart in his own way. He had ambition and plans to start his own practice. But the main thing was that he supported Tara getting her master's and ultimately her PhD in astrophysics. That was all that mattered.

"Which is how you describe a sweater in the mall," Mayuri said. "You haven't said love."

Tara couldn't look at her best friend, not even in the mirror. "You know how our moms say that first comes marriage and then comes love. That's how it was for my parents and yours."

"Mine can barely stand being in the same room with each other," Mayuri said. "You don't always fall in love with your husband."

"Maybe I don't need that." Unless it was with Ben. Maybe he was somewhere thinking about her, knowing, like her, that they weren't meant to be anything more to each other than one night of lying side by side, palm to palm. She hugged Mayuri. More because Tara needed the anchor. "Just help me get through this." It was the most she'd ever asked of her friend.

Mayuri gave her a squeeze, then leaned away. "I got your back. Nothing is forever, not even marriage, even though it's supposed to be. If you ever need it, just remember, I'll always be Louise to your Thelma."

"Or Cecilia to my Hillary."

"I promise to sing 'Wind Beneath My Wings' as you walk slowly down the aisle."

Tara laughed, then blinked away the wetness in her eyes. She moved slowly, carrying the heavy weight of her cultural accoutrements with her as she joined her maternal uncles for the long walk toward the mandap. Devon stood behind a tall sheet awaiting Tara for the seven turns around the fire that would tie their fates together.

CHAPTER ELEVEN

Change from the inside is 10x more effective than on the outside.
—*YNLIN*

Jamaica Plain, Massachusetts, present

It wasn't like Tara to pop in unannounced. Something must have happened. Nikki made sure she was decent before she shut the bedroom door. Then she straightened her messy hair before opening the front door.

"Mom? Is everything okay?"

Tara came in, her hands in her coat pockets. "It smells nice in here. Am I disturbing you?" Her mom always dressed well. No leggings or sweats for Tara Parekh when leaving the house. Tonight she had on forest-green wide-legged slacks under her camel-colored wool coat. A silk scarf in green and gold was draped around her neck. Her mother was a striking woman. Nikki appreciated that she'd learned that it was important and a form of self-care to dress well and be put together even while running errands.

"It's fine. I'm surprised to see you." Nikki went around and blew out the rose and cedar candles she'd lit. "Is everything all right?"

Tara stayed in her coat but sat on the edge of the chair in the living room. "Yes."

"Your voice is shaking." Nikki sat on the coffee table in front of Tara.

"I don't know what happened," Tara said. "I mean, I do. I wasn't planning on coming this way or knocking on your door, but I was driving and then I was here."

Nikki began to worry. "Is it Dad? Was there an accident?"

Tara had a blank look on her face. "Maybe. No. He's fine. It's me. It's good. Necessary. It was you, what we talked about the other day. Choices. Consequences."

Nikki thought back to that day in Tara's study and couldn't remember what she'd said. "You're not making any sense, Mom."

Tara looked into Nikki's eyes. "I'm divorcing your father."

Stunned, Nikki felt her entire body freeze. Of all the things that she'd imagined in a few seconds, this wasn't one of them. "I don't understand."

"You're going to get married." Tara touched Nikki's shoulder. "You're making a choice. I need to do the same. I *want* to do the same. I must."

It was as if Tara was speaking to herself. Nikki shook her head. "What's happening?" She stood and paced. She couldn't think, it was all jumbled in her mind. "Did you and Dad have a fight?" Her parents had a steady marriage. Sure, sometimes Devon threw little barbs at Tara, but for the most part they seemed to be fine.

"No," Tara said.

"Then what's going on?" Nikki shouted. "This isn't like you."

"I know."

Nikki saw a soft smile on Tara's face, as if her mother was proud of herself.

"Everything okay?" Jay came out of the bedroom.

"Oh, Jayesh." Tara rose. "I didn't know you were here."

"Auntie?"

"Mom, what did Dad say?" Nikki turned to Jay. "My parents . . . I don't." He took her hand, and she could breathe again. "Divorce. She said they're breaking up."

Tara touched Nikki's shoulder. "It's fine, Nikita. You don't have to worry about anything. I only wanted to let you know. I should have waited. I didn't mean to disturb your evening."

Nikki reached for Tara. "This isn't like you left the water running and flooded your bathroom. Mom, we have to talk about this."

"There is nothing more to say," Tara said. "I've spoken to your father. Now I'm telling you. I'll call Heena on my way home."

Nikki stood frozen as her mother left, with no explanation or conversation. Not even a single look back toward Nikki. "Did that just happen?"

Jay wrapped her in his arms. "It's going to be okay, sweetheart."

Nikki let him hold her, too numb to figure out the sudden turn of events. In less than five minutes, her mom had come in, scattered Nikki's entire past on the floor, and left as if she'd come to drop off a casserole.

"She's divorcing my father?" It would be more believable if her dad had been the one to decide. Tara wasn't someone who took any action. What was her mother doing? Sure, her parents weren't demonstrative or very loving, but they had been together for three and a half decades. They had grandchildren. Something had to have happened.

Nikki pulled away from Jay. "I need to talk to my dad."

He nodded.

She reached for her phone. It rang on the other end, then went to voicemail. "He's not answering."

Jay rubbed his face. "Maybe that's why she wasn't so enthusiastic about our news. She was considering divorce."

Nikki stopped pacing. "This is the point you want to make right now? My mother just announced that she's leaving my father."

"I'm saying that maybe it's not sudden for her," he said. "Yeah, it's a surprise to you, but it could be something she'd been planning for a while."

Nikki walked away from him and went to the bedroom to change her clothes. "I need to go see him."

Jay followed her. "If he doesn't want to talk, let him be."

She whirled around on him. "I can't do nothing. It's not your family that's falling apart."

He sat on the bed. "Fine. Go over there."

She threw her hands up, angry and upset at the same time. "You're such a big help. Thank you."

"What do you want from me?"

She looked directly at him. "Nothing. Never mind. I need to deal with this right now. Maybe you should go to your place tonight."

He shook his head, then got dressed. She was already in her kitchen, phone in hand. She needed to call Heena before she went over to her parents' house. Jay passed her, kissed the top of her head, then let himself out.

She stared at the closed door. Tears rolled down her cheeks, and since no one was there to see her, she let them fall. He'd left her. He didn't see that she hadn't wanted him to go. She wasn't being fair, the rational part of her brain knew that. She hadn't used her words. But she didn't have any.

Nikki wiped her eyes. With shaky hands she called her sister.

At least Heena picked up. "Mom just called me."

"Did she explain?" Nikki paced back and forth in the small space between the wall and the coffee table.

"Does she ever?" Heena said.

Nikki squeezed her eyes shut, then opened them. "I don't get it." Heena stayed silent as Nikki poured herself a glass of water. "What should we do?" Nikki stared at the glass, unable to drink. Her throat was too tight to swallow.

"Nothing," Heena said.

"I'm going to go home," Nikki said. "Make Mom explain. Talk to Dad. They must have had a fight. This isn't, I mean, it's not something that comes out of nowhere. I can help them through it."

"You're not *their* life coach," Heena said. "You have to sit this one out."

Impossible. "They are our parents."

"And it's their relationship," Heena said. "Not ours."

Nikki hung up without saying goodbye. It was immature, but Nikki didn't need yet another person to tell her that this wasn't her problem. Because if not, then why did her heart feel like it was breaking? She couldn't catch her breath. She didn't know why it was so important, but Nikki needed to know what had happened between them. How could her mother just decide this, after all this time?

CHAPTER TWELVE

Andover, Massachusetts, 1989

Newton's first law of motion is inertia. As an object, she was placed wherever her parents needed her to be, and right now, she was at her own wedding reception while her mother and father held court at the head table, receiving congratulations from their guests. Kamla's gold-and-purple sari gleamed under the glimmering multicolored lights. She was regal and graceful in ways Tara could never imagine being herself.

Tara had expected to feel some sort of way, but as she watched her now husband and his friends dance to bhangra and Bollywood music, their sweat dripping freely on the small wooden floor, she was numb. His kurta was unbuttoned and exposed to his undershirt as he danced as if this was the best night of his life. It had nothing to do with her, likely because of the shots she'd watched him take at the bar with his friends. It seemed like a fancy frat party except everyone was in saris and kurtas and drinking out of glasses instead of red cups. Just as frat parties hadn't been her scene, neither was this.

She wanted to be back on her small green patch of land overlooking the Charles River. She missed going to class, her notebooks, and Ben. This wasn't his scene either. Their wedding would be small, only the two of them, with Mayuri as her bridesmaid. On the beach, under the night sky. Tara glanced at her henna-covered hands. She now wore a small gold band with three tiny diamonds on her ring finger. It was a newer tradition, added to the mangal sutra, which young girls didn't want to wear as a symbol of their marital status. It had been chosen by her mother-in-law, approved by her own mom. Nothing about today was Tara's choice, not the flowers or the menu. Her mom had gotten Tara's wedding sari from India, brought over by an aunt on her dad's side.

The reception outfit was from a shopping trip to Edison, New Jersey, with her mom, where Kamla had chosen the deep-purple lengha. The long-sleeved top was fitted and bedazzled with little gold dots; the silk skirt covered her gold high-heeled sandals. Tara didn't like any part of her outfit but wore it because she was now a zombie who was led here and there. If only she could live on Ben's boat in the middle of the ocean and gaze at the stars.

She didn't have the courage to call him. His number, now committed to memory, was still in the secret pocket of her wallet because it was the only thing she had from him. Tara had created so much meaning from the way he stacked circles for the number eight, as if it were a secret code. If she could decipher it, she might learn more. She'd often wondered if he'd waited for the phone to ring, if he'd been disappointed to not have heard from her. She'd had months between that night and today, but Tara had stayed inert.

I'm not brave, she remembered telling him. Calling would have meant ruining her future. She'd heard a few stories about children being disowned for choosing a path not approved by the family. If she'd been more like Mayuri . . . Tara stopped at the painful thought. She was an obedient daughter who didn't believe she could survive on her own. She would lose MIT because she wouldn't be able to afford it. She couldn't see herself in cubicle jobs. Her ambition required this of her.

Tara watched from the edge of the dance floor as people celebrated her inaction. She'd done what was necessary. Now she would live with it.

"Come get out here." Her cousins dragged her toward the thick crowd. "Your husband has moves. Show him yours."

Tara resisted. "I am not much of a dancer."

"Just try," they pleaded.

Tara declined, pulled out of their grasp, and sent them off toward Devon.

"Here." Mayuri thrust a glass in her hand. "It looks like Coke, but I had the bartender sneak in a shot of rum."

Tara thanked her friend and took a sip. The bitter and sweet made her think of cough syrup, but she gulped. Her small rebellion. "Thanks."

"So, listen," Mayuri said. "Wedding night. Any questions?"

For the first time in what seemed like weeks, Tara laughed. "I paid attention in health class. Unless things have changed in the last few years."

Her friend nudged Tara's shoulder with hers. "I'm talking sex with a stranger."

Tara was worried about that. She wasn't unattracted to Devon, but she also didn't want to jump his bones. "I've gotten to know him a little. We've had a few dates."

"What's his favorite food?"

"Um, anything with sugar." Tara had watched him eat sweet after sweet at every prewedding event. "Which is ironic because he's a dentist."

"What's his favorite band?" Mayuri kept going.

Tara pointed. "Whatever he's dancing to, I guess."

"This song is from *Dil Diwana*. You know, songs on the radio," she said. "Bon Jovi, Tears for Fears, Simply Red, or even Metallica."

"It doesn't matter," Tara said. "I'm not that picky."

"I'm worried about you." Mayuri's voice was soft and low. "It's like you're going through the motions of what's expected. There is no you here. Remember when we pranked the guys on the floor below us our sophomore year? I don't remember the last time I saw you truly happy. It's like you're disappearing."

"This is what us Desi girls do, right? We graduate; we get married. And Devon is a good match. He's okay with me continuing my studies. And we'll live with his parents while I'm in grad school, so it's not like

I'll have to cook and clean all day long. And as far as the sex thing, we'll take it slow until we know each other better."

"'Sex thing'?" Mayuri asked. "If you had ever experienced it, that's not how you would describe it. As if it was an item on a to-do list."

Tara shrugged. "It's not that important to me. I'm not like you. I've never been boy crazy or had posters of actors on my walls."

"I know," Mayuri said. "It was weird seeing a giant picture of Albert Einstein above your bed every day freshman year."

"You had one of Mae West," Tara countered. "With a quote that said, 'Give a man a hand and he'll run it all over you.'"

"She was my hero," Mayuri said. "Hopefully, Devon knows how to use his hands."

Tara blushed. "If it's comfortable and nice, there's not much more I can ask for. I'm just happy to be getting out of my parents' house and to start my own life."

"By moving in with his parents," Mayuri said.

"Temporarily," Tara said. "Until we find our own place in the city. Hopefully, Cambridge near MIT."

Her friend sipped from her own glass. "Do you think you'll fall in love with your husband?"

The *no* was so visceral and clear that she physically reacted by placing her hand on her stomach. She loved someone else. Another man she didn't know well, but she remembered the feel of his palm against hers. The vibrato in his voice. The heat that emanated from his body as they lay side by side under the night sky. "Maybe," she said. It was the right thing to say and only slightly less honest.

"What are you thinking about?" Mayuri said. "Or who?"

Tara jerked her mind back to the present. "What do you mean?"

"You have a goofy look on your face," Mayuri said. "One I've never seen."

Tara held up her drink. "It's the rum."

Mayuri didn't believe her. Tara turned away. Ben was her secret. She would keep him only for herself so no one could take him away from her.

"Come on." Her friend tugged her toward the middle of the room. "Let's go dance."

Tara felt the effects of the rum and agreed. The crowd parted as Tara awkwardly moved to the beat. Then Devon took her hands and moved her around like a rag doll as their guests formed a circle around them. Tara closed her eyes as the room spun. This was her life now. She had to accept it. It would be okay. She kept repeating it to herself as she pasted a smile on her face.

CHAPTER THIRTEEN

Your figurative spoons-to-commitments ratio should be 1:1.
—*YNLIN*

Newton, Massachusetts, present

Nikki found a seat and worked on her laptop as she waited for Bijal auntie. Jay's mother had wanted to meet at a coffee shop in the village center so that they could get to know each other better. Nikki had arrived early because she didn't know how to be late. It wasn't a problem because there was always work to be done. Her current priority was to finish a blog post for a national lifestyle magazine about gaining control by letting go. If only she could follow her own advice. It wasn't that Nikki was trying to control Tara . . . but it was infuriating that she wouldn't even respond to calls or texts. Nikki had even invited Tara to come to this planning session with Bijal auntie. But her mom had gone silent, and there wasn't a way for Nikki to get her to be more involved.

It had been over a week since Tara's surprise visit and announcement, and while Nikki continued to send both parents links to articles about resolving relationship issues, they responded only with thumbs-up emojis.

At least she and Jay were doing well. Though he was still against a lavish engagement party, he understood that this was a chance for Nikki to bond with his mother. He'd urged her to keep it simple. It was a new side to Jay. He was an extrovert with a big group of friends and close to his parents, but she hadn't realized how hands-off he was, especially when it came to cultural traditions. Nikki loved the Indian side of her. It was ironic because Tara had never focused on it. Going to Desi events, learning to wear a sari, knowing when the major Hindu holidays were . . . Nikki had learned these things from her two grandmothers. She wasn't all in, though. Bollywood movies went over her head for being unrealistic. And some Hindu rituals could become overwhelming. She'd created a nice balance for herself in what parts of her Indian identity she leaned into.

"Nikki." Bijal came up. "What a quaint table."

She glanced up from her laptop. Jay's mom was dressed in black yoga pants and a loose white sweater with a puffy vest for the cool spring weather.

"Hi, Auntie. It was crowded, but if we need more space, we can move when a bigger one is free."

"It's fine. I'm getting a latte," Bijal said. "Can I get you anything?"

Nikki pointed to her mug. "I'm fine. I'm maxed out on caffeine for the day."

Nikki kept a smile on her face as Bijal headed to order. She shut down her computer and put away her work notebook. She slid them into their appointed slots in her tote, then pulled out her life notebook. She was determined to show Bijal auntie that she'd already done a lot of planning to make up for Tara's lack of involvement. Jay's parents would be her in-laws, and it was important that Bijal auntie see Nikki as a capable and self-made woman who would seamlessly fit into their family.

Bijal sat across from her, a paper cup in her hand. "You are so industrious, Nikita."

Nikki couldn't tell whether it was a compliment or a dig. Bijal auntie had a lilting tone to her voice, and it was hard to infer. She decided to take it at face value. "Thank you. How are you? I hope this time is good for you."

"It's right after my Pilates class, so it's perfect. And now that I've stopped working, I'm figuring out how to fill my days," Bijal said. "There are only so many books to read, and watching television all afternoon doesn't interest me. Of course, my work on various boards keeps me busy."

"I imagine it's hard to adjust after decades in finance."

"Yes." Bijal unwrapped her wool scarf and slid out of her puffy vest. "I can always consult if I miss it."

"Working for myself is what I always wanted." Nikki wanted to show Bijal that she was ambitious and accomplished. "I'm fortunate that I am able to do that."

"Yes," Bijal said. "I signed up for your newsletter."

Nikki was surprised. "Thank you! I hope you're finding it useful."

"It's a bit pithy for me," Bijal said. "It could use more substance. You have good research, but condensing it in such a way loses something."

Nikki wanted to push back. The average *YNLIN* subscriber was a woman, aged twenty to forty. Her target was drowning in information; attention spans in that demographic were eight to ten seconds. She offered bite-size information and an opportunity to dig deeper. "I appreciate the feedback."

"I hope you're not insulted," she said.

Nikki shook her head. "Of course not. I'm a big believer in improvement."

"Though you position yourself as an expert," Bijal said. "That is very commendable."

It wasn't just in her head. Bijal didn't approve of Nikki. She would have to work harder to get Bijal auntie to like her. "I'm excited to plan this engagement party. I already ordered my outfit. It's a pale yellow with gold embroidery."

"Isn't your mother joining us?"

Nikki folded and unfolded her paper napkin. "She couldn't make it. But I have done quite a bit. I'm so glad you liked the invitation designs; we can finalize that. I want to make sure I get yours and Uncle's full names as well."

"Yes, of course." Bijal scanned Nikki's notebook. "There are so many decisions to make. I have a list of venues. We need to schedule a day to go look. Then there are caterers and decorators. Perhaps we can divide up the items. Kirit and I will need to meet with your parents about the ceremony and who is bringing what for the different customs."

Jay's parents had no idea there might be a divorce—it wasn't public. And it wouldn't go over well, as Bijal auntie cared a lot about social standing in a community where divorce was frowned upon. Nikki refused to risk the party. She would talk to her parents, make them cooperate, to fake it if they had to. But she didn't see a meeting of the four parents happening. "If you tell me what we need to bring, we'll make sure it's covered," she said. "I know the dowry will be for symbolism, with fruits and nuts. Jay's already put in an order for barfi."

"There is no food my son can say no to. It's a good thing he's a runner with a good metabolism." Bijal leaned back against the wooden chair. "I remember when I was engaged to Kirit. Of course, ours was semiarranged. We went on a few dates before deciding. Back then both sides of the family were very involved."

Nikki nodded. "Dad and Kirit uncle have been texting a lot," she offered.

"I knew your mother a little in high school," Bijal said. "She never blended. At least not with the Desi students."

"She's always been shy." Nikki did not want to make this about Tara.

"*Reserved* is a more appropriate word for a sixty-year-old." Bijal laughed to defuse the insult.

Nikki didn't correct Bijal. It was a dig against Tara's actual age, but she would let it pass. "Tell me what your wedding was like." Nikki had learned a long time before that people often opened up when they were the center of the conversation. "You and Kirit uncle were set up?"

"In a way," Bijal said. "We met at a matchmaking event at the mandir. It was based on being like-minded and deciding to build a family together. Kirit and I were evenly matched in looks, education, and financial prospects. We met a few times before agreeing to get married. But we didn't have a romance until after we were married. Even then it took a few months for us to become comfortable with one another."

"You and Kirit uncle get along well, from what I've seen."

"It took about a year for me to realize I cared for him," Bijal said. "Kirit doesn't tell me his feelings for me, but he shows me, always has. He is kind, supportive, and loyal. He's a good father and husband. Love is secondary."

It seemed so clinical and detached, yet they seemed secure and content. The few times Nikki had been with Jay's parents, she'd noticed that they were in sync. Unlike her own. Devon and Tara seemed more like friendly acquaintances. "How did you do it? Make the marriage work for this long? I mean, you and Kirit uncle seem happy," she asked. She knew it was a personal question but couldn't help asking.

Bijal sipped her coffee. "We are. Kirit doesn't talk about his feelings, but he does say that once we made the decision, that was it. There was no other option than to commit to building a life together, raising our children. It was that mindset that helped us with decisions like where to live, when to buy a house, when to have a child. We also did things together to get to know one another as people. I used to go watch horror movies even though I hated them, I did that for him. It took a few years of feeling comfortable before I stopped going with him. And he used to go bowling with me. Then it changed to us doing things separately and then we had different topics of conversation. Now, I would like to ask you a sensitive question, Nikita."

Nikki held her breath.

"I haven't been able to reach your mother," Bijal said. "I've called and messaged. Is there something I should know? Does she disapprove of Jay as a match for you?"

"Of course not! She likes Jay and she's always been the kind of mom who lets me decide what's best for me. She gets like this when she's preoccupied with a scientific issue." Nikki felt bad for exaggerating. "I'll make sure she reaches out. And like I said, planning and all this isn't her thing. My sister is also helping, I'll have her reach out to you as well."

Bijal leaned over and patted Nikki's arm. "I don't want to upset you. But there has been some talk. Kirit knows one of your father's golfing friends. It seems that your father's business partners' wives are sending him food. Tara is not at home?"

Nikki had forgotten how people knew each other in their small community. Secrets were hard to keep, especially around Bijal auntie, who knew almost everyone in the Greater Boston area Indian American community. "My mom hasn't been feeling well, so she's away getting rest. I'd really like for us to keep it in the family. Now that we're also going to be related." Another exaggeration, this one bordering on an outright lie.

"I see. Tara did seem off during our dinner. I hope she gets well soon," Bijal said. "The engagement party is less than a month from now. Should we talk centerpieces and flowers?"

Nikki had never been more grateful for a reprieve.

CHAPTER FOURTEEN

Newton, Massachusetts, 1989

Two large suitcases and four boxes. That was everything she owned. There were no tokens or mementos. She'd taken down the empowerment quotes and posters of Einstein and Marie Curie a long time ago, when she'd moved into her freshman dorm. Her small room had been converted for guests. For the few months before the wedding, she hadn't fully moved back in. What would be the point?

She was nervous, scared, and sad but tried to stay positive. Keep your eyes on the prize; she recalled the old poster on the closet door that she'd used for motivation as she'd studied for her SATs. That's what she needed to do; this was one step.

"Hey, almost done?"

Devon stood at the threshold of her bedroom door. She'd never had a boy in here, yet this stranger was ready to carry her things to his house, his room. Not a stranger, her husband. "Doing one last sweep."

"This is cute," he said. "My room, I mean ours, is bigger at my parents' house."

It was still awkward between them, so she pointed to a taped box he could carry down to the car.

She was now his wife, not that she knew what that would mean. She'd been trained in all that was required in this new role, from cooking to cleaning. She'd been given lectures on behaving respectfully toward Devon's parents and relatives.

She'd listened to all the lessons but refused to give them any weight. This would be temporary, and she would do her part. She would miss this year because the wedding had been scheduled for after the start of the semester. In a year, she and Devon would move into their own apartment, and she would be in her first year at MIT. She didn't hide the small smile on her face because there was no one to see her. Both her parents and Devon's were downstairs in the living room while Tara packed her things.

She sat on the edge of her bed, her hand atop her most precious box, the one containing her physics and astronomy books. Faded from her turning the pages. It was finally happening. In a few years, she would be Dr. Tara Rajput. She didn't know how Devon would react, but for now she wasn't going to legally change her name to take his. Her diplomas would match from bachelor's to master's to PhD. Professionally, she had her own identity. Her success would be hers alone, not the Parekh family's. Every paper she authored would be in her birth name.

Devon came back. "What's in there?"

"Books," she said. "From undergrad. I don't want to be behind when I start next fall."

"Right," he said. "I married a brainiac. Go figure."

She didn't like that description. She preferred the simple moniker of scientist. "I can bring this down if you want to take the suitcases."

He nodded and grabbed both black Samsonites.

Her marriage would be worth it. Her father always said that to get something, you had to give something. She would put up with Devon's goofiness and rough edges. As long as he was respectful and supported her, everything would work out between them. Tara had sacrificed love to have a profession. She had a passion for atoms, energy, gases, and mass. It fulfilled her in ways that romance would not. If she occasionally thought of Ben, that was fine. She wouldn't let thoughts of him overwhelm her. Tara nurtured the slight pang she felt whenever she thought of that one night under the stars. It allowed her to know that she had a heart that not only beat for survival but was capable of feeling.

Devon was attractive, though she didn't feel that spark and wasn't drawn to him. She rubbed her wrist, worried about tonight. They would share a bed, and she wasn't ready to take it further yet. She didn't know where he was when it came to sex, but . . .

"Okay, all set. Just the last box you're holding."

She stared at him and knew she needed to say something. "Devon, um . . . your room. We're going to share a bed and I'm . . . I want us to get to know each other better."

He sat next to her. "Yeah. Me too. It's fine. I'm not going to force you or anything."

She exhaled. Relief relaxed her. "Thank you."

"I'm not a bad guy," he said. "It's going to work out."

She nodded and stayed at the edge of the bed, unable to push herself to her feet to leave.

"If . . . uh, if it matters," he continued. "I haven't before. With anyone else."

She didn't care if he had but liked that in this he was as shy as she. "Me neither."

"We'll figure it out," he said.

She liked that he was seeing them as a team. "We will. Did everything fit in the minivan?"

"Yup," he said. "My dad is an expert at loading the car. Ready?"

She nodded and, with determination, Tara stood, grabbed her precious box, and followed him out of the room that would never again be hers.

She was not as fearful and almost looked forward to getting to know her husband better. If he saw her as a partner and not a servant, there was hope for them to have a happy life. She dreamed of living in the lab, them hanging their matching white coats on the hooks in their future home and chatting about their day. With one last look at her room, she said a silent goodbye to the young girl who had lived so quietly. She was ready for her future.

CHAPTER FIFTEEN

If someone loves you, let them.
—*YNLIN*

Jamaica Plain, Massachusetts, present

Nikki's eyes were so tired from looking at lists that she was starting to see double. She closed her laptop and rubbed her temples. One thing she'd learned in the last month was that she hated event planning. She would rather conduct a financial audit for an insurance company than decide what to feed people while considering more than a dozen dietary restrictions. And everyone thought Indian food was easy.

Jay came in, sweaty from his run. "Done?"

She wanted to throw the candle near her arm at him. "We're having three kinds of spinach. Palak and potatoes for the dairy free. Palak paneer for vegetarians. And palak chicken for the nonveg who are also lactose intolerant. This is a nightmare. Hope you enjoyed your run while I was cross-checking how many gluten-free guests we will need to feed."

He rubbed her shoulders from behind. "I voted for the beach."

She twisted away from him. "Walk away right now." She had tried to involve him, hoping that maybe if she was enthusiastic, he would become interested. Instead, Jay would throw out unrealistic options, make a joke, or tell Nikki it was up to her.

She ignored whatever he muttered as he went into the bedroom to shower in the en suite bathroom. Tired, she lay on her side on the sofa. With work, planning this event, dealing with Jay's mom and dad, who wanted to be part of every decision, and managing her own parents, who would talk to Nikki only one-on-one and still refused to discuss their divorce, she was ready for all this to be over.

Tara had moved into a hotel for a bit after she announced to Nikki and Heena that she was leaving Devon. But after a direct talk wherein Nikki explained that she needed her mother to be there for her, Tara had moved back into the house. She and Devon were in separate rooms, but it worked to quiet the gossip. Nikki had also noticed a few changes in Tara, such as when she'd caught her mother singing two weeks ago. An oldie from the nineties. She had paused to make sure that sound was coming from her mom, then seen the smile on her mother's face. And all Tara was doing was peeling potatoes. Last week, Tara had stopped by Nikki's to help with the centerpieces after spending an entire day at a spa, which was not an activity Nikki had ever imagined her doing.

For as long as Nikki could remember, Tara had had one haircut: long, parted in the middle, and curly. Her mom usually wore it in a bun. But now Tara wore a bouncy layered bob. With bangs. Nikki was too shocked to comment. But if Tara's newfound lightness helped her and Devon stay in the same house, she wasn't going to interfere and accidentally upend whatever was going on.

Fresh from the shower, Jay sat on the other end of the sofa and pulled her legs over his lap. "Just think, a week from now, it'll be over."

"Did you pick up the kurta vest from your parents? Or are you going to get ready there?" It had taken her two hours to find one in the exact shade of her lengha.

"My mom probably has it. You're too wound up, relax. It's all handled."

She closed her eyes and prayed for patience.

For tonight, she would let it all go. She didn't want to argue with him; instead she and Jay got up and went into the kitchen. He began slicing cucumbers, and she cuffed his wrist to stop the knife from clacking against the cutting board. "Let me do that."

He leaned over and kissed the side of her head. "Don't slice off a finger."

"Fine, you finish." Nikki grabbed the lemons from the fridge, along with the smoked salmon.

"No, I was joking." He handed her the knife again.

Nikki tried to shake off the irritation. "Did I tell you my mom bought a new sari for the party? It's purple, which is my dad's favorite color."

"Hmm." Jay turned his back to her and stirred something on the stove.

"I'm just happy she's going to be there. She gave Heena a list of the things we must bring to present to your family too. She's coming around."

"Good for her," Jay said.

She kept chopping. "Oh, and her sari matches my dad's vest. Heena and Caleb will also match. Your parents too. Complementary colors, too, so we'll all look good together."

"Can we not talk about this?" Jay said.

"I'm making conversation."

"There are a thousand other topics," he said.

"Why do you get so annoyed whenever I bring up the party? It's yours too," she said.

"I don't want to fight," he said.

"This is a discussion." Nikki took two plates from the cabinet. "I want to know."

He said nothing.

"You proposed. This is all part of it."

He sighed. "I made it clear that I wasn't into all the ceremony stuff, but okay, I'm going along with it. And I'm glad you're excited and happy. I'm on board. Honest. Yellow vest and all."

"Then what's the problem?"

"If I tell you," Jay said, "you're not allowed to get angry."

She made an X across her chest.

"This last month, you've been busy with your work and this party. Fine, I get that. But the hardest part has been watching you take on everything that's going on with your parents."

"They're in a tough spot. My mom's going through something."

"And you don't have to fix it for them. Cut the cord," he said. "Your parents are grown-ups, so are you. You let what your mom's going to think determine whether you should do something or not. It's like you live for her sometimes."

"If your parents were in this position, you would do the same," Nikki said.

"No. I'd check in on them, but I wouldn't call them five times a day." Jay added the diced cukes to a bowl. "I've watched you cajole Tara auntie into being involved with our engagement. You run every detail by her, and you're constantly watching what you say, how you say it. You shouldn't have to walk on eggshells with your own mother."

"That's a bit of an exaggeration." That was not what she was doing. Jay didn't know what it was like to have a mom like Tara.

"You don't like roses," he said. "What's going to be in the middle of every table? A vase of roses."

"They're red and a symbol of love," she said. "Your mom likes them too."

"But you don't," he said. "That's my point."

"It's called compromise," she said. "Not everything is about us. It's a family event."

"I knew I shouldn't have said anything." Jay tore open the package of salmon and added slices to their plates before dishing out the salad.

"No, I'm glad you did," she argued. "It's good to know that you would put yourself first over family."

"No, I am trying to put us first. Us." He served their food and added olives only to his plate. "I want you to enjoy this, that's all. You're pretending. That's what I don't like. This stopped being about the two of us after the dinner at Ostra."

She grabbed her plate and a fork and sat on a stool. "Yes, there are times I am accommodating our families, but I'm also doing the same for you. I ask what you want and you say you're good with my decisions."

"I told you what I wanted. Maui." He nudged her shoulder with his as they sat side by side at the counter. "Am I getting tricolored barfi? And cashews? Because that is a must."

She smiled. "You know that's all food coloring. There is no difference in the taste."

He put his hand on his chest and gasped in exaggerated shock.

She laughed. "And the bar is going to be stocked with your favorite beer."

"I just hope that yellow goes with the undertones of my skin," he said. "I want to look good in the pictures."

"Do you even know what that means?"

He laughed. Put his arm around her and kissed the side of her forehead. She popped a tomato in his mouth. He gave her a wink. Their discussion was over.

"Shut off your brain and eat." Jay pointed to her plate with his fork.

"Don't tell me what to do." She took a big bite.

"Always and forever."

CHAPTER SIXTEEN

Andover, Massachusetts, 1990

Daughter to daughter-in-law. Woman to wife.

Tara existed, reliving the same day over and again. The frenzy of pre- and postwedding activities was over, and she'd settled into a different routine these last five months. Space and time were now bent in a way that made her feel like she was in an unending time loop. In the morning, she made chai, laid out nasto for her in-laws, and filled a thermos for Devon to take to work. She cleaned the kitchen. Prepared a hot lunch for her in-laws and a tiffin for her father-in-law to drop off for Devon. With the few hours she had to herself in the afternoon while her mother-in-law watched soap operas, Tara would review her textbooks and anticipate the future when she would be on campus. Around four thirty, Tara would start making a full Gujarati dinner: dal, shaak, bhat, and fresh rotli, cooked only when her in-laws and Devon had taken their seats at the table. Each round, flat bread, generously brushed with ghee, served to them on demand. They ate their fill; only then did she cook the last two for herself before starting her own meal while the three were almost done.

Afterward, she would clear the table and do all the dishes because, as with most Indian American homes, the machine was reserved for special occasions, like after a large dinner party. Once the kitchen was clean, she would join them for an evening in front of the television.

They liked sitcoms over drama, watching others live vastly more interesting lives than their own. She would retreat into her thoughts. Quantum theory, colliders, particles, Tara would review the articles she'd studied. Retreating into her head became Tara's salvation. In her thoughts, she didn't have to accept the reality of her present. In her mind, she wasn't stuck or stagnant, but a change agent who wanted to understand the universe.

During undergrad, Tara had thought she would focus on unifications of particles, but lately she was becoming interested in dark matter and dark energy. The invisible over the visible. Like her existence. She would stay in this constant for six more months. Another sacrifice toward her goal. She'd mentioned MIT to Devon a few times as she prepared her financial aid forms. He'd nodded along. The only thing that made it bearable was that Devon had finally talked to his parents and let them know that she and he would move closer to Boston by late summer.

At least Tara had grown to like Devon. He was different, gregarious and quick to laugh, even-tempered and nice to his parents. He had a lot of friends and cousins, who had welcomed Tara into their social circle. It was awkward because she didn't enjoy being out every weekend, but she knew compromise was important, so she would go along, at least until the start of her semester.

When it came to sex, he'd let her set the pace. He wasn't demanding or demonstrative. Mostly he was comfortable with routine, a creature of habit, and he was determined to be successful for himself. He and his two closest friends from dental school, Kiran and Hiten, often talked about having their own practice. Their wives, Hetal and Shefali, were nice but satisfied with being homemakers who looked forward to motherhood.

Tara stayed in touch with Mayuri, even though her friend had moved to Los Angeles to pursue documentary filmmaking. Tara was excited for her, but selfishly, she wished her friend wasn't so far away. Even though there were more people in her life than ever before, Tara didn't have anyone to lean on or confide in. Sometimes, not too often, she would dial Ben's number, but not the last digit, just to remind herself that night had been real. It made her feel better when she let herself believe that whenever he looked up at the stars, he would think of her.

"Tara, beta. Do you like this show?" Devon's mother asked.

"It's good." She nodded absentmindedly.

His parents were as talkative as Devon. There was nonstop chatter about other family members, work drama, and general stuff. His mother, Varsha, thrived on gossip and spent most of her days on the phone. His father liked to lecture and guide, telling Tara the optimal ways to do anything from auto repair to gardening. They didn't talk to each other. It was like the way Tara had grown up. No intelligent discourse, merely retelling of stories and cataloging of daily events. There was little in terms of meaningful conversations. Devon didn't confide in his parents regarding his worries or anything personal. He discussed career-related topics.

Once they all retired to their rooms for the night, Devon would chat with her about stuff he didn't discuss with his parents. Tara now knew which of his friends was planning to break up with his secret girlfriend, stories from past parties, and everything else that was on his mind. Tara listened with one ear. He didn't expect her to join in, and she didn't have an active life or a past that would be of interest to him. She'd spent most of her college years in labs and the observatory. He never asked her about her day or what she'd read. He often told her physics was boring or wondered how much a physicist made.

Like matter, they coexisted.

"I have some awesome news." Devon took off his watch and put it on the nightstand. It was a Movado, a gift from his parents when he got his DDS. It was also what his friends had, the same white gold with a black face and a single silver dot.

Tara closed the book she was reading, her back against the wooden headboard of their bed, her knees up. She wrapped her arms around them. "Okay." It was likely something about getting on a list for a private party or a guys' trip to Atlantic City. She hoped for the latter because then she could have a few days to herself. Maybe she could stay with her parents while he was gone. No one would bother her there.

"Our loan was approved," Devon said. "Hiten, Kiran, and I are going to get our own practice. Earlier than we thought, DHK Dental Associates is finally going to be real."

Tara was surprised. Last she'd heard, they'd discussed a five-year plan. "I didn't know you had already applied."

"I'm sure I mentioned it." He waved her off as he came out of the bathroom, the faint smell of toothpaste lingering. "It was a few weeks ago. Remember when I asked you to get all the papers together, taxes, bank statements, and your own accounts?"

"Right. I thought it was for my financial aid stuff." She had given him all the information except about the one account that was just hers. A secret from even her parents. One where she saved birthday and Diwali cash, her earnings from her campus job, and money from returned textbooks. She'd opened it in high school. Her own savings she'd kept secret. It was Tara's safety net. That was why she had been filing her own taxes since age eighteen. The total was up to ten thousand dollars with interest, and it made her feel secure.

"You know I never planned to stay in my job for long, we talked about it from before we got married. I hate working for a franchise. There's more money in private practice. It's something the three of us have been planning since our UConn days."

Yes, Tara was aware. It was his biggest ambition. "I'm happy for you." His independence could lead to hers in the sense that they might be able to move out on their own sooner. "Congratulations."

He patted her on the shoulder as he passed her, then jumped into bed next to her. It was such an annoying habit. Like he was a child. Why couldn't he simply slide in on his side without making the whole bed shake? At least he wasn't very affectionate, which was a relief. Give and take, she reminded herself. He'd been good in respecting her requests around sex. They'd waited a month. Then it had been a simple "Do you want to?" from him and an "I guess" from her. After all, it was what separated friendship from marriage. Now it was a weekly occurrence, in the dark, and with as much silence as possible because his parents' bedroom was separated from theirs only by a small shared bathroom in the middle.

It wasn't bad, the sex. Not that Tara had a basis of comparison. She didn't consider herself a sexual person; she didn't yearn or pant like some women she knew. Occasionally Tara would remember the touch of Ben's hand, the brush of his lips, and something would stir at the bottom of her belly. It helped when she wanted it to be over quickly. If she needed a cuddle after Devon turned away from her, she would bunch up the side of her comforter. Tonight, however, was not Thursday, so she was under her own blanket, and he was under his. Which meant a better night's sleep.

"We're going to go look at some sites this weekend," Devon continued.

Tara tuned back in. She'd become used to Devon's running commentary and knew that if she didn't pay some attention, he would get frustrated. It was her wifely duty to listen and acknowledge. She'd read that in a gag wedding gift from Mayuri—a book from the 1950s that was an instruction manual on how to be a good wife.

"That's great," Tara said.

"An agent has a list of places that might work for the practice," Devon said.

His words broke through her thoughts. "I can come along." It would be nice to get away from his parents for a few hours. Whenever she could take time for herself and spend a few hours at Barnes & Noble, her mother-in-law frowned and passive-aggressively made her displeasure known to Tara.

"I . . . um . . . it's just us guys," he said. "None of the wives are coming."

"Right, it's just that when you said we—"

"No, yeah," he cut her off. "I didn't mean to, like, I should have been more specific. But for sure, once we have a place, we'll get you girls together and do the puja and stuff. Our parents too."

He fumbled for words. But Tara knew that this was another reminder that she was an appendage to his life, one that was necessary because society deemed it so. He didn't see her as anything other than the person he'd chosen to take care of his needs, support his decisions, and stay where he put her. Necessary, but not useful, like a pinkie toe.

She nodded.

He was quiet for a few minutes. "We want something closer to Boston. It would be good to go where there are more people. Andover has too many dentists anyway."

A burst of excitement fluttered in her chest. "Where are you looking?"

"Somerville, Cambridge, Arlington area," he said.

"That's amazing." Tara clasped her hands. It was finally happening. "If we move near there, it'll be an easier commute to MIT. Especially if we move near the T." The tiredness from the monotony of her day faded, and she thought about their own apartment. He would work; she would be on campus. They could finally start their life. This was why she'd gone through with the seven circles around a fire that tied her to Devon for life.

"Oh, right," he said. "MIT."

She turned her head to look at him propped up on pillows next to her. "Yeah. We can get a one-bedroom apartment, even if it's not on the bus line. I won't mind." She would be willing to walk a few miles each way if it meant they would be on their own.

"No, yeah," he said. "I just think, well, it's going to be tight, you know, financially. The first year of the practice, I don't know how much of a salary I'll be able to draw."

Tara kept her face neutral. "I can apply for loans. And we can get something affordable. We can cut down on eating out and other unnecessary expenses."

"Except it'll be harder to get another loan when I have the business one," he said. "It doesn't make sense to add more debt."

He was wavering, and fear settled in her chest. "I can take one out myself. Keep our finances separate."

"That won't work," he said. "We're married, and if we share income, then we share debt."

"I don't understand." Tara tried to keep her voice from shaking. "We agreed."

"We did. You can still go back to school, but maybe in a couple of years," he said. "Honestly, once I get established, you can do whatever you want."

"Not whatever. I'm getting my PhD," she said. "If I don't use my deferral in the next two years, I'll have to reapply. And chances for admission become more difficult."

"The thing is," Devon said. "You don't need one. I mean, I'll be making money, so you won't need to work."

"That's not why." She put her hand on her heart to calm the rapid beat.

"It's unnecessary, Tara," Devon said. "I mean you don't need to impress anyone with a big degree. And my doctorate is going to give us a better return than yours."

"You get to pursue your dream," she whispered. "Not me."

"This isn't my dream," he said. "It's a profession. I fix people's teeth so we can be well off, not have to struggle like our parents did. You should be happy about this. Shefali and Hetal are planning to help in the office initially, office manager stuff. You can do that, too, if you want something to keep you busy. It'll be a group effort. In a few years, we'll be solid financially. Until then, I'll support us by staying in my current job while we have a steady client base. We can also keep saving by living here for a couple of years. Then we'll buy a house instead of renting, especially for when we have kids."

With each word, each sentence, the future she imagined for herself floated further away from her. This was not the agreement between them. She'd believed Devon when he'd told her he supported her. Instead, he'd betrayed her. *First get married. Then you can do what you want.* Her parents had said it so many times once she'd told them she'd been accepted to a graduate program. She'd believed them too. She'd thought it was the right path, the only one.

She'd done everything they'd asked of her. She'd let them find her a husband. She'd gone along with moving in with Devon's parents. She'd trusted that they would keep their promises. "We agreed. You were supportive. You know how much I want to keep studying. It's the only thing I asked from you."

Her need wasn't about ego or to impress anyone. Tara lived an unassuming life. She wasn't the type to be noticed. And while she never wanted to be onstage or the center of attention, Tara wanted to matter, leave her mark on this world. She wanted to contribute to the field of physics that would shape future understanding. Her dream was big, though not for fame or fortune. She wasn't looking to be the next Marie Curie, she merely wanted to publish a theoretical paper in a well-regarded journal. Something future physicists could refer to in a citation. This man, the one she had chosen to rely on, was taking that away from her.

"I know girls have to say that before marriage to show that they're smart," Devon said. "Then after, it's on the man to make it so they don't have to work. I'll take care of you and our future family, so you don't have to worry."

She didn't know why he'd chosen her. She'd never asked. Tara turned away from him to hide her tears. She hadn't cared about his reasons. Anger, frustration, helplessness, and now guilt stirred inside her. Her hands trembled and her chest ached. It was all slipping away. And she didn't know how to save herself or her future.

Tara shut down, locked herself up. She'd worked so hard to get accepted into MIT. Now she was an unnecessary appendage. Pinkie toe. That's what she'd become.

"Don't sulk," he said. "I'm not saying no, but right now, we have to focus on getting the practice set up."

He thought she was throwing a tantrum. The fact that Devon couldn't understand the pain he was inflicting on her furthered her resolve to stay still. She resolved to never trust his word again. She'd been prepared to make a life with him on the promise of mutual ambition. Six months into their marriage, she'd learned that he would never be someone she could love.

"Tara, I know you're upset," he said. "You'll feel better tomorrow. We can discuss it in a few years. If not MIT, there are other schools you can go to if you want."

Tara scooched down, folded her blanket into a mound to hug it close. Then reached up to turn off the lamp on her side. He'd lied. So had her parents. Her life wouldn't start after marriage. It would end.

CHAPTER SEVENTEEN

Your yes can be someone's no, and that's okay.
—*YNLIN*

Bedford, Massachusetts, present

Several hundred people mingled at a rented-out Indian restaurant in the Boston suburb of Bedford, not far from the trail carved by the minutemen of the Revolutionary War over two hundred years ago. The high-pitched clarinet from the speakers mingling with the volume of the conversations made Nikki's nerves more frazzled. For over an hour, Nikki had been led around by Jay, who'd introduced her to his large extended family, most of whose names and relationships to Jay she would never remember, even with her favorite technique of creating an acronym around the name. It started well with Karan who was CCK for "California cousin Karan." After the fiftieth person, though, Nikki's brain rebelled and decided it was officially over the alphabet and its limit of twenty-six letters.

Once she'd met everyone from his side and greeted the guests from her side, she and Jay were led to the center of the room, where a small portable firepit was set atop a stack of red bricks. There were pallets on the floor holding red-and-gold silk cushions. Nikki, dressed in a pale-yellow sari, was helped into the low chair by Heena so as not to step on the pleats and have the whole thing unwrap. As the maharaj performed the ceremony in Sanskrit, Nikki executed the rituals as ordered. Offering a coconut marked with red kumkum powder, draping a floral haar around the framed photo of the gods Ram and Laxmi, and performing other tasks that ushered in blessings for both her and Jay.

Nikki's focus was not on Jay, but on her parents, who were to the right of her. Her mom looked beautiful in a purple sari and a diamond necklace with matching earrings. Her father was dressed in a purple silk kurta with a silver vest. She was grateful that they were standing together, united, even if it was for show. Her parents were a stark contrast to Jay's. His parents were more regal as they displayed their status with ornate gold jewelry and Rolex watches. It was an obvious ploy to display the caste disparity between Nikki's and Jay's families. Nikki hadn't paid attention to any of those things. They were terrible holdovers from previous generations. And Jay's stance was very much against inequality of any kind. He preferred off-the-rack suits for court. His favorite items in his closet were his cargo shorts and baseball cap.

When they'd walked in, Jay had complained about how unnecessary it was, but he'd gone along with Nikki's need to please their families. As she sat across from him, the small fire for the gods between them, she appreciated his casual elegance and the way Jay carried himself. In his three-piece suit, he was so handsome that she lost her breath. In her kitchen, with bare feet and backward cap, he was accessible. In this setting, she saw another side of him. Here he was formal, reserved.

Nikki had been so focused on her problems and issues that she'd forgotten to consider him. Okay? she mouthed to him. Jay winked and gave her a tight smile. If she hadn't been paying attention, she would infer that he was fine, but now Nikki wondered. How much of his laid-back, low-key approach to life was natural, and how much of it was an act to get through the moment?

The priest asked Jay to tie a red thread around Nikki's wrist, a precursor to the one that he would tie at their wedding ceremony. It felt snug even though it wasn't, as if a cuff were now attached to her.

Binding her to him. Her heart wouldn't settle as she suffocated in the crowd and the noise. The heat from the fire made her lightheaded.

Jay said her name. She snapped her eyes back to his. He took a deep breath, then asked her to do the same. She matched him. Breath for breath until she was steady again. Together, they showered Ganesh with rice, kumkum, water, and flowers in worship to bless the occasion. They repeated the Sanskrit phrases and prayed.

"We've finished with the Ganesh puja," the maharaj called out to Jay's and Nikki's parents. "What gifts will be presented?"

On cue, Tara turned to Heena and a few of Nikki's cousins, who held stacks of red boxes tied with gold ribbons in various sizes. Tara took them one by one for the priest's blessing, then offered them to Jay's mom. The symbols of an evolving tradition of dowries from the bride's family to the groom's. Once the gifts were distributed, Bijal brought out two small red velvet boxes and presented them to the maharaj, who blessed them with splashes from a wet betel leaf, presented them to the small statues of Ganesh, Ram, and Sita, then returned them to Jay's mother.

She then presented the flat, square box, opened, to show the attendees the collar necklace of diamonds and 24K gold being given to welcome Nikki into a family of wealth and status. The second box was small. Jay's mom handed it to Jay, who opened it toward Nikki.

It was the biggest and brightest emerald she had ever seen. So clear she could see the purity from four feet away. The rectangular beveled stone would cover her finger from knuckle to base. The gem was set in step-cut facets on a thick gold band. Jay held it out for Nikki's hand.

She felt the cool band slide up to the base of her ring finger. The ring was simple and heavy, gaudy in its size. Uncomfortable, she could imagine it getting caught in sweaters and blankets. She wouldn't be able to have full function of her left hand while wearing this ring, and it was not one she would choose for herself. It was loose, as her fingers were smaller than the band. She'd never been much of a jewelry person, preferring only her smartwatch and a thin gold chain with a small N that rested between her collarbones. This didn't feel like her, and she was relieved that when Jay let go, the ring slid down. Luckily Jay caught it in the palm of his hand. Nikki let out the breath she'd been holding.

"It's too big," Bijal said.

"It's fine," Devon said. "We can get it resized."

Nikki saw the worry in Bijal's eyes. "If anyone has a bandage," Heena offered, "I can loop it around and secure it until we adjust it."

"That's not possible," Bijal said. "We can't alter it in any way, it's an heirloom that has been in our family for hundreds of years."

"Then why offer?" Tara asked. "Or was it that you wanted to show off?"

Nikki couldn't hide the shock on her face quickly enough. She glanced at Heena, who was just as surprised by their mother's comment.

"It's fine," Nikki said quickly, recovering. "It's not meant for every day anyway. It is a lovely ring, Bijal auntie. You're right, it should stay as it is."

"It's Nikki's now," Jay chimed in. "She and I will figure it out. For now, the bandage Heena suggested will work. Let's get through the pictures."

"Beta, we can't take the risk," Bijal said. "I can keep it with me for now."

"It's an engagement," Jay argued. "Nikki is the most responsible person in this room. The ring is safe with her."

Nikki tried to catch Jay's eyes to tell him to let it go. Right now, the rest of the guests were not paying attention to the ceremony, busy with drinks, appetizers, and conversation. Though it was only her, Jay, the two sets of parents, the maharaj, and Heena in the tight circle, if things became heated, their guests would become curious and pay attention. "Jay, please," she said. It would take only one auntie to notice the tension and make it known.

"This is not a big deal." Devon stepped forward. "They have those inserts; we can pick one up at CVS on the way home. See? Problem solved!"

"I'm going to put it away for now." Bijal grabbed the ring from Nikki's finger. "Let's finish this up."

The maharaj argued that the ring had been blessed, so if they switched it, the next one would need the same treatment. Jay's dad assured the priest that it would all be taken care of while Bijal put the box in her purse.

"What's the point of an engagement ceremony without a ring?" Jay loosened the knot of his tie.

Nikki reached for his hand while stuck in her chair. "It's okay," she whispered.

"We went through all this, weeks of planning, bickering, for what?" Jay reached for Nikki's hand but kept his eyes on his mother. "I told you a dozen times that I would buy a ring for Nikki, but you insisted that it had to be done this way."

Nikki squeezed his hand, then tugged. He looked down at her, then sighed and let go.

"The drama. I am here for it." Heena inserted herself into the conversation.

Nikki reached both arms out. "I can't get up. Help me before my sari catches on fire from the puja."

Jay reached down and grabbed Nikki's arm, hoisting her from the low chair. She leaned into him and put the flat of her hand against his chest. "It's okay."

He nodded, then glanced at his mother.

Nikki moved around him and took hold of Jay's hand. "Let's get something to drink, we're all overheating from the fire." She led him toward the bar.

They found a private corner and asked for water. She handed a glass to Jay. "Is your tie too snug?"

He finally smiled, and she could see his shoulders relax. "A little. I'm also not a fan of the vest."

Nikki rested her head on his shoulder. "In two hours, we'll be home. This outfit is beautiful but so heavy. I'm ready to get out of it."

"I can't wait to unwrap you."

She laughed and stroked his cheek. "This is held together with a dozen safety pins. Your fantasy isn't going to work out the way you think."

"Oh, how you underestimate me."

His parents interrupted them with Kirit uncle leading Jay away to talk to his friends. Nikki turned to rest her elbows on the bar. It was mostly over. The buffet was being laid out, soon people would stuff themselves and then head to their cars. Nikki ordered a glass of wine and went in search of her parents. She found her father among her uncles, laughing while munching on a pakora.

Then she spotted Tara, in a heated conversation with Bijal. A few aunties were inching closer, straining to hear. Nikki moved to intervene.

CHAPTER EIGHTEEN

Newton, Massachusetts, 1993

The arrival of her second child sealed Tara's fate. The pregnancy had been a surprise, thanks to failed birth control. She hadn't wanted children but had given in to Devon's wishes for one and had given birth to Heena. That pregnancy had been awful, and she'd decided to never spend another nine months in that kind of physical agony ever again. Then Tara had found herself pregnant again. And as Devon and his parents were overjoyed with hope for a boy, Tara had carried this child with numb indifference. This sealed her fate. She knew she would never be able to make peace with Devon's original betrayal. Each fall, when students started another year, Tara's pain would deepen; her heart would become more bitter. She would live with it, have to, because now she had two daughters.

She would smile, but there would be no joy, no contentment, no happiness. When she'd gotten pregnant with Heena, she'd been scared and worried, but Devon had shown her that he cared. He'd found them a home so that she didn't suffocate with her overattentive mother-in-law. He worked hard and still managed to care for her. Tara had softened toward him. Now, she felt the impossibility of it all. She would never be able to escape or live a life of her own.

Devon loved Heena, he was a good father who was attentive to their baby. Instead of weekends partying with his friends, their life now revolved around family gatherings. In brief spurts, Tara accepted that it wasn't all bad. She'd asked him to be okay with having only one child. She didn't want to go through another pregnancy. He'd agreed. Fate had other plans, and now Tara, once an aspiring physicist, spent her days in weighted exhaustion among never-ending diaper changes, sleep trainings, potty trainings, and laundry. The early days of her marriage had been easy compared to what she now endured.

She'd lost her ability to think, couldn't remember when she'd last gone to the library or opened a book. The shackles of marriage were light compared to the chains of motherhood. The idea of going back to school felt so far away she didn't know if it had all been a mirage. In the last few years, she'd forgotten more physics than she'd learned in the whole of her life.

Devon, on the other hand, became more driven, obsessed with wealth and success. He wanted to provide a luxurious life for his daughters. He used possessions as a measure of how well he was doing. He exchanged his Toyota Camry for an Audi. His Movado watch had company with Rado and Omega. To fund all this, he worked six days a week. On Sundays, he golfed. His time with his daughters was precious. She saw a new side as Devon became attentive toward his daughters. With Heena and Nikki, he was a present father. At first, Tara was relieved to not have to be the main parent; however, she vowed to ensure that her daughters learned to be independent, nontraditional.

A few days earlier, in the middle of the night, as Nikki suckled on her breast, she'd dialed that last digit of Ben's phone number. He'd faded in her memory, but at times she could recall how she'd felt that one time she'd lain next to him under the stars. She'd believed that in letting him go, she was choosing a future that would see her on the other side of the Charles River. His number had been disconnected. She shed silent tears for hours. Hope for what could be was gone.

As she stared out the bay window of their suburban house in Newton, Tara no longer hoped or wanted. She was back in the town where she'd grown up. She'd dreamed of exploring the universe, yet she found herself three miles from her childhood home. It would have to wait for her next life. This one had been decided. Nikki screamed in her arms and Tara paced, bouncing the baby to calm her.

"I wish I could do the same," she whispered to the infant.

She thought about Mayuri. If she'd run away with her instead of getting married, where would she be now? Maybe in Los Angeles with her best friend. Instead, they settled for phone calls once every few months, exchanged birthday cards and letters. Mayuri was living the life she'd dreamed of, and Tara owned that the distance between them was mostly the result of her jealousy of her friend's bravery.

She had no one. Except for a toddler and an infant. And they needed around-the-clock care. Shefali and Hetal always offered to help. They were friendly but not friends. Tara knew that it was out of obligation that they reached out. Her own parents had given her away in marriage and only showed up for milestone events. They did their duty with their initial visit after each birth but often skipped social obligations. Kamla had no interest in being an active grandmother. Devon's mother would bring food but only his favorites. She'd never been asked if she liked bhakri shaak or aandhvo. She didn't. Tara wanted only soup. And had enough energy only to open a can of Campbell's.

Tara turned away from the window to scan the chaos around her feet in the form of padded toys and blankets. The couch was covered with an old sheet for protection. The coffee table had rings from people not using coasters. The stale stench of baby vomit mixed with the Glade plug-in air freshener. In the reflection of the mirrored wall clock, Tara didn't recognize herself. Her long hair was frizzy, her T-shirt stained.

"It's temporary." That's what well-intentioned people told her. If they only knew.

Her shoulders slumped. Tara hated whom she'd become. Resented her lack of spine, her passiveness, her inability to go after what she wanted.

Nikki slapped her tiny fist into Tara's face. She glanced into her daughter's dark-brown eyes. The same as her own. "I deserve that."

The baby mumbled nonsensically. Tara mustered a bitter laugh. Amused at nothing and everything. At least she didn't hate her daughters. There was some grace in that. It was a statistical probability that biology would take over and a woman's brain would instinctively care for the children she'd birthed. Tara had never wanted children, yet she couldn't deny the love she felt for them. She would protect them, nurture them. "I promise you a different life. You will always live on your terms. You will know to not count on anyone. You will be free."

Tara sank into the couch, cradling Nikki as Heena slept in the playpen next to the coffee table. These two people, who made her cry and weep for her unwanted life, had given Tara the most precious gift. She'd learned what it was to love. She experienced a kind of joy she'd never known when they smiled at her or clung to a finger. There was protectiveness and fear. It was as if her heart now lived outside of her body. With them.

Nikki shoved her pudgy fist into Tara's mouth. Tara pretended to nibble with her lips, then moved the baby hand out of the way. Tara looked from one daughter to another. "I'm going to teach you about Nikola Tesla, Einstein, Curie, and Oppenheimer. I'm going to make sure you are independent, able to choose your own path, and that you will never be an accessory in someone else's life."

Tara felt silly having a conversation with an infant and a sleeping toddler. She put Nikki on her shoulder and patted her back. Once Nikki's head was heavy against her shoulder, Tara slowly lowered her into the small cradle near the playpen.

She looked at both. "I will make sure you don't follow in my footsteps and marry a person who is not worthy of you."

CHAPTER NINETEEN

People pleasing is the biggest barrier to personal freedom.
—*YNLIN*

Bedford, Massachusetts, present

As Nikki walked toward Bijal and Tara, they separated. Nikki followed her mom back to the bar. "Mom, what was that about?"

Tara ignored Nikki. "Rum and Coke, please, with a wedge of lemon."

Her mother never drank more than one glass of wine. "Are you sure that's a good idea?"

"Aren't there other people you want to see? Your friends from school are over there. Spend time with them," Tara said.

It's what Nikki wanted to do, but she couldn't leave her mom alone. Not when Tara was being unpredictable. The knot in Nikki's stomach grew as the bartender served the cocktail her mom had ordered.

"The last time I had one was . . . never mind." Tara stared at the glass in her hand with wonderment. "It was bitter back then and had this smell that made me think of medicine, but I read somewhere that it tastes better with a squeeze of lemon. Like a compound. Atoms and molecules bonded together creating deliciousness." Then she finished the drink in several gulps and ordered another.

The more her mother acted unlike herself, the more Nikki worried. Maybe she was having a medical event of some sort. "Let's go outside and get some fresh air."

"I don't need you to keep me company. This is your party," Tara said. "Go have fun."

"I'm worried about you." Nikki wanted to tug the glass out of her hand. "Were you arguing with Bijal auntie?"

"She hasn't changed in the least. She's offended." Tara waved her hand dismissively. "She wants me to apologize for what I said about her showing off with that ring. She acts as if she's the only descendant of royalty. As if such things matter anyway."

Nikki didn't understand. "It is unlike you. I've never heard you care about these things."

Tara took another swig. "Maybe I do. I overheard her bragging, showing off that gaudy ring to her friends. She was worried about you losing it. Then she makes a fuss because it is so precious she couldn't risk it. It's as if we're still in high school. I had to say something."

Since when? "It doesn't matter to me."

"You deserve so much more. I always believed you were born for a reason. When I first heard you cry, it was loud. When you were born, your first cry was a roar. I knew then that you would be someone who left a mark on this world. You shouldn't have to settle for less. You deserve to be respected. Bijal should be grateful that you are choosing her son, who is not your equal."

Nikki winced. "Jay and I fit well together. Please don't say things like this. He's a good man."

"You can have any life you want." Tara waved her hand around the room. "This is you going backward. It may be fruit and nuts, but the idea of a dowry, a bribe for their son to marry you. That's not you. They should be the ones falling at your feet, instead they're behaving like you can't be trusted with a gemstone."

Just then, Devon approached. "My lovely daughter." He wrapped his arm around Nikki. "And my beautiful wife."

"Hi, Dad. Having fun?" Nikki hugged her father but kept her eyes on Tara.

"Who doesn't enjoy a good party?" Devon signaled the bartender for another drink. "Your mother and I didn't have one, you know."

"We did. You don't remember," Tara said. "It was a small ceremony at your parents' house. Only immediate family. My mother gave you twenty-one saris, gold bangles, and cash. You used the cash for your partial down payment on the building lease for your practice."

"My memory is not great." Devon tapped the side of his forehead.

"I'd love to see pictures," Nikki said. "What color was your sari?"

"I don't remember." Tara looked directly at Devon.

Nikki regretted the line of conversation.

"Let's not do this here," Devon whispered to Tara.

"Because you decide what I do and don't do." Tara didn't back down. "I'm tired of it."

"Mom, let's go get some air." Nikki reached for her mother's hand.

"No." Tara pulled away.

Devon pointed at Tara. "This is not the time or place to make a scene."

Tara shook her head. "I don't have to listen to you anymore. I said I would stay until this party for Nikki. It's over. I'm leaving."

Nikki grabbed her mom's arm. "What does that mean?"

"She's talking nonsense," Devon said. "It's the drinks."

Tara turned to Nikki. Clasped their hands together. "Promise me that you won't lose yourself, that you won't waste your potential."

"Mom, what are you talking about? Where are you planning to go?"

"Tara, let's leave Nikki to enjoy the party," Devon said. "We can say goodbye to our guests and head home."

"No. I am staying. You can go. Besides, they're your friends and family. It's your house," Tara said.

"Mom, stop." Nikki put her hand on Tara's shoulder. "You're upset."

"No." Tara shook her head. "For the first time in a long while, I'm not."

"You're ruining Nikki's evening," Devon said. "I don't understand why you're doing this. I have never treated you poorly. I have provided everything for our girls and you. You've been treating me like I'm your enemy for months now. Whatever you're going through, stop it." Devon finished his drink.

"You're right," Tara said. "I will. This is the end."

Devon left his glass on the bar and walked away. Tara ordered another drink.

"Mom, let's go get some food. It smells great, and I'm starving."

Tara reached up and cupped Nikki's cheek. "You are beautiful. Sometimes it's hard to believe you come from someone as plain as me."

Nikki hugged her mom. "What are you talking about? I take after you." She saw the sadness in Tara's eyes before her mom cleared them. They were the same dark brown as her own. She and Tara shared features—a small nose, the widow's peak that slightly protruded from the hairline, the sharp chin, and ears that stuck out. As a teen, Nikki had hated her ears and thought they made her look like an elf. Now she covered them by wearing her hair down. "Let's go." Nikki led her mom by the elbow. "There is no line at the buffet."

Tara followed.

With plates filled with paneer tikka, saag, tadka dal, and chicken korma, they found a seat at an empty table. After a few minutes of silence, several aunties descended upon them, some relatives and some friends of her parents. Everyone chatted about how great the food was, how pretty Nikki looked, how handsome Jay was, and how they all couldn't wait for the wedding.

"We haven't set a date yet," Nikki responded to an auntie whose name she didn't remember.

"She's been saying that for weeks." Jay's mom took a seat at the round table across from Tara. "Nikki has decided to not even think about the wedding until after the summer. Maybe she has doubts."

"Bijal auntie!" Nikki protested.

"Good," Tara interjected. "Maybe she'll change her mind."

"Mom!"

"It's good that the emerald didn't fit," Bijal said. "Maybe it's a sign."

"No!" Nikki said. "Stop this, both of you, please. I'm not sure what is going on, but Bijal auntie, I love Jay. Mom, Jay and I are going to get married. It's just that we want to enjoy the summer and not stress over all the details."

Nikki looked around the room and spotted Jay. He was relaxed and laughing with a few friends in the corner. She stared long enough to see if he would look her way, see her eyes pleading for rescue. He stayed with his back to her.

"Nikki doesn't need your son," Tara said.

Nikki covered her mom's arm. She didn't want to be in the middle of another battle.

"Jay is a lawyer. He has a kind heart and a sweet disposition," Bijal countered. "Nikki is the one in a career that could go away. Canceled, right? One wrong email or social media post and everything you built could topple. Maybe that's why you were so quick to marry my son after a few months of dating. He has stability."

Tara raised the ante. "Then let's call it off."

"Okay, enough," Nikki said. "None of this is up to you. Mom, stop it. Bijal auntie, I'm not using Jay. We are partners in every aspect of our relationship. I'm sorry that you're suspicious of me, but please know that I would never take advantage of him."

"Then tell your mother to act better," Bijal added. "Show some interest, lift a finger or two in support of your match instead of walking around in judgment and a sour disposition."

Nikki reached for her drink and was disappointed that it was just ice water. "Please, Mom, you need to eat. Have some naan," she said, even though her stomach no longer wanted what was on her plate.

Bijal fixed the pallu of her coral-and-cream silk sari to make sure the pleats were crisp against her bodice. Her hair was done up in a tall, thick bun with little gold pins. The heavy gold necklace and earrings showed the world their wealth. "You should have some naan, Tara. It will soak up the alcohol."

"You should have a drink," Tara replied. "It'll make you less uptight."

Nikki wanted to be anywhere but here. Maybe it had been better when Tara was indifferent. "How about the three of us have lunch next weekend? We can talk it out. You're both upset with each other, but we're all going to be related soon, so let's resolve it all before it gets worse."

"I'm busy," Bijal said.

"So am I," Tara added.

Nikki wanted to rub her face and pretend this was all a fever dream. Except she had on too much makeup and they still had more pictures to take. Whatever midlife crisis her mom was experiencing, Nikki wanted it to be over. "I'm going to find Jay." She got up and left the table. She wanted him to give her a hug. Take her away.

"Having fun?" Heena stepped into her path.

"No," Nikki said. "Mom is buzzed, maybe drunk. First she fought with Dad, now she's bickering with Bijal auntie. Who is she? I regret ever wanting her to be more sociable. Aloof and ambivalent was better."

Heena shrugged. "Hey, these events bring out another side of people. Remember Dad getting trashed at my wedding reception and breakdancing with his bow tie wrapped around his forehead?"

"I'm not having a wedding." And seeing how uncomfortable Jay had been, he would agree. The pins holding her hair back dug into Nikki's scalp. She leaned her head on Heena's shoulder. "Jay will get his wish for a beach in Belize. Make sure your passport isn't expired."

"Oh. We should go zip-lining for your bachelorette's," Heena said. "Caleb's parents can handle the twins."

Nikki laughed. "Thanks. The image of you hanging on for dear life as you slide across the forest is just what I needed."

"You're welcome." Heena hugged Nikki.

Suddenly a scream pierced the air. "NO! It's gone!"

Nikki spun around to see Bijal looking terrified. "The ring! I had it in my purse. It's not in here."

Nikki and Jay both rushed to his mother's side.

"What are you talking about, Mom?" Jay put his hand on Bijal's arm.

She handed him the purse. "The case. I had put it in my purse. Where is it?"

"Did you leave it somewhere?" Jay asked.

Bijal frantically searched the floor. "No, I've been holding my purse. The only time I set it down . . ." Bijal's gaze landed on Tara. "It was her. She stole the ring. I'm sure of it."

Nikki and Heena flanked their mother as Devon came around to the small group. Jay and his father guided everyone toward the back corner, away from the curious eyes of guests. Nikki saw her mother stare curiously, as if she were watching from above instead of an active participant. It wasn't possible. There was no way that her mom, the unassuming, quiet woman, could be a thief.

CHAPTER TWENTY

Newton, Massachusetts, 2000

They survived Y2K. Tara was slightly disappointed that there was no chaos or war as predicted by doomsdayers. All because of a date change in the systems that ran the world. For months it had been the topic of every conversation as the news spoke of a possible apocalypse. Tara didn't believe that the Earth would cease to exist, and she secretly laughed at those who mentioned Nostradamus. It would take another big bang or an asteroid for the planet to be destroyed. She trusted in science. Even though she was no longer a practitioner. Another century. Same life. She'd hoped that in the new millennium, she would be different, but she remained the constant, the control group. There had been discoveries, mainly in technology, but Tara's day-to-day was no different. Though Devon carried around a BlackBerry and he had an email address. For Tara, the new year was merely a reminder of putting a 2 and a 0 instead of a 1 and a 9 in the year whenever she wrote checks.

She was still a wife and mom. The latter she didn't mind as much anymore because Heena and Nikki became her projects. They were out of their toddler years, and the tantrums and helplessness had turned into independence. Yes, there were backtalk and battles over studying, but Tara was up for the challenge. She would make sure her daughters never felt helpless or needed anyone. Her job was to make sure they made their own choices and solved their own problems. She never wanted them to feel obligated to do their duty, stay within the confines of their conservative culture, or marry.

They would not live Tara's life. She was determined to ensure that Heena and Nikki pursued their passions without the burdens of their culture. They would never feel dependent on anyone for anything. They would be stronger than Tara. Her daughters would become successful in their chosen fields. They would experience freedoms Tara hadn't—living on their own, financial independence, self-determination. That would be Tara's contribution now that science was no longer a viable choice. She had given up her own happiness so that Heena and Nikki could thrive.

She would teach them to question everything. Asking why, using the scientific method in life, would build their ability to think critically. It frustrated Devon, there were times when he expected blind compliance. Tara gave him that so the girls could challenge him. Tara was wiring their neural networks to ensure they had the ability to adapt and change.

"Do you have the Manuel Diaz file?" Devon came through the short hallway and into the reception area of their small dental practice.

Tara shuffled the papers on the desk, found the name, and handed the folder to Devon. "Here you go."

"Thanks." Devon barely glanced her way as they swapped manila folders.

So much for graduate school. Her original GMAT scores had expired along with any hope of continuing her education. Every time she'd mentioned to Devon that she was sending out applications, he'd asked her to delay. Again. The dental practice had grown, but Devon and his partners continued to be cost-conscious. The wives still filled in at the office. Instead of being able to pursue her dreams, she was her husband's support staff.

She had lost faith. Even worse, Devon knew it. He openly teased her among his friends about buying textbooks instead of expensive purses. "My wife is a professor, and her only student." Tara didn't argue.

He was right. She hated it, but the runway was getting shorter. Even if she started now, she would be in her late thirties by the time she got her PhD. A job in academia or doing important research? She wouldn't be able to compete after being out of the field for more than a decade.

Tara accepted her linear existence. In this timeline, she added administrator, bookkeeper, and appointment scheduler to the list of roles she played.

"Before you leave, can you organize the paperwork for Hetal?" Devon came to the reception area again. "She's working on insurance billing this evening."

"It's in this box." She pointed to the tray of files. She didn't expect please or thank you. They weren't part of his vocabulary when it came to her.

"And we're having dinner next weekend with Piyush and Anjoli." Devon scanned another file as he prattled on about his younger brother. "I think they're going to announce their engagement. Hopefully, the wedding will be in the fall. We already have a dozen weddings, receptions, garba, Vidhi, and all that through this whole summer."

It was a never-ending cycle. Mother. Maid. Office manager. Wife.

Devon continued to linger near her desk. "Do you need something else?" she asked.

"No," he said. "I was thinking, maybe we could go out to dinner this weekend. There's a new restaurant, a hibachi place. Hiten told me he took Shefali there on a date night."

Tara glanced up. They'd never gone on a date. "We're married."

He laughed. "I'm aware. Just that we don't do anything, just you and me. And Heena can babysit Nikki. Or I can have my mom come over and watch them."

Tara didn't respond, kept her eyes on the black-and-white computer screen. Her mind flashed back to that morning in front of the Charles River. As she and Ben were saying goodbye, she'd silently pleaded with him to ask her out. He hadn't.

Tara glanced up at Devon. They had been together for over a decade, and she saw that he had aged into his looks. At thirty-six, he was attractive. She'd witnessed women give him second looks. The young interns giggled over him. She didn't mind. Tara did not claim any ownership of him.

"Do you want to think about it?" Devon asked.

She didn't have an immediate answer to either of his questions.

"*Opphhooo*, even after all these years you're still shy around me whenever I try to romance you." Devon leaned down. She felt his breath on her cheek. "It's sweet, but unnecessary, janam."

She rejected the endearment. That was part of his version of marriage. Not hers. To end the conversation, she agreed. "Okay." It was the role she was playing, and she would do her part.

"Great. Let's dress up. Do it right. I'll serenade you in the car." Devon was a big fan of Bollywood movies, and he would belt out songs whenever he was in the mood.

Without looking at him, she gave him a single nod. Finally he left her to go back to his office. She could breathe again. She wondered what made him want to add dating and romance to their relationship. They worked together, parented, did their social obligations with family and friends. Neither of them was physical with the other. While their friends held hands or flirted, Tara and Devon resembled their parents. Rarely did they sit on the same sofa or touch each other. There were no endearments or sentences prefaced by "honey." They had sex once or twice a month.

Over the years, Tara had learned that she didn't need it. Shefali and Hetal talked about famous men their husbands would give them hall passes to be with, but Tara's brain wasn't wired that way. Her libido was low, and she liked that she wasn't driven by physical desire. In that way, she and Devon matched well. In return, she'd go on date nights to accommodate him.

CHAPTER TWENTY-ONE

Numbness is the opposite of happiness.
—*YNLIN*

Bedford, Massachusetts, present

Nikki, Jay, their parents, and Heena sat at a round table as two officers from the Boston PD finished up their investigation. After a thorough frisking and going through all his bags and items, the police had let the priest leave, but they'd asked the immediate family to stay for further questioning.

"Shouldn't we have a lawyer?" Heena had removed her earrings and was playing with them. Caleb had left with the twins, as he was not needed for questioning.

"That would be me," Jay said.

"But you're a suspect," Heena retorted.

Jay opened, then closed, his mouth.

"No one has been accused," the policewoman reiterated.

"She did it." Bijal pointed across the table to Tara.

"Is this slander or libel?" Tara said.

"Neither," Jay answered.

"Have more alcohol," Bijal said. "It'll jog your memory."

"That's enough, Mom."

Nikki sat between her parents. "It's missing. We can't assume it was stolen."

"Agreed," Jay said.

"You're taking her side?" Bijal asked.

"He's being reasonable," Nikki offered.

"They're engaged." Heena looked at the policeman. "Even though she doesn't have a ring on her finger."

"Heena!" Nikki shouted.

"She's not wrong," Tara said.

"Since when do you and Heena agree on anything?" Nikki rubbed her forehead.

"Jay, your mother thinks Nikki only wants to marry you for your money," Tara said.

Jay raised his brow. "It's the other way around since I have a hundred thousand dollars in student loans."

"This isn't the time for jokes," Nikki said.

"Why not? This whole thing is a farce," he said.

Everyone began talking at once. The two dads talked about the importance of celebration. Bijal taunted Tara. Her mother and Heena argued over something Nikki couldn't decipher. She and Jay looked at one another. She closed her eyes when she saw the hurt and disappointment in him. It took the police officers several minutes to get them all to be quiet.

Then there was silence. Kirit and Devon stood and hovered over the table.

"Tonight, we joined our two families," Devon said.

"We have to make peace," Kirit added. "For the sake of the children."

"I will only support this marriage if the ring is returned," Bijal said.

"That's fine with me," Tara said.

The headache that had been mild for the last hour gained power. Nikki closed her eyes to keep it at bay. This was not the time for a migraine. "Please. Everyone."

"We're adults," Jay said. "Not kids. And you don't get to give us ultimatums. Officer, unless you're filing charges or making an arrest, can we go? You've gone through all our things. It's safe to say that no one has the ring."

"Jay, please." Nikki whispered it, though in her head it was a roar.

After this, the officers handed them the police report and advised them to send it to the insurance company. Then they backed away from the table and left the restaurant while mumbling something into their radio. Nikki kept her eyes on the cloth stained with splatters of tikka masala and dal. The votive candle floating in the floral centerpiece had burned down. From the outside, the table resembled a still life of what had been merely a few hours before.

The smell of oil, spices, and cologne caused her headache to worsen. She needed to get home before her migraine reached its peak.

Jay came around and stood behind Nikki. "Let's go."

Nikki pushed back her chair, grateful for the escape. Nausea would be next, and she needed to be in her bedroom with her blackout curtains and sleeping mask to avoid the pain of light.

"You can't just leave," Bijal cried.

"We've looked everywhere, it'll turn up. Maybe the cleaning crew will find it," Jay said. "We're all tired."

"Jay is right," Devon said. "Tara?"

Nikki was relieved to see Tara follow Devon out the door.

"I can help you with the insurance paperwork for the ring, Bijal auntie," Nikki offered.

"It's priceless," Bijal said. "A family heirloom. It's been in the family for hundreds of years. You're all acting callous."

Nikki closed her eyes as the stabbing knives began to poke her skull. "You're right. I'm sorry, Auntie. Let me help look again." She would crawl on her hands and knees at this point.

"That won't work," Bijal said. "Your mother has it. She's hidden it somewhere."

"Okay, guess it's not only my toddlers that need a time-out." Heena stood. "Everyone, go home. Sorry for your loss, Bijal auntie."

"No one died," Jay called out to Heena. Then held Nikki at his side. "Okay?"

"Headache." He didn't know about her migraines because they didn't happen often and she'd managed to handle them on her own. "I'm fine. You should stay with your mom. She's upset and rightly so, it's important. Don't worry. I'll call a rideshare."

"I don't want to leave you like this," he said.

She took his hand. "She's your mother. She needs you."

He disagreed but let her go. She knew he was upset, but right now all she needed was her bed and her pills. Nikki waited outside. The air was cool for June, and she was grateful. In two months, Boston would be a steam bath, so it was necessary to enjoy it now. She scanned the empty parking lot. There was no sign of her parents or their car. She needed her bed. It had been a while since her last flare-up, so she didn't have her medicine in her purse. Forty-five minutes. She would get through the ride and pray that she made it into her apartment without throwing up.

What a mess. Tomorrow, with a clear head, she would reflect. Then she would go see Bijal auntie and help. The woman deserved consideration. The heirloom was meaningful to her. Then there was Tara. Nikki didn't want to suspect her, but Tara had been acting out of character. Could Bijal be right? Could her mom have taken it?

CHAPTER TWENTY-TWO

Newton, Massachusetts, 2003

Tara parked the minivan and came around to let the girls out of the car. The warm September day marked the start of another year. Nikki would begin fifth grade and Heena seventh.

"You're growing up so fast." Tara helped Nikki out of the car. Nikki let go of her arm and heaved her heavy backpack over her shoulders.

"Grow your brains." Tara waved to them.

"I will." Nikki waved back.

"I won't," Heena grumbled with her back to Tara.

Tara closed her eyes to calm herself. Heena and Nikki were different. While her younger daughter was well behaved, eager to learn, and sensitive, her firstborn was becoming more challenging. Devon excused Heena's average grades and stubbornness, which felt like betrayal. Her husband was an intermittent parent, prioritizing his work, yet the girls loved him more. She tried not to be jealous of the way Heena and Nikki were always cheerful and loving toward Devon when Tara was the one who put more energy into their well-being.

Tara tried to let go of the resentment, but then Devon would do something like take the girls to Six Flags for the day, just the three of them, because "Mom was no fun." They shared jokes that Tara didn't understand or wasn't included in. Tara didn't know how to relate to her own daughters, and with each passing year, she could feel their distance.

Once the girls were in the building, Tara headed to a café in the local bookstore. She planned to make it a ritual starting today. The next sixty minutes were hers. Errands, dinner prep, paperwork for Devon's practice, paying bills, and everything else she had to do would wait until she did something for herself. She'd planned it meticulously. Five hours each week, and she could restart her quest to relearn all that she'd forgotten.

She cradled the warm mug and opened her own notebook, then stroked the blank page, traced the college-ruled lines. Excitement vibrated through her. She was finally executing her plan. Reaching for something. Tara was embracing her adulthood. She was in her mid-thirties, too old to stay stuck, to let others define her existence.

With determination, she opened the GMAT study guide.

"Hi, can I join you?"

Tara glanced up.

"It's crowded, and I need five minutes of peace. I'm Mona." She sat before Tara could speak. "Oh, you're studying. Are you in college?"

Tara laughed. "No. I'm going for my PhD."

"That's great." The woman crossed her legs, the hem of her skirt hugged her thighs. "I couldn't do it. I barely made it through Washington State. I'm such a bad example of Indian." She laughed, and her white teeth gleamed against her painted red lips. "You are too. Right? I'm never wrong about this."

Tara nodded. "Gujarati."

"Me too," Mona said. "We must have common friends."

"I'll let you enjoy your coffee in peace." Tara wanted to get through one section of the practice test before her hours were up.

"You're shy. It's okay, I'm an extrovert. Oh, I am thinking of starting a women's club, a way to make friends." Mona closed Tara's book. Her manicured nails tapped the cover. "You're officially joining. We're going to do all sorts of events like seeing plays, dinners, weekend getaways, dancing. A community of women who support each other in everything from in-law problems, kid issues, and everything else."

"I'm single." She said it to get Mona to leave. But saying the words made her happy. This was a stranger. It didn't matter. Still, she mentally apologized to her daughters.

"I just assumed since you look older than me."

Tara widened her grin. "I probably am. I prefer a career. I'm in the astrophysics field." As she talked, she became different. Felt alive, interesting. An alter ego.

"You must be smart," Mona said. "I stopped after chemistry."

She straightened her posture, lifted by the compliment. "Thank you. It's my passion."

"Shoes are mine." Mona laughed.

Tara joined her. "I own exactly five pairs, two are sari champals."

Mona gave an exaggerated gasp, then leaned forward. "Seriously, we have to fix that."

Tara couldn't help but like her. "Do you live in town?"

Mona nodded. "We moved here a few months ago. My husband got a job with New Balance. Originally, I'm from San Francisco. Have you been out west?"

"Once." It had been her first flight without her parents or relatives. "San Diego for a conference while I was in college." She'd left the hotel by herself one morning and secretly gone to the Pacific Ocean just to put her feet in the water. The image of Ben flashed through her mind. He had probably sailed on it, more than once.

"You might be single, but the look on your face screams love," Mona said.

Tara snapped her eyes to Mona. "What?"

"You were dreaming about someone," Mona added. "I'm an expert in romance."

Tara laughed. "It's nothing like that." It was time to confess her actual life.

"Don't be shy," Mona protested. "If you can't tell a stranger, who can you tell?"

Tara opened her mouth and the words that should have come out changed. "I was thinking of my ex." What was she saying? Tara didn't even know she could act this way. Her alter ego was Mr. Hyde.

"I knew it." Mona smacked her hand on the study guide. "Spill."

"We met right before college graduation." Tara tried to stay close to the truth. "It was magical."

"And you never forgot him," Mona said. "Was he cute?"

"Very. In a boyish way." Adrenaline rushed through her as she went back to that night. "Did you ever see *Good Will Hunting*? He was a taller Indian American version of the blond genius. And with black hair." When she saw the commercial for the movie, she'd seen Ben in his face. He was paler than brown-skinned Ben. Still the smile, the forehead, and the jaw were familiar. It was one of the few movies she'd seen twice.

"Matt Damon! Amazing. How did you meet?"

Tara launched into the memory. "The grass was freshly cut, and whenever lawns are mowed, it takes me back to that spot." She didn't share the details of the conversation; she wanted to remember the way she'd felt. Seen, acknowledged, appreciated. "He supported my goals and dreams. He didn't laugh when I talked about stars."

"Sounds like a dream guy." Mona held her chin in her hands. "Is he the inspiration for getting a PhD?"

No. "Yeah. He already has his. He's teaching at a university." Probably. "I want to catch up to him."

Mona clapped her hands. "Wouldn't it be so romantic if you went to the same college, and you were walking on the same path on campus? You immediately recognize each other, then start running toward each other. He picks you up and kisses you and then you can live happily ever after."

Tara laughed at the fairy-tale version of a reunion even as she yearned for it. *Two daughters*, she reminded herself. "What about you? Do you have this amazing love story?"

Mona twisted her diamond-and-platinum wedding ring. "Oh, we had the classic story. Our parents didn't approve, we fought to be together, got married, and now everyone gets along. Last week was our ten-year wedding anniversary. He gave me a card. I gave him a pack of screwdrivers. Romance fades, right? Anyway, back to you. What was his name?"

"I actually have to study." Tara picked up her pen.

"I understand." Mona scooched her chair back. "It's just that I don't know anyone here and it's nice to talk to someone other than my eight-year-old."

Tara felt bad. "Ben. His name was Ben." She moved the books out of the way. She would start her reading ritual tomorrow.

Mona's beautiful face glowed with happiness. "That is a romance novel name. I devour those. Are you still in touch with him?"

Tara shook her head. "No. It's been a while."

"Maybe you can put his name into Yahoo," Mona offered. "If he's famous."

Devon had a computer at the office, but they didn't have one at home. It would be nice to know where Ben might be, have a way to connect with him. "He probably doesn't remember me." Most likely he had a family of his own.

Mona glanced out the window as they sat at the small table. "Idea! I have a lot of cousins that are single." She tapped her nails on the table again. "Let's see . . . who is smart and likes science? And is also cute? Because you're beautiful, and fit is important."

Tara blushed. She couldn't remember the last time someone had said something nice about her appearance. She took care of herself by going to the gym and ate well because proper nutrition was rooted in science. "Thanks, but I'm not, um . . . I need to focus on my plans. Fix-ups aren't for me."

"Because you're still not over him."

Because I have two daughters and a husband. "Something like that."

Mona took the pen from Tara's hand and wrote her name and number on the back of her coffee receipt. "This is mine. Write yours down and I'll call you. We can do this again."

Tara handed Mona her home number. Then, without thinking, added, "I'll be here from nine to ten on weekdays."

"Perfect," Mona said.

They chatted a little while longer before Tara's time was up. She had to go to the bank and then the supermarket. They said goodbyes, and as she drove off, Tara found a little bit of her old self. She'd been so wrapped up in Devon's life and world that she'd forgotten that she was an individual. Taking charge of her future with GMATs and grad programs, now a possible friend, she was at a turning point. Tara was an object in motion that had stopped when she'd married Devon. Now she was turned around, going in the opposite direction. Maybe it would lead her back to her spot along the Charles River, the night under the stars.

CHAPTER TWENTY-THREE

You can't fix what others have broken.
—*YNLIN*

Jamaica Plain, Massachusetts, present

After a restless night, Nikki woke up needing caffeine. The worst had passed thanks to medicine and water, which she'd had to force down at the risk of throwing it back up. She was sore and groggy but thankfully pain-free. In her silk robe inspired by a Jackson Pollock print, she brewed a strong cup of Earl Grey. She wasn't much of a coffee or chai person, but she found that tea was less bitter and offered more flavor variety. With a warm mug cradled in her hands, she sat on her structured sofa, curled her legs under her, and let her mind rest. She wondered how it had all gone wrong. The new Tara. The missing ring. The police! She couldn't focus on a single thought as they all swirled together.

After a few sips, Nikki reached for her small red leather Moleskine and her favorite serviceable Pilot fountain pen. The emotional chaos within her needed an outlet. She needed to journal in order to understand before she went to work on fixing it all.

First she wrote Jay's name. She didn't believe in soulmates, so why had she rushed to agree to his proposal? She'd seen a new side to him these last few months. Instead of discovering ways they were compatible, it seemed as if they were finding more differences. Particularly when it came to family. She'd believed him to be carefree and relaxed, a counterbalance to her ambition and structure. But there was also a detachment to him that lay beneath his guileless expression. He supported Nikki, but she wasn't sure he understood her. When it came to addressing serious issues, Jay wanted Nikki to either brush it off or deal with it later. Same as Tara. Would she have to spend her life managing his emotions the same way she did her mother's? She drew a heart but left one arc unconnected.

Tara. Or whoever this person was who was acting so unlike the mother Nikki had always known. She sipped more tea and stared at the abstract painting on the wall. Inspired by Kandinsky, it was patterns, shapes, and lines laid over each other. The intensity of emotion had drawn her to buy it. She let it wash over her to access her own feelings. Nikki waited for them to surface. Anger. Frustration. Heartache. That was the core of what her mother made her feel.

From the AP courses she'd taken in high school to the colleges she'd applied for admission to, she'd always done as Tara had wished. Tara made a big deal out of wanting her daughters to make their own choices, but they never had a doubt as to what *she* wanted, and that was what Nikki always did. Her mother had pushed her out and away even as a child. Tara didn't hover or helicopter parent. There were only a handful of times when Tara had helped with homework or a move. Even then, Tara had pushed her own agenda. Nikki drew a half heart.

The ring. She truly felt for Bijal auntie. The woman had looked stunned and defeated when they'd decided to give up the search. She hoped Jay had been sympathetic to his mother's feelings. She knew that sometimes he didn't value the things his family did, especially when it came to their wealth. She kept her gaze on the painting. She'd often used it as a way to feel her feelings, find release. There was something about it that made her feel as if the artist was in the throes of an emotional breakdown, and it allowed Nikki's tears to flow. Heena used to tell her that Nikki would make a great soap opera actor because of her ability to cry. Nikki saw it as a gift to be able to release all that was blocked so that she could function. It took a full ten minutes until she was done and able to clear her stuffy nose and take a shower.

Once dressed, she was calmer, though she knew that the sadness she carried would be a part of her for a long time. With a heavy sigh, Nikki went to her desk and pulled the phone from its charger and tapped the screen to wake it up. She had close to twenty messages. Nikki checked to make sure she'd grabbed her personal cell and not her work phone.

Jay: Text when you're home.

Jay: Checking in. Hopefully you're sleeping.

Jay: How's your headache? Need anything?

The next series was from Devon. Rows of texts five to fifteen minutes apart.

Dad: Nikita, answer your phone.

Dad: Did you get home? Where are you?

Dad: Call me! It's very important.

A few more of the same. Which left Heena with the last of them.

Heena: Um . . . you need to call dad.

Heena: Hey, so I don't think it's a big deal but dad's kind of freaking out.

Heena: Look, if mom is with you, just let dad know.

Nikki's heart raced as she called her father. He answered on the second ring.

"Is your mother with you?" Devon shouted through the speaker.

"No," Nikki replied. "What's going on?"

"She left." Devon sighed. "We came home. I went to my room. She went to hers. I don't know where she is."

Nikki sat in her desk chair. "Maybe she went out for coffee."

"I called her, she's not answering," he said. "I checked the Holiday Inn, she isn't there. Heena thought she might be with you. I messaged

Kiran and Hiten, and neither of their wives have heard from your mother. Now they're concerned too. I called the police. They said it hasn't been long enough. And umm . . . I think she packed."

"Wait. Dad." Nikki rubbed her forehead. "Why are you so frantic? She might be ignoring her phone. That's all."

"Her duffel bag that she kept in the bedroom closet is missing," he said. "It's her go bag."

She heard the strain in his voice. "What? Is there a zombie apocalypse or something?" She couldn't imagine Tara being a prepper.

"I can't get into it right now," Devon said. "She's gone. And not like last time."

"What last time?" Nikki couldn't comprehend the words coming so fast from Devon.

"This is different," he said. "Just take my word."

"Okay." Nikki had never heard her father sound this desperate. "Do you share a credit card? Can you see the last charge? Maybe she used it."

"Beta, you're freaking brilliant," he said. "One sec."

Nikki waited. What was she thinking of, taking off like that, and no messages? Nikki texted her mom while on speakerphone with her dad.

"What the . . . ?"

"Dad?" Nikki said. "What is it? Is there a recent charge?"

"Yeah." Nikki heard the puzzlement. "Maybe she lost her purse and someone used her card because this doesn't make sense."

"What's the name of the business?" Nikki raised her voice to get her father's attention.

"Airstream Marketplace," Devon said.

"I don't get it." Nikki quickly searched online. "She bought an RV. With a credit card?"

"The business Visa," he said. "It's joint and has a pretty high limit."

"What is Mom doing?" Nikki murmured.

"If I only knew," Devon said. "One minute everything is as it always was, then she wants a divorce, now she's run away. I wanted to keep you girls out of it, but I don't know what to do anymore."

Her father's voice broke. She heard him hold back his tears. He was more a man who laughed and joked. She'd never seen him cry. It made her own throat clog.

She cleared it and kept her voice calm. "Nothing happened between the two of you, right? No big fight?"

"No, beta," Devon said. "Nothing like that. Only that she's been different lately. Not like herself. I admit, I haven't been the best husband. I paid more attention to work than I did to your mother. But I did my best to give us a good life. There were times when she tried something like this before."

"Wait, more than once? What are you talking about?"

"No, just . . . forget it, it's never gotten this far," he said. "It's the duffel bag. She doesn't know I know. Now it's gone and so is Tara."

She rubbed the back of her neck. "Okay, Dad. Hang in there. I'm going to go and see if I can track her down. I'll call you as soon as I find her." She ended the call with more assurances that everything was going to be fine. More for her than him. First she had to find her mother. Who'd run away. In a camper van.

CHAPTER TWENTY-FOUR

Newton, Massachusetts, 2004

"Mom, did I do this right?"

Tara scanned the paper Nikki slid across the kitchen table toward her. They were working together on Nikki's extra credit project, and Tara had thought it would be fun to have Nikki illustrate an atom, one of the building blocks of all matter. She hoped Nikki would show an interest in science. "It's ellipses, not circles." Tara redrew the structure with long concentric ovals. "You did great with the three rings—proton, electron, and neutron. But you must be exact."

"Positive, negative, and neutral," Nikki said.

"Not neutral," Tara said. "They are absent of charge."

Nikki furrowed her brow. "Then why are they in there?"

"Because it helps determine mass."

"Like church?"

Tara prayed for patience. Nikki needed to be more attentive. "No, it's the amount of matter in an object. Different atoms have different particles." She saw Nikki's confused look. "We can get to that later. For now, let's focus on atoms. And everything we touch and see, even things we can't spot with our eyes, is made up of these particles."

Nikki stroked the table. "You and me too?"

Tara nodded. "Hydrogen, oxygen, carbon. All the things that keep us alive."

"Interesting. But it also makes my brain hurt," Nikki said. "I like math."

"There's a lot of math in physics," Tara said. "Maybe you'll be the next Marie Curie."

Nikki shook her head. "I already know what I'm going to do."

Tara rested her elbows on the table. "Tell me."

"I want to be a boss," Nikki said. "Like Dad."

"It's too early to decide," Tara said. "Give this a chance. There are so many areas to explore. Biology. Chemistry. You can oversee experiments."

Nikki looked at Tara for a few seconds. "Okay. I'll try to like science."

Tara wanted to reach over and hug Nikki. Her younger daughter was becoming more attached. She'd accepted that Heena would never understand her, but Nikki noticed Tara's wishes and tried to please. Nikki resembled her in discipline and ambition. However, where Tara had caved to the pressure of her family's expectations, she made sure Nikki would be courageous. Her daughters would know they were supported in their achievements.

"Did you ever want to work, Mom?" Nikki said. *Mom.*

"Let's finish this homework." Tara cradled her mug. She watched as Nikki concentrated. *Mom.* That's all she was to them. She'd never shared her ambition with either of her daughters. But how could she? She'd never done the things she was trying to instill in them. She was too ashamed.

"Heena is better at drawing than me," Nikki said. "She can make perfect circles."

"You're both amazing."

"I guess." Nikki kept her eyes on her work. "Do you like being a mom?"

Sometimes these innocent questions became existential. She couldn't tell Nikki the truth. Her visceral reaction was to say no.

Which she wouldn't. Ever. She loved her daughters. But she would never glamorize motherhood or romanticize being a wife. Tara took the coward's way and merely smiled and said, "What a silly question!"

"Dad says being a dentist wasn't what he wanted to be," Nikki said. "But he does it because it's his job to take care of us. And he loves being a father more than his job."

She had never asked Devon what path he would have chosen if he hadn't been so obsessed with making money. She knew she was ungenerous with him. He was a good provider and a great parent. "Hold your pencil straight." She watched as Nikki adjusted her grip.

"Mom, why don't you do science? You have a lot of books about it."

Tara couldn't hold the words back. "I let other people decide for me. That's why it's important that you stay strong. To make your own path. No matter what."

"I will," Nikki said. "I promise."

"Let's clear the table so I can start dinner," Tara said.

Nikki gathered up her notebook and papers. "Are we having Indian?"

Tara shook her head. "No. Enchiladas."

"Cool."

While Nikki headed up to her room to put things away, Tara clutched the back of the dining table chair. So much was happening in physics, so many gains had been made in the last decade. Top quarks, the tau neutrino, the accelerated expansion of the universe. In a different life, she would have been a part of that work, made gains. She would have felt alive and excited.

She picked up the kitchen phone. For a few minutes, she wanted to live her other life. The pretend one. "Coffee tomorrow morning?" she asked her friend.

"Bookstore?" Mona answered. "Ten o'clock?"

Tara agreed and hung up. At least she had an escape. With Mona, she could be someone else. No longer guilty that she hadn't told her friend the reality of her life, Tara reveled in the fantasy. She had concocted all sorts of details about Ben, their past and the love they'd shared. It wasn't real, Tara knew that, but it comforted her. And she'd made Ben into someone who didn't exist by giving him characteristics, style, personality traits, that were likely false. She'd shaped him to be her big love.

The following day, Tara arrived early. She got two coffees and sat at their usual table. As she stared out the window into the parking lot, Tara realized this was the only thing that was hers. She would savor these moments. For an hour or so a day, she was free.

"I have a surprise for you." Mona grabbed the chair opposite her at their usual table. She was in skinny jeans and high heels.

Because of Mona, Tara made more of an effort with her appearance, wearing makeup and styling her long hair with rollers to give it body. These past six months, she'd learned that Mona was a big personality with a generous heart. The guilt of not sharing her true self with her friend warred with Tara's need to live outside of the life she'd chosen. "I don't want to know," she said.

"I found Ben."

Tara almost fell out of her chair. This was bad. Very bad. "What are you talking about?"

"Internet."

"I'm sure there are many Bens out there." Tara's voice trembled.

"Yours is still at the University of Maine." Mona shoved a printout in front of Tara.

She was afraid to look. And desperately curious. It was there, in black and white. "Ben Anand, Research Associate, Oceanography Department." There was no picture. She wondered how he had aged, whether his hair was still thick. Was his body still lean? Did his smile change? "It could be a coincidence."

"There's a phone number there," Mona said. "Call it. See if it's him."

Tara hung her head in her hands. This had gone too far. "It was a long time ago."

"What if he remembers you?" Mona insisted. "You're beautiful. And what you feel for him is so strong that you can't get over it. This is your chance. I want this for you. You can't let him go again."

Tara shook her head. "Stop, Mona. It's not . . . you don't know."

"Come on," she pressed. "You have nothing to lose. Call, you're no worse off. But it's not going to be like that. I guarantee that he still thinks about you."

Tara saw the hope and earnestness on her friend's face. *I'm a terrible friend.* "I need to think. It's too sudden. Give me some time."

"Okay," Mona said. "I did shock you. But seeing your reaction tells me that you still love him. He's your true love. You need him."

Tara folded the printout and put it in her purse. "Why are you so determined?"

Mona looked away. "Because I want to believe that happily ever after is real."

Tara reached over and clasped her friend's arm. Mona and her husband were on uneven ground. "It's still rough? At home?"

Mona's typically manicured nails were bare and uneven. "He moved out. For a few months, at least that's what he says. Our families don't know. He said he's crashing with a friend. I didn't ask who."

Tara went around and hugged Mona. "I'm so sorry."

"I'm the one who had to tell our son. How selfish can he be? He only thinks about his happiness, no one else's."

She listened to her friend as Mona poured her heart out. After they'd gone their separate ways, Tara sat in her crumb-filled minivan. The back seat was cluttered with snack wrappers, toys, blankets, a single shoe, all indicators of her two children. She glanced at the paper. This was likely the same Ben Anand from that long-ago night. She traced his name with her finger.

It seemed that he finished his PhD in oceanography. The printout held a simple biography of his academic achievements. There was no mention of his personal life. She wondered how his face had changed in the last decade, whether he had his own boat. Tara closed her eyes and leaned back against the headrest. If she drove north, in a few hours she could be on campus. Stare at him through the windshield. She would know, firsthand, how time had treated him.

She folded the paper and put it back in her purse. She was many things, including a liar. She had it in her to be as selfish as Mona's husband. The only reason she headed to her house instead of the highway was that she now lived for Heena and Nikki. This little fantasy she'd created for herself and presented to Mona had to end.

CHAPTER TWENTY-FIVE

A map isn't directional, it's static. Redraw yours every year.
—*YNLIN*

Quincy, Massachusetts, present

Nikki hopped out of the rideshare and found her mother in the driveway of a small Cape Cod–style house in a town adjacent to Boston. It had taken seven phone calls before Tara answered. Two conversations before Tara gave up her location. Her mom was twenty minutes southeast of Boston, meeting with a stranger. Nikki had been frantic.

"Mom!" Nikki ran through the grass. "What are you doing?"

Tara was in the driver's seat of the vehicle, an unfamiliar older man in a blue trucker hat sitting next to her. "Nikki. I told you I'm fine. You didn't have to come here."

"Get out of this—whatever this is. Get out now. This isn't okay," Nikki heard herself screech.

"It's an Airstream. Isn't it beautiful?" Tara said. "Green and silver. Your favorite colors."

She preferred gold, but now was not the time. Nikki leaned over to catch her breath. Tried to count to ten and made it to two. "First, you need to come out. Second, we're going to have a long talk." Her mother needed a parent and Nikki had drawn the short straw.

Tara turned to the person next to her. "I'm sorry, Jack. This is my daughter, and she looks like she's hyperventilating."

Jack handed Tara a water bottle from a cup holder. Tara passed it to Nikki through the window.

Nikki uncapped it and gulped half. "Cancel the transaction. She can't buy this camper van."

"Actually, it's a motor home. And it's too late for that." Jack got out of his side and walked around. "The title is signed, and the website said the payment was already transferred into my account."

In this moment, she didn't care about the technical term. "I'm sure there's a law. Buyer's remorse or something."

"I'm not changing my mind," Tara called out.

Nikki waved her off. "She doesn't know how to drive anything larger than an SUV," Nikki said. "Doesn't she need a special license?"

"Only for vehicles longer than thirty-five feet," Jack said. "We went for a spin earlier and Tara handled it okay."

"Nikki, get in," Tara said. "You'll like it. It's fun."

Nikki stared at the large metal tube with tinted windows on the side. It was as long as the short driveway. She circled around and hoisted herself into the passenger seat. "What is going on, Mom? You left. Now this. We're worried about you."

"It's not necessary." Tara turned the ignition on.

Nikki reached over and turned it off. "Talk to me. Are you having a breakdown?"

Her mother twisted her body toward Nikki, the seat belt keeping her mostly in place. "Enough. Stop treating me like I'm helpless, like I can't do anything for myself. I'm free."

"In a motor home?"

"Yes." Tara gripped the steering wheel. "Do you know that this is the only item that has my name on the title? Two in one." Tara laughed. "A home and a car."

"That you paid for with a credit card. From Dad's business," Nikki reminded her.

Tara's smile faded. She turned away from Nikki and stared out through the windshield. "I earned it. I worked there on and off for decades. Helping when business was bad or they were short of staff."

"I didn't mean to say that." It had been a slip because she always saw it as her father's practice. Her mom had been a homemaker. She'd never thought about her mom as a woman with ambition or a profession, but Tara had contributed to their family. Nikki felt guilty for not acknowledging it.

"It's true," Tara said. "Your father worked, paid for everything. It's his name on the sign and on the business registration along with Kiran and Hiten. This is a loan. I'll pay it back."

"That's not what I meant," Nikki said. "You and Dad share finances; it's not my place to say anything. This, however, is an irrational purchase."

"It doesn't have to make sense." Tara stroked the dashboard. "A 1982 retro Airstream Excella. I was a teenager when this was made. Jack said it's rare to find one in as good a condition."

He probably saw Tara as an easy mark and had said it to get a sale. Nikki looked through the driver's-side window, and the previous owner of this metal black-and-white-leather monstrosity was nowhere to be seen. "Did you have it checked over by an independent party? You can't take the seller's word."

"You got an award for being most diligent in fifth grade and made it your entire personality," Tara said. "Jack told me he'd spent a lot of time refurbishing it. His wife designed the interior. I believe him."

Nikki scanned the back of the motor home. There was a long bench along the side behind Tara. The fabric on the seat was brown with yellow, red, pink, orange, and white flowers. "She must have been a fan of the seventies."

"It's funky," Tara said. "Flower power."

Nikki groaned. "Please don't say that."

"We need to play ABBA," Tara said. "My phone is almost out of juice. Do it on yours."

"This thing doesn't even charge phones!" There was a panel that jutted out behind Nikki, flanked by two benches facing each other. A quaint little dining table that reminded her of a retro diner. Behind that was a small stove, sink, and counter. At the far end were two twin beds, behind which looked to be a tiny bathroom. The bedding was in the same fabric and design as the bench seat. "It's bare bones."

"And perfect," Tara said. "An empty canvas. I'll add to it over time."

She frowned. Her mother was missing an important piece. "Um . . . where are you going to park it? I don't think you can just keep it on your street."

Tara laughed. "Don't be silly. I'll find RV campsites along the way."

"What?" she shouted. "You're planning to live in this thing? Where will you go?"

"Nowhere, everywhere," Tara said. "Anywhere the mood takes me."

Nikki fished out her phone. "We're going to find you a therapist."

Tara covered Nikki's hand. "I'm fine. I promise. I'm doing this with a clear head."

Nikki tightened the grip. "How can you take off? You have responsibilities, a family."

Tara let go. "I did that, fulfilled my obligations. Everyone is settled and on their own paths. It's my turn."

Her mother spoke as if they didn't need her. As if she didn't want them. "You can't just take off. You need a map, a route. What are the details? Do you even know what type of gas this thing takes?"

Tara gripped the steering wheel. "What good is a plan if you never act on it?"

Nikki looked behind her again, spotted the black duffel bag, recalled the conversation with her father. "Mom? For once, tell me what this is all about. I'm worried. You're still my mom."

Tara stared through the windshield. "You're right."

Her mother's tone changed. The familiar sadness seeped through Tara's pores. "It's okay. I'm right here. I'll support you."

Tara turned and faced Nikki. "Your father betrayed me, and I can't forgive him."

Nikki sat back against the seat, stunned. "Tell me." Even though she didn't want to know the details. Part of her felt guilty because she could see why her father would have chosen to be with someone else. Tara had never shown him affection.

"Your life isn't like mine," Tara said. "I made sure of it. I had to be a dutiful daughter, which meant marriage and children. I chose Devon because he promised me that I would be able to pursue more."

Nikki didn't know where this conversation was going. A dozen questions rose in her mind. She stayed silent. This was the most her mom had ever spoken about what was going on inside, and Nikki didn't want to give her any reason to stop.

"I was accepted into the graduate program in physics at MIT," Tara said. "That was all I had ever wanted. To be a contributing experimental physicist. I was going to start the year after our wedding. Instead, he opened his practice. I thought once his business was stable, I would start again. Every time I tried, he didn't think it was necessary. It was either too expensive or unnecessary. He said I was selfish for wanting another degree when he would be the provider for our family. I was the caretaker."

This was worse than any of the things Nikki had worried her mom might reveal. She'd known her father to be loving and supportive, Tara to be cool and indifferent. The people in this narrative were strangers to Nikki. She glanced at Tara with wet eyes. Her mother's were clear and dry. "This was so long ago. Did you ever talk to him about it?"

Tara nodded. "I tried for a few years, planned, applied. Something always came up. He needed help with the practice. I had babies. You and Heena had to be raised. Then I accepted that too much time had passed. The opportunity was forever gone."

Nikki swallowed her tears with a gulp from the water bottle. Guilt warmed her face. She'd blamed Tara for all her mother's faults, but she'd never considered why Tara was that way. In this new light, all Nikki saw was how alone Tara appeared.

"I'll go with you."

Tara whipped her head toward Nikki. "What?"

"Wherever you're going, I'm coming with you." Nikki didn't know what she was saying. It was impulsive and rash. She looked at her mom again. She couldn't let Tara go alone.

"Are you sure?" Tara turned the key, and the engine started up.

No. "Yes," Nikki said.

Tara kept the Airstream in park.

"Come on, Mom. You want an adventure, it's the summer. We can go on a road trip." Adrenaline coursed through her. Nikki's to-do list began to scroll through her mind: deadlines, projects, posts, videos. She shoved them away. Her heart raced. "A mother-daughter road trip." No sane person would volunteer to do this. But she would. Because her mother needed her. And this was who Nikki was.

"Don't you have work?" Tara said. "A wedding to plan?"

She did. And yet, at this moment, none of that mattered. Fear enveloped her. This was her bungee jump, her skydive. She was going to take off in an Airstream from the 1980s. With her mom. Cocooned in this tiny space, it would be hard for her mom to avoid conversation. "I'm not letting you go alone."

"I don't know what is happening, but okay. For now, you can come." Tara shifted to put the van in reverse. Slowly, she backed it down the drive. After a few hitches that forced Nikki to clutch the edges of her seat, Tara slowly rolled down the street. Nikki tried to calm her breath. She was excited, scared, and, as reality crept in, sad. She was doing the thing she hated her mom for. Avoiding the talk she needed to have with Jay.

CHAPTER TWENTY-SIX

Malden, Massachusetts, 2005

In most of her life, Tara thought in terms of eons, light-years, and infinity. Ways that time could be calculated and determined. Rarely did she wonder about human mortality. Her mother had lived for seventy-five years. The fraction so small that it was incomprehensible. Yet the marks of her life were there on her embalmed face as she lay in the open casket.

The crematorium was filled with mourners who had come to pay their final respects to her last parent. Everyone was dressed in white, the men in kurtas, the women in saris. She didn't recognize the many faces of extended family or her parents' friends. Family had always been a burden, something she'd been born into but never needed. She'd always thought of her parents in terms of limits. They had been the keepers of how she lived her life until she'd been handed over to Devon and his family.

"Tara, we're going to start."

She nodded from the front row, her daughters on one side and Devon's mother on the other. Devon and Tara's uncle would perform the puja ritual to prepare Kamla for the fire, which would release her soul. She would find a different incarnation, the next life, one that would be determined by the way she had lived this one. Tara hoped her mother would find joy and satisfaction in her search to become one with God.

Devon moved around the body, performed the rituals as guided by the maharaj. It fell upon him as the son, even if by marriage, to carry out these duties. Devon placed a small vial of water from the Ganges River inside the casket to cleanse her mother's sins before the soul departs. On the other side of forty, Devon was still youthful. He was active and made time to work out. Over the years that she'd come to know him, she'd learned that he cared about his appearance. His thick hair was tamed with gels and mousse. He was meticulous with his beard, which made him look rugged and serious at the same time.

"Let's go early tomorrow," her mother-in-law whispered. "We can sort through her things for what goes to charity and what can be thrown away."

Tara ignored the woman. Her mother's body was a few feet away, coated in flowers, ghee, and other items that would help incinerate the body faster. Tara didn't want to think about having to clear out her childhood home, where her mother had lived on her own after the death of Tara's father a few years back. Devon had started to deal with the legalities, and Tara would take care of the rest. She didn't need her in-laws' involvement. She'd never seen them as a second set of parents. They adored Devon. He was their perfect son. She'd heard comments from her in-laws about how they wished Tara would be a better wife. They wanted Devon to be with someone as social and personable as their son.

Her husband was that and more. He was critical of Tara, telling her she wasn't as good a cook as his mom. He would speak for her when they were among friends. He would make jokes at her expense, telling everyone that they had better wives than he did. She heard it all but didn't laugh along with the others. The more he wanted from her, the less she gave him. It was her only power.

"The saris can go to an Indian women's shelter," her mother-in-law continued.

Tara turned away. She had made peace with how her parents were. They had done what was needed to survive. They'd fed and housed and provided safety for Tara. In return, she'd had to ensure that she stayed on the proper path, got good grades, and married an appropriate man.

Her mother's body was prepared for the cremation chamber. Tara, along with Devon and his parents, was invited to toss a handful of flowers in the casket. As she passed by the casket, panic and fear made Tara's breathing erratic. She began to calculate. If Tara's lifespan mirrored Kamla's, she had already lived more than half of her life. Devon placed a hand on her shoulder. She shrugged it off.

"Mommy, you're hurting my hand."

Tara loosened her grip on Nikki as they stood near the photo of her mother. Well-wishers greeted them one by one, but she paid no attention. She inventoried the first half of her life, memories, moments, achievements, victories. Skipping rope in the courtyard of the apartment complex they'd lived in when Tara was a tween. The giant shoulder bow of her purple satin prom dress that made her and her friend roar with laughter. Hugging the acceptance packet from Boston University. The night with Ben. Fear when she'd learned she was pregnant with Heena and again with Nikki.

"Tara?"

She glanced over at Devon.

"They're taking the casket to the incinerator," he said. "The girls can stay out here with my mom."

She let go of Nikki's and Heena's hands and followed Devon behind the casket. They were led into a small room with a glass wall. They watched as the now-closed casket was placed into the furnace. She winced as the metal door clanged shut. The whir of the machine pierced her heart as she shed her first tears. The woman who had given Tara life was becoming ashes that would be scattered in a river.

She would be remembered only by the hundred or so people here, and once they had their bodies burned, it would be as if Kamla Rajput had never existed. Tara knew that unless she did something, she was on the same trajectory.

CHAPTER TWENTY-SEVEN

Travel isn't about sightseeing, it's for memory making.
—*YNLIN*

Boston, Massachusetts, present

Nikki's small Samsonite was stored in the back next to her mom's stuff, and they were on the road after a hasty trip to her apartment. She'd texted her dad and Heena that Tara was okay and that Nikki was with her. She'd left out a few details and kept it vague as to when Tara would be home. She sent Jay a message that she'd call him in a bit. She'd already sent him a *Feeling much better, will call in the evening* text. She'd sent another message off to her assistant to reschedule her appointments and revise due dates on pending projects.

The Airstream was unwieldy, and Tara needed to concentrate, especially on turns. Nikki believed they were going to run off the road and crash because Tara could barely stay in her lane. "What's the first stop?"

Tara grinned. "Let's take 93 North and see where we end up."

"That's very unspecific." Nikki forced herself to go with the flow and not open her maps app to find a spot that would allow RVs. She turned to look at her mom. Tara was relaxed in a way that Nikki had never seen. There was a lightness to her that made Nikki wonder if Tara was faking it. She would find out.

Her mom was in jeans and a white sweater with a printed kerchief tied around her neck. Her more-gray-than-black curls bounced as her mom bopped her head to the radio. Tara rarely wore any jewelry, but the glass sailboat pendant dangled from the chain around her neck.

"You're wearing that necklace," Nikki said.

Tara nodded.

"Can you tell me about it?"

"I bought it for me," Tara said.

Nikki waited to see if Tara would say more.

After a few minutes, Tara spoke again. "It sounds silly. It was two weeks before my wedding, and I was out shopping, and I saw this at an arts and craft market on Newbury Street. Ten dollars. Which was expensive back then. I bought it."

Nikki had seen a few pictures of Tara when she was young, but she rarely saw her as anyone other than her mom. "Why a sailboat?"

"It was something I thought I might do one day. Sail," Tara said. "Nikki, you don't have to come along. I am fine on my own."

"Maybe I want an adventure too." Nikki stared through the passenger window. "I've been so busy lately. It'll be good to get away."

"You're not spontaneous," Tara added.

"Neither are you. We're both exploring a new side."

"Maybe this can be research for your newsletter," Tara said.

Nikki laughed. And there was the Tara she knew. It was comforting to know that her mother hadn't completely changed. "I texted Dad to let him know we're fine."

"Who?" Tara said.

"Mom."

"It's a joke. I sent Heena a message to not worry," Tara added. "Do you know that this is the first time I've run away?"

"I don't think that's what it's called when adults do it," Nikki said.

"Figuratively, then. When I was young, I would think about doing it," Tara continued. "I was too scared. One time, in high school, I decided to not go home after my last class. I went to the library, then church. Around seven thirty, I didn't know where else to go, so I went back home."

"Were Ba and Dada worried?"

Tara shook her head. "They were still at work. They never knew."

She'd known that Tara hadn't been close to Nikki's grandparents. The idea that they hadn't known Tara's urge to run away was surprising, though. "I never even considered it. Running away." She wondered if her mom would have stopped her, searched for her, or merely wished Nikki well.

"I never worried when it came to you," Tara said. "You never did anything without diligence. You would have a plan, your finances would be in order, and you would have left a note. Heena was the difficult one. You were the well-behaved, perfect-grades, never-late child. And a peacemaker."

"Yeah, I guess."

"I'm surprised that you wanted to come along," Tara said. "Or is it all part of a master plan to offer to drive and then turn this van back toward Boston?"

Nikki stared out of the passenger-side window. "Now that you mention it."

"Then I'll make sure to not hand over the keys," Tara said. "Enjoy the moment, isn't that what your business is about? Look up at the blue sky, appreciate that there is no traffic. It's perfect weather, too, not hot, not cold. Look at the trees! There are little buds. Nature is restorative, don't you think? In a few weeks, leaves will blow in the breeze, flowers will bloom, and the grass will glimmer under the sun."

Nikki braced her hand on the dashboard as her mother took a wide turn to get onto the Riverway. The camper van was too big for the small, tight lanes in Boston. "If we're still alive."

"It's the other cars," Tara said. "Once we're on the highway it'll be better."

"Do you know the height on this thing?" Nikki asked. "If you're taking Storrow Drive, we might be too tall and get stuck like all those moving vans at the start of fall semester."

"We should be fine," Tara said.

"That's not reassuring!"

"Look in the glove compartment. I'm sure there's a manual in there." Tara zigged to avoid hitting a MINI Cooper. "That might make you feel better."

Nikki shuffled through the brochure to look for the dimensions of this giant metal tube on wheels. "I think we can clear the overpasses." The initial rush of adventure was beginning to fade as the reality of what she was doing began to settle in. A woman who filled her days studying physics and astronomy wouldn't be able to navigate a spontaneous road trip in an RV. If this car/house got a flat, her mom would be able to calculate the force needed to remove the lug nut but wouldn't be able to change the tire. She had few to no life skills outside the home.

"Do you know how to hook this up to a generator or water?" Nikki asked.

"Jack said I could find any answer I need on YouTube." Tara concentrated on the road.

"Mom, what's a go bag?"

Tara glanced over. "I don't understand."

"Dad mentioned a black duffel bag. The one that's over there in the back." Nikki kept a tight grip on the door handle as her mother switched to the right lane and onto the 93 North ramp. At least the midday traffic was light.

"I didn't realize your father had noticed," Tara said. "He rarely paid attention to anything that had to do with me."

"Why?"

"Some arranged marriages don't work," Tara said. "We're leaving the city behind to go explore and have fun. That's all I want out of today. I don't want to think about anything back in Boston."

"Yay, road trip!" Nikki faked enthusiasm.

"That's the spirit." Tara didn't acknowledge Nikki's sarcasm.

"How long will we be gone for?" Nikki asked.

"That's up to you. You can be with me for a day, a week, a month . . ." Tara changed to the middle lane as they exited the tunnel and drove away from Boston toward New Hampshire.

"What?" A month? Tara was not serious. "I thought a few days, a week at most."

"You can do whatever you like," Tara said. "This is my life now. On the open road. Like Jack Kerouac."

"Yeah, well, we're not in the 1950s and you're not a bored white dude," Nikki said.

"Who says middle-aged brown women can't appreciate jazz and drugs?"

Nikki stared at her mother, jaw all the way open. "Therapy, Mom. That's what you need right now. Not LSD."

Tara laughed. "I've never tried anything. Not even pot. Have you?"

"No," Nikki said. "I took a gummy once but got so paranoid that I never wanted to do that again."

"We should stop at a dispensary." Tara eased back as they crossed the Zakim Bridge and left Boston behind. "It was too bad that the pro-psychedelic measure didn't get enough votes in Boston. Live and let live, I say."

A stroke, an alien abduction, or maybe she'd done a *Freaky Friday* with someone. Nikki would believe anything that would explain Tara being this out of character. "You barely handled a few glasses of rum and Coke last night." How had the engagement party been less than twenty-four hours ago?

"I am only slightly hungover," Tara said. "I had two glasses of water before bed. And I slept better than I have in a long while."

"More like passed out," Nikki muttered. "Do you remember being questioned by the police?"

Tara laughed. "It was fun, wasn't it? I mean the way Bijal accused me. I have never been seen as a bad girl. I got a kick out of it."

Tara's voice had changed. It was giddy and sly. "Mom?" It wasn't possible. There was no way. Except she had to ask. "Do you know what happened to the ring?"

Tara glanced over, then back to the road. She laughed. "Now you think I'm capable. I'm flattered."

"Mom! Did you take it?" Nikki turned her body toward her mother. "We're about to cross a state line. If you have it, turn around right now."

"Can you imagine it? Tara Rajput, a woman who has never done anything of note, commits a felony." Tara changed lanes. "Or is it a misdemeanor?"

"This is serious," Nikki said. "Why? How? Where is it?"

Tara sighed. "Calm down. You're not an accessory to a crime; I'm teasing you. It's fun to think about. Your mother, the thief." Tara reached over and turned on the radio. There was static until she found a station, and Kelly Clarkson's voice filled the cab of the Airstream. Nikki watched the road and her mom.

Tara hadn't denied it.

CHAPTER TWENTY-EIGHT

Boston, Massachusetts, 2006

Each year Tara accompanied Devon to the annual chamber of commerce dinner. It was important for him to network among his peers and be visible as a small business owner. Among the three partners, Devon was the face of their practice. He liked to be involved in everything. He filled his days with work, his evenings with their daughters, and his weekends with things like this. Rarely did Tara join him. Tonight, he was being recognized with an award, the first one for their practice's contribution to the community.

She was uncomfortable in her high heels, but she loved the short, twirly yellow dress she'd bought for tonight. Tara had spent time on her hair and makeup, and she felt beautiful. When Devon walked into their bedroom to straighten his tie, she could see his eyes take her in. His lips parted.

"You." He had to clear his throat. "That's a nice dress."

She'd never initiated a touch in all their years together. Tara had made him responsible for any intimacy between them. But the way he froze, his tie half done, she approached him. Straightened his tie and then stroked his cheek. The silky beard added a depth to him. She could barely remember what he'd looked like beforehand. She was braver now.

Having a friend like Mona had made Tara appreciate the positive in her marriage. She wasn't in love with her husband, but she was trying to be kinder to him.

He had covered her hand with his. Once she stepped back, she felt something, a little spark that had not been there before. It shocked her enough that she busied herself with gathering her purse, then grabbed her shoes and ran down the stairs to make sure the girls had everything they needed for their night with Devon's parents.

The room was crowded with local business owners and town leaders. She'd decided that she would not be jealous of Devon's achievement. He deserved this accolade, as he'd put in a lot of work to gain it. She'd helped, but only slightly.

"Mr. Parekh." A man with gray hair and a tweed jacket approached them. "I'm Philip Baird. I'll be presenting you with the plaque. There is time if you want to say a few words."

"Thank you. I promise to keep it short," Devon said. "This is my wife, Tara."

She shook hands with the man. Devon was taller than most in the room. One of three men of color. She followed him from group to group and saw him in his element. Not much different from when they were with their friends, Devon was gregarious, could converse on most topics, and was never shy or nervous. Tara spoke only when she was asked a question, uncomfortable with attention.

"You must be proud of him." A woman she'd been introduced to spoke to her while their husbands chatted.

"Yes," Tara said.

"Are you a dentist as well?" she asked.

"No," Tara replied.

"Oh, then what is it that you do?"

"She's a fantastic mom and a great wife." Devon put his arm around Tara.

"Ah," the woman said. "How conventional."

Embarrassed, Tara glanced down at her feet as heat rushed to her face. She stopped listening. Once they'd moved on, Devon asked if she wanted a glass of wine. Tara said yes, if only to get a minute to herself. She found a spot near the tall windows; the heavy brown curtains gave her some cover to prevent people from talking to her. She wanted to disappear. It was Devon who would be recognized for his hard work while her physics degree was buried in a box in the garage.

"No way."

Tara glanced up at the familiar voice. "Mona?"

Then she was wrapped in her friend's arms. "I can't believe it!"

Tara looked around to see where Devon was. "What are you doing here?"

"Rahul," Mona said. "He's networking." Mona's husband had moved back in and was looking for a new job.

"I was just leaving," Tara said. She would pretend to be sick and get a taxi home. "We can catch up next week."

"What brings you here?" As usual, Mona ignored her attempts to deflect. "Are you representing MIT?"

Tara mentally kicked herself. "No, I came here with someone."

Mona grabbed her arms and jumped excitedly; her silver jumpsuit shimmered with movement. "A date. Yes. Finally. Who is he?"

Tara didn't know how far to take things. She had only added a few lies, relied on Mona's ability to fill in gaps with her assumptions, but she couldn't pass off Devon as a date. Or could she? No. That would be too far. "It didn't work out. Like I said, I was just leaving."

Mona kept holding her hand. "I'm going to give you some tough love. You need to move on. You can't keep pining for someone you don't even want to see again. You're smart, pretty, and you have your life together. You're a research assistant at MIT. Any man would be lucky to be with you. I'm serious."

"Mona, it's not like that." Tara couldn't keep up the charade anymore. Yes, it would cost her the only friend she had, but that was the consequence for what she'd done. "I have to tell you something."

"Tara." Just then Devon came up and handed her a glass of white wine. "Who is your friend?"

Mona's eyes widened as she took in Devon in his navy suit. "You are gorgeous."

Devon gave Tara a wide smile. "Thank you."

"Well done, Tara."

Devon laughed. Then put his arm around Tara's waist. "I'm actually the lucky one."

Mona gave Tara a thumbs-up. Tara closed her eyes to the scene in front of her. This would be humiliating.

"How do you know my wife?"

The words made the room spin. Tara braced herself on Devon's arm. Mona looked at Tara, her expression confused. "I don't understand."

"We met in the café at the bookstore," Tara whispered. "A few years ago."

"You're married?" Mona asked.

"You didn't know?" Devon turned to Tara.

She didn't know what to do. "It was a misunderstanding."

Mona looked confused, then furious. "That's a long word for lying."

Philip Baird stood at the podium and called Devon forward.

"You never mentioned me?" Devon asked.

"I can explain."

Devon didn't reply but abruptly turned and left her. Mona scowled, then walked away as well. Tara stayed glued to the floor and watched.

A few minutes later, Devon kept his expression neutral as he spoke about doing work in underserved areas, part of the mission of his practice. He thanked his partners but didn't mention his family. Once he was done, he mingled a little before they left the event.

The car was silent as they rode home.

Tara finally spoke. "I didn't mean to hurt you."

He gave a bitter laugh. "You don't think you can."

She glanced at his profile. "What do you mean?"

"Forget it," he said. "I don't exist, right?"

She was ashamed. How could she do this? A grown woman acting like a five-year-old playing make-believe. "I'm sorry."

He said nothing. The silence continued as they pulled into the drive. Once inside, he checked on their sleeping daughters while she ushered his parents out of the house. Tara waited for him in bed. For the first time in their marriage, Devon slept in the guest room.

CHAPTER TWENTY-NINE

Time moves in a single direction—forward.
—*YNLIN*

Massachusetts–New Hampshire state line, present

Nikki and Tara found a rest stop once they had crossed into New Hampshire. Serviceable, not scenic. Nikki clutched her phone to gather herself. She couldn't put it off anymore—she needed to call Jay.

Next to her was a metal garbage can. Someone had missed, so Nikki picked up the trash from the ground and dropped it in the bin. She leaned back against the window of the rest stop's market and called.

Jay answered right away. "Where are you? Caleb said you were with your mom." Jay's voice in her ear was muffled by the wind and the passing highway traffic.

She nodded. Realized he couldn't see her. "Yes." Her voice soft.

"Why?"

"She bought a camper van," Nikki said. "She's running away."

"And you're what? Trying to stop her?"

She heard the frustration in his voice. "I'm trying to understand what's going on with her."

"How? By enabling her?"

Her mouth fell open. "I know you're mad, but that's not fair."

"I'm trying to understand, babe," he said. "But you just left without even talking to me."

She hadn't considered that. "It all happened fast."

"Maybe you're running away too," he said.

"What does that mean?"

"Nothing. When are you back?"

She closed her eyes. "I don't know."

"Seriously?" Jay's voice was strained, as if he was trying not to yell.

"As soon as possible," Nikki rushed to assure him.

"We have tickets to Leon Bridges next week," Jay said. "Maybe you'll consider coming back by then."

Nikki cleared her throat. "Please try to understand."

"That's all I do," he said. "Your mom comes first, right?"

"If it was your mom? You would do the same," she said.

"No," he said. "Because she's an adult, capable of making her own decisions. I wouldn't drop everything and take off without talking to you about it."

"I'm sorry," she said. "You were in court."

He snorted.

"Okay, you're angry with me," she said. "I don't know what else to say except I'm sorry I crossed the state line without your permission."

"Don't," he said. "You know that's not what I mean."

She rolled her neck. "Jay. I will get back as soon as I can. Please don't be upset with me. I just want to help my mom. I'll call you tonight from a quieter place and we can talk about it."

"Fine," he said, and sighed loudly. "Love you."

She said it back. Three months into their engagement and the phrase had become rote, a thing they said instead of goodbye. She ended the call and took a few deep breaths, stood, and rolled her shoulders back. He would come around. Hopefully.

Nikki went to the Airstream and waited for Tara. She busied herself by looking for places to stop and mapping out a route for them. Franconia would be a good area to spend a few days, then they could keep going north, cut east toward Maine or west toward Vermont. She would make the most of this opportunity, use the time not only to help her mom but to maybe understand why Tara was doing this.

"I can't remember the last time I shopped in a gas station supermarket." Tara climbed into the driver's seat and handed a large paper bag to Nikki. "Did you finish your phone call? Were you updating your father, telling him where we are?"

Nikki shook her head. "What did you buy?" Nikki looked through her mom's purchases. "Iced tea, a bag of potato chips, cheese puffs, and . . . pork rinds?"

"Chicharrones," Tara said. "Road trip snacks."

"For twelve-year-olds," Nikki said.

"Loosen up," Tara said. "We're having an adventure."

Nikki uncapped the iced tea. "Is this because you're postmenopausal?"

Tara laughed. "I am, but no. I've never done this before. And my parents wouldn't have let me have these kinds of snacks, especially in the car."

"There are trans fats, a lot of sodium, and chemicals in these things." Nikki put the plastic bag behind her seat.

"Deliciousness," Tara said.

"We never ate those things growing up. My after-school snack was sliced apples and peanut butter."

"Which is what the other moms were feeding their kids," Tara said. "I tried to do what they did."

Yes, she had. Thinking back, Nikki remembered Tara's presence, but there had been a detachment to her actions. Her mother never hugged them hello when they came home or kissed them good night. At most she patted their shoulders when she approved of them. Tara had done obligatory things. Affection was handled by her father and sister.

Nikki wasn't sure whether being a self-soother was a badge of honor or a by-product of the way Tara showed love. Maybe both.

"I wanted different for both you and Heena," Tara continued. "You are meant to conquer the world in your own way. Heena could have been a world-renowned artist if she hadn't attached herself to Caleb at such a young age."

"And now I am choosing to marry Jay," Nikki said.

"When you started your own business, I was so proud. I have all your writings and appearances, the podcasts you've been featured on. You're on your way to becoming a household name by making a meaningful difference in people's lives. Marriage will limit you."

Nikki turned her face away from the road and stared at the phone in her hands. She wondered if that were true. "Are we driving toward somewhere specific? The sun is about to set."

"We should look for those brown signs," Tara said.

"I found an RV park near Franconia," Nikki offered. "We can stay there and figure out the next few days."

"Let's see if we can find something near a lake or a river," Tara added. "I'd love to go for a hike, put my feet in the cold water."

"We're outdoor people now?"

"We don't know who we are," Tara said. "That's the whole point."

Except she knew who she was. It was Tara she no longer knew.

CHAPTER THIRTY

Newton, Massachusetts, 2006

A month after the chamber of commerce event, the uneasy silence between Tara and Devon had created a chasm in their home. Tara had apologized for not mentioning their marriage. She'd kept the lies about Ben a secret. That was only for her to know. Devon kept his distance. She hoped the girls didn't notice, but they were intuitive. Heena overcompensated by talking mostly to her father, making him laugh, checking on him. Nikki shared her snacks with Devon, brought him treats.

Tara did everything to reassure the girls that things were fine. Even if they weren't. Devon, on the other hand, didn't do the same. He was good with the girls, but he'd run out of pretense with Tara. He treated her the same as before, but he didn't smile toward her, didn't tease her if the soup was oversalted. He saved his laughs for Heena and Nikki.

She was an outsider in her own family. She'd done everything to be a good mother to her girls, she had even accepted that Devon would be their favorite. Tara told herself that it was more important to ensure that Heena and Nikki did not repeat her own mistakes. But it was becoming more difficult. Heena's room was covered from wall to wall in posters of actors and boy bands. She'd caught Nikki giggling over a boy in her class. Tara was tired of fighting with Heena over test scores and grades. While Nikki was a good student, Tara noticed that she had less influence over her younger daughter.

The large black duffel bag was on the bed. She'd bought it with her own money. It had been painful to take the hundred dollars from her precious private account. But it was time. Heena was in high school and Nikki two years behind. They were old enough to adapt to change. Devon was the favored one. They might even be relieved to be left with just him.

She'd done her best to make them self-sufficient, and she hoped that over time they would become more resilient. She wasn't leaving them, Tara reminded herself. She would find a way to be in their lives, if they forgave her. She'd accepted that she was a selfish person, but she couldn't continue to live this life she'd never wanted. She'd stayed too long. She no longer had any parents, whose reputation and standing she would have had to worry about.

One item at a time, she began to fill the empty bag. She would take only what she needed for a few weeks. There was a cheap hotel in Watertown that she could afford. That would give her and Devon enough time to separate their lives.

"Hey."

Tara jumped at the sound of his voice behind her. She was caught. She'd planned to leave a letter, let him know where she would be, and give him space to come to terms. "What are you doing home?"

He sat on the side of the bed. "I'm not feeling well."

"Oh." She took the bag from the bed and shoved it in her closet before closing the door. "Do you need anything?"

He looked at her, his head propped on the pillows of the bed she'd made that morning. "A little concern would be nice. But you don't know how to do that."

She paused. "I just asked you if you needed anything. But I've also been apologizing to you for weeks. I don't know what else to say. It was unintentional. Harmless."

"What were you putting in that bag?"

She didn't answer.

He turned his head away from her. "We've been married seventeen years. I've learned a lot about you. One thing that frustrates me is that you never answer a direct question."

Tara stopped at the foot of the bed. Hands clasped. "A few things. I was putting them away to make room in the dressers."

"Whose stuff?" He leaned against the headboard, one arm supporting his neck.

"Would you like some tea? Or chai."

"No. Whose stuff?"

"Mine." She didn't want to do this in person. It would be too difficult, and she didn't know how she would explain herself. Say that it wasn't him. She was the problem.

He nodded. Kept his gaze on her. She tried to stay still, not shuffle her weight because of his scrutiny. Then he sat up and rubbed his hands over his face.

"Let me bring you medicine," Tara offered.

"Took some."

She needed to get away from his stare. "Are you hungry?"

"Stop, Tara," he said. "Just stop."

"I'll leave you alone."

"That's not what I want." He stopped her with his words. "I don't want you to go." Devon patted the bed, gestured to her to sit. "We don't talk. You and me."

She sat at the edge, her hands in her lap. "I don't usually have a lot to say."

"Your parents told me that you were shy, preferred dreaming over participating in the world," he said. "I thought it was cute. I believed that would change once we became more comfortable with one another. I was wrong."

She didn't want to hear any more. "I'll make soup for you."

"There are pockets when I think, *Oh, that's who she is*," Devon continued. "When you think no one is looking, you give yourself a pat on the back when you finish a hard crossword puzzle. The way your real smile shows up when Nikki or Heena get honors for their accomplishments. How excited you get when you buy a new book. And then I realize, none of it has anything to do with me."

She closed her eyes against the ache in her chest. "I'm sorry." She didn't know what else to say.

"We've been in each other's orbit for a long time." He scratched his beard. "But we never got close. I'm sure there's a physics or astronomy word for that."

"Co-orbital configuration," Tara said. "Not exactly, but it's the closest to what you're saying."

"Right," he said. "That first year, I was so intimidated by you. You were beautiful and so much smarter than me. I thought you might be spoiled or demanding, but you carried yourself with grace. Quiet, shy, and you made do, accepted, adjusted. It wasn't easy for either of us."

She'd never asked why he'd wanted to marry her. She was stunned at his read of who she had been, that he had seen more than she'd believed.

"We settled in, and I don't even know how fast time has gone," he said. "Until that night at the chamber dinner, I thought we had a typical marriage. You support me, I provide for us. And if we didn't hold hands, if we weren't affectionate, that was fine. My parents were the same, and it's what I thought I wanted."

Past tense. She let his words wash over her. She'd gone through the motions, and he'd been deprived of a true wife. He'd had to deal with a body in motion. One without a heart.

"And now," he said.

She finally looked at him.

"I shouldn't have iced you out this past month," Devon said. "I was frustrated and annoyed. I needed time to take inventory of our relationship."

She swallowed. He was going to do what she had been putting off. He was going to let her go. One more person she'd made responsible for a decision because she didn't have the guts to go after what she wanted. Worse, she didn't know what that was anymore. The dream of academia was gone. She knew only that she couldn't stay here. Like this. On repeat every day.

"All those thoughts going through your head." Devon circled his index finger in her direction. "I can see them. Maybe you could try saying them out loud."

She channeled strength. For once in her life, she was going to say what was on her mind. Fight for what she wanted. "You want to end this. Our marriage."

"No," he said.

She glanced up.

"The opposite," he said. "I want us to try. I want us to figure out what sort of relationship we have. We have a family, Tara. Two girls who need us."

She gave a glance toward her closet. The duffel was half full. She could disagree. Leave as planned. Tell him instead of leaving a note.

Instead, she chose different words. "I don't know how to do this. I never have."

He scooched toward her. Touched her arm. "Then let's work on that. We've done a few things right along the way. Two incredible ones. We have a good life, the kind our parents wanted for us. They made it work. We can honor that by trying ourselves."

She smiled through her pain. He was asking her to live the kind of life she'd never wanted. Except it was all she had. Sometimes dreams stayed in the REM state, life was lived in consciousness. "If it doesn't work?"

"It will," he said. "I have faith in us. I don't even think our problems are that big. We need to talk more with each other. Share what you're thinking instead of assuming what I'm thinking or implying."

She didn't know if she could give him that much. It wasn't in her nature to share the messiness of her mind. "For Heena and Nikki."

"And for us." He tugged her toward him and lay them both down, her back against his front. She hoped he wasn't contagious but didn't say what she was thinking. Merely lay there in the warmth of his arms. It had been a while since she'd been held. Tara closed her eyes and let herself relax. She should have been in a cab by now, full of nerves and fear. This was better. A reprieve of sorts. A restart. Maybe Devon would be right. She slept.

CHAPTER THIRTY-ONE

Not all mountains should be climbed.
—YNLIN

Green Mountains, Vermont, present

For women who primarily worked out with Peloton bikes, choosing the Haystack Mountain trail was not the smartest idea. A thousand feet up for two miles and then back down seemed doable. But thirty minutes in, Nikki deeply regretted going along with her mother's suggestion. She checked her watch. "We've done a mile, maybe we turn around?"

"No, we can do this." Tara navigated the exposed roots and rocks as she continued upward. "Pretend it's Everest."

"God, no thank you," Nikki mumbled. Halfway was the top and then back down. "P.S. Mountain climbing isn't on my bucket list."

"What did you say?" Tara called back.

"Since when are you into this stuff?" Nikki picked up her pace and got closer to her mom. "You never came with Heena, Dad, and me when Dad took us out on his free weekends."

"Maybe I should have," Tara said. "It's refreshing in this forest."

"Cold and damp," Nikki said. "And I never knew how loud birds were."

"You're just in a bad mood," Tara said. "You haven't been sleeping well."

"Because we're sleeping in a van. On a cot. With a teeny-tiny bathroom behind our beds." She missed her apartment. And Jay.

Tara stopped. Put her hands on her hips and breathed deeply. "Amazing. This is so intoxicating. And clean. Try it. It'll help you stop panting."

"Are you sure you're not on drugs?" Nikki asked. "You can tell me."

"We've already had this conversation. If you're going to be grumpy, let's do this in silence." Tara started walking again. "Like a meditation."

They'd been on the road for three days. Nikki had tried to get Tara to open up, but her mother was too busy being excited for every experience from diner french fries to sunsets. It was as if Tara had never seen nature before. She took pictures of leaves, trees, and mushrooms that sprouted along trails. Nikki had to admit that seeing her mother like this was better than seeing the Tara who rarely spoke and wore a sad expression all the time.

On their second day, they'd had plans to go up Mount Washington, but it was closed because of high winds at the top. Instead of reverting to silence, it was Tara who had cheered Nikki up with a spontaneous plan to cross another state line into Vermont's Green Mountains and make an overnight stop at another campground.

"How are things with you and Jay?" Tara huffed as she climbed.

"I thought we were doing this in silence," Nikki replied.

"How are you feeling about marriage?"

"Why don't you tell me? You're the one who is walking away from one. What happened?"

"Is that why you've been in a bad mood this whole time?" Tara kept walking. "It shouldn't matter to you. You're an adult, you don't have to worry about custody battles or who you're going to live with. Get over it."

Nikki bumped into an exposed log and navigated around it. Had her mom just said that? "It still affects the family. Especially since you are being like this."

"Like what?"

"Mom, we're freaking climbing a mountain in the middle of nowhere. On a weekday. And you're happy about it. I heard you humming this morning. *Humming.* I didn't even know you knew how."

Tara waved with her back to Nikki. "You're being dramatic. But you're right, I am happy. For the first time in, well, I honestly can't remember."

"Maybe mention the birth of your two children," Nikki murmured under her breath.

Tara kept her pace and trudged up the trail. Hiking might not be their thing, but her mother was fit. Daily walking had been her mom's routine, thirty minutes in the morning and thirty in the evening. Nikki remembered how, when she was in high school, her parents would go together after dinner while Nikki cleaned the kitchen.

"When you married Dad, were you nervous that you were so different from one another?" Nikki caught up to Tara.

Tara stayed silent. Nikki didn't push.

"I didn't know him well enough," Tara said. "I hadn't thought about compatibility. I hoped he would be kind, respectful, and supportive."

"Did he tell you what he was looking for?"

Tara stopped to catch her breath. "I think he wanted someone like his own mother. A stay-at-home wife and mother. He has a lot of pride. He saw himself as the sole provider."

"And you wanted more." Nikki could understand how something like what her father had done could eat away at Tara. But thirty-five years was a long time to hold on to anger and resentment. She couldn't understand why Tara had never done anything about it. Lost in thought, Nikki tripped on a rock and was smacked in the face with a damp leafy branch.

"Are you okay?" Tara whipped back around. Her face full of worry as she checked on Nikki.

"No," she said. "I hate hiking."

"Me too," Tara said.

Nikki stopped, out of breath. "Then why are we doing this?"

Tara walked back and offered Nikki a sip from her metal water bottle. "Here, drink. You're probably dehydrated. Do you want a snack? I have some trail mix in my fanny pack."

Tara took a gulp and offered her mom a drink. "No. That heavy breakfast of bacon, eggs, and toast is expanding in my stomach. I hope the van is aired out by the time we get back."

"It was a good experiment," Tara said. "Now we know that the stove works, but the tiny oven doesn't. I can use it for storage."

"You can't live in that thing permanently," Nikki said.

Tara recapped the bottle and led the charge upward. Forty-five minutes later they reached the summit. The sky was heavy with clouds, but sunlight peeped in through gaps in the thick white puffs. Nikki looked around. In the distance, she saw the small mountaintops that looked like round hills. A tiny blue lake in the valley below gleamed when a ray of sun touched its surface. "This is pretty. I mean, I'm sure I'll appreciate it once I'm able to breathe. Or maybe I'm dead. Either way, the way down has got to be better."

Tara was silent and still. Almost in prayer as she faced the vista before them. Nikki gave her a minute and found a large rock to sit on.

"I wasn't nervous to marry your father," Tara said. "I was sad, lonely, and heartbroken."

Nikki's eyes filled. "Because your parents pressured you?"

Tara nodded. "It was what was expected of me. Do you know this is the first time in my life that I'm doing something of my own choosing?"

It broke her heart to hear this from her mom.

Tara patted Nikki's hand. "I let life happen to me. Your father broke his promise to me. He made us live with his family until we had Heena. Then he bought a house without me seeing it. He said it was a surprise.

And it was. I had no idea he had the money to pay the down payment and mortgage. He did the same with the car I drove all these years. I didn't even get to choose the color much less the make and model."

Nikki hadn't known any of this. She couldn't imagine Jay making all their decisions. Then she understood why he'd been frustrated that Nikki had left without talking to him first. "It's hard to believe."

Tara grabbed a bag of trail mix and held it out for Nikki. "He's a good father. I won't take that away from you."

"You raised us too," Nikki said. "Helped me learn about molecules. Carried boxes up to my first apartment."

Tara stared at the vista. "I love you and your sister. I am lucky to have you. But I never wanted to be a mother."

It was a gut punch to hear. Wanting your parents to be honest and hearing the truth were vastly different things. "Then why did you?"

"Marriage, for a woman, is like being slowly squeezed until the shape of you changes into someone you no longer recognize. Your grandparents, your dad, family, friends, they all expected children. So I delivered."

"You couldn't have said no?"

Tara shrugged. "I didn't know how. I was raised to be someone's wife, a daughter-in-law. I had an obligation to ensure my parents were respected."

"But when you and Dad were on your own," Nikki asked, "did you talk to him about this?"

"No," Tara said. "I accept that it's my fault. I was not a good wife. I am solely to blame for this divorce."

A relationship by its definition involves two people. Her mom had been twenty-one when she got married. Nikki remembered how young she'd been at that age. "I'm worried about you."

Tara patted Nikki's thigh that was covered in sweaty workout leggings. "We just climbed a mountain; I can handle things."

Nikki wasn't so sure. "What if we go back to Boston? You and Dad can talk."

"No," Tara said. "I have some things to do first."

"Like what?"

Tara stood and stretched. "I think we've tested the stove enough today. How about we find a nice place for dinner tonight?"

"Mom, please don't change the subject," Nikki pleaded.

Tara stared out at the vista. "Do you know why I enjoy physics so much? Because it is the ultimate understanding of all things. From how we came to be, to our existence, time, motion, energy, force. It's all-encompassing. The answers are there. There is certainty and assurance in the calculations."

Nikki accepted that Tara had opened up as much as she'd been comfortable doing and that now she needed to shut down.

"You know what it can't explain?" Tara said. "Love. There is no formula that solves that specific emotion. We feel it. Know when it's there and when it's missing."

"And it's missing between you and Dad." Spending three and a half decades with someone without love was unimaginable.

Tara touched Nikki's shoulder. "Don't be sad. I care for him as he does for me. We have a friendship. There was contentment in that."

"But it's no longer enough." The air was cool and dry. A soft breeze played with her hair.

Tara closed the zip on the bag of trail mix and shoved it back in her fanny pack. "I don't know if there is such a thing as enough."

CHAPTER THIRTY-TWO

Newton, Massachusetts, 2006

Tara waited for Mona at their usual table. Her stomach in knots, she toyed with a sugar packet. Her untouched chai latte sat lukewarm at her side. She had made six calls to Mona before her friend finally answered. Tara asked for one more meeting to explain, even though there was no rational answer for Tara's actions. She had built a friendship on a lie. Mona was the better person because she'd agreed to meet. Tara checked her watch again. She'd been early and hoped Mona would show. If Mona stood her up, Tara deserved it.

Tara had never been surrounded by loads of friends, never part of a clique or a team. One. That had been her pattern. From elementary school to now, Tara had one friend at a time. First grade, Kamila. Fourth grade, Lisa. Seventh grade, Dana. Ninth grade, Vicky. Then Mayuri. One for each finger on a single hand. She couldn't count Mona, who didn't know the real Tara.

Through the window, she watched as Mona got out of her car. She was bundled up against the freezing temperatures. The parking lot was icy, and Mona walked gingerly to avoid falling. Tara straightened the table. There was nothing there but her mug and the packet of sugar, but still, Tara wiped it with a small paper napkin.

"Hey." Mona removed her tan wool coat and slung it over the empty chair between them.

"Thanks for meeting me." Tara stood. "Coffee or tea? My treat."

Tara's rhetoric professor at BU used to say that if you're nervous it means you care. That was the crux of it. It wasn't only about an apology. Tara didn't want to lose her only friend. Mona chose to get her own coffee. Tara waited, her head down. She had thought over what to say, but her mind was blank. How did you start a conversation like this?

Mona sat again, a mug of coffee held between her palms. There were dark circles under her eyes. She didn't wear any makeup today, and her long black hair was tied up. This was unlike her, as Mona was always camera-ready. Worse, this was the quietest Mona had ever been. Tara was nauseous. Her friend was taking Tara's betrayal hard. "I'm sorry."

Mona didn't respond.

"I didn't mean to lie." She told Mona everything, starting with the impulse she'd had to pretend she was someone else with someone she'd never see again. "I wanted to live a fantasy for a few minutes. Then we became friends, and I didn't know how to undo it." That was a lie. "I was afraid to tell you the truth. Embarrassed. I thought if you knew the real me, you wouldn't want to be friends."

Mona's silence was unnerving.

"There were so many times I wanted to tell you, then too much time had passed. I let you assume a lot of things, and while that's not an excuse, I didn't know how to get out of it. I was ashamed of my real life. And I don't know how to make it better. I'm making you cry."

Mona wiped her cheeks with a paper napkin. "Stop."

Tara listened. Stayed quiet as Mona sipped her coffee.

"My marriage is over, permanently," Mona said. "Rahul moved out."

Tara saw the anguish on Mona's face.

"It's fine," Mona continued. "We've been trying to make it work for the last two years. Sometimes love isn't enough. Maybe it dissolved. I'm sure you have some physics word for it. Or maybe it wasn't what I thought."

Evaporation. But Tara held her words. Instead, she reached over and placed a hand on Mona's arm. Tara wasn't a demonstrative person and wasn't one to initiate touch, but the urge to comfort her friend made her act instead of think.

Mona pulled away. "I'm fine. I will be."

Tara fumbled for words. She wanted to be there for Mona, but maybe it was too late.

"Inelastic collision," Tara said. "We were two objects in motion. When we met, there wasn't equal energy. You were bright sunshine, and I was dull, gray rain. I absorbed your energy, became lighter. I didn't give much back. I'm mixing it up. I just want you to know that I wanted—*want*—to be your friend. I can be a true friend to you, especially now."

"You're not dull," Mona said. "It's your wardrobe."

The tension eased. "Maybe we can go shopping."

They sat in contemplative silence for a bit. Tara got them another round of beverages.

"There are so many things going on in my head," Mona said. "My parents will gloat because they were against us marrying. I'll be the first one in my family to have a broken marriage. I'll have to get a job, and I'm not qualified for anything."

"One thing at a time." Tara understood. She'd considered similar issues when she'd been packing her bag. Now, talking to Mona, she was glad Devon had stopped her.

"Can I ask you something?" Mona said. "Was Ben real? Or did you make him up?"

Tara hadn't been prepared for the subject change. She looked out the window and watched someone slip and catch themselves by grabbing the hood of a parked car. "Real. Though it's been so long that I'm not sure how much of him is what I created from my fantasies."

"Did you love him?"

Tara closed her eyes to remember those feelings. "I'm not sure that's what it was. I called it that because I was consumed by him. I didn't know him well enough so I created someone that became lodged in my heart. I can remember his voice, but don't know if I would recognize it if he said something. I'm not making sense. There are things I associate with the memories I relived or created. I'll smell fresh grass or see the ocean, and Ben is my first thought. I know part of it is that I've spent so much time with those moments that they are now hardwired in my brain. Neuroplasticity."

"But you're married to someone else."

Tara nodded. "I'm not the type of person to go against convention. It was expected of me. At twenty-one, I was making an adult decision. But I never considered that it would be for the whole of my life."

"What do you mean?"

"My aim stopped at being able to go to MIT. A means to an end. I never thought beyond that in terms of a relationship. It was platitudes. We'd be kind to each other; we would support each other. I didn't have examples or experience in what that would mean."

"Rahul and I were so in love," Mona said. "Us against the world because our parents didn't approve. I thought about forever with him but in a childish way. I dreamed of getting 'just because' flowers. I never imagined daily disappointments or how small problems can become so huge that they become impossible to overcome. I never understood what it meant to grow apart."

Tara reached out again and put her hand on Mona's wrist.

"I think it's good that you didn't end up with your first love," Mona said. "You can keep it pure in your heart."

Tara sipped her now-cold chai. "He's perfect because I gave him all the characteristics based on spending one night with him. I made him be a person who is calm under pressure. I made him intelligent, not simply smart. Ben is a real person, but I only know my version of him. The past is just a lie we tell ourselves."

"Wait," Mona said. "One night? That's it?"

Shame made her face burn. "It was real and imaginary. Mostly, Ben was an invention of what could have been. You asked about love. Can you love without ever knowing if you've been loved? No one besides my daughters have said those words to me. Not my parents. Not Devon." She didn't add Ben because he hadn't known her. "Pathetic, right?"

Mona didn't say anything. And Tara refused to look at her and see pity in those eyes.

"Do you want that? I mean in the future."

"I can't think about it," Tara said. "I have to stay in the present because I can't bear the thought that this might be how it is until I die."

"That is dark," Mona said. "There's still a lot of life left, you know. You have things to look forward to, like your daughters, their weddings, having grandchildren."

Tara wanted Mona to know the real her. "That is my nightmare."

Mona stared at her. "Really?"

"See? I'm a hard person to be with," Tara said. "My dream is to be in a university setting, learning from great minds. I would have an office with a whiteboard and plenty of markers. I would spend my days lost in research and experiments."

"Then go back to school," Mona said.

Tara shook her head. "It's too late for that. Devon wants us to work on our marriage, and I agreed."

"Even though it's not what you want?"

Tara stayed silent. It was too late. She was too behind. It was better to live the life she had instead of reaching for something that might never be achieved. "Is there anything you need? I want to help."

Mona shook her head. "My friends are coming in from San Francisco this weekend. They're helping me with lawyers and all that. Once the school year is over, I'm going to move back to the Bay Area with my son."

And there it was. Mona didn't see Tara as one of her friends. This proved her hypothesis, that going after dreams wasn't for her. "I will miss you." She meant it. Mona would be another person who had come in, touched her heart, and left. She would count her as a friend. The first finger on her second hand.

CHAPTER THIRTY-THREE

What's meant for you will arrive for you.
—*YNLIN*

Bennington, Vermont, present

Nikki's fingers traced the delicate filigree of an antique silver picture frame.

The antique shop in Bennington, Vermont, was a far cry from her usual shopping expeditions at Wrentham Outlets or the Prudential Center mall.

"Oh, Nikki, look at these cute bud vases." Tara was on the other side of the aisle.

Nikki nodded as her mom held them up. Brown and teal, they were worn and chipped. "Since when are you into dust catchers? You hate clutter."

"People change."

If she hadn't witnessed it with her own eyes this past week, Nikki would not have believed Tara was capable of such a thing. Her mother had smiled. Genuinely. When they couldn't maneuver the Airstream out of a tight parking spot, Tara had laughed so hard at their attempts that tears rolled down her face. It no longer seemed unbelievable that Tara would buy knickknacks.

In the evenings they would sit under the stars, and Tara would talk about interstellar bands, and Nikki would summarize an Anne Hathaway movie. When their temporary home became a place for calamities, from a backed-up sink to lack of ventilation in the bathroom, Tara took it in stride. She had no buyer's remorse for the $75,000 impulse purchase. Nikki, meanwhile, had gone down the online research hole of lemon laws. Still, she'd started the trip believing it would be torture and it had blossomed into understanding. She was seeing her mother as a person in her own right.

"What are you going to do with those?" Nikki pointed to the bud vases in Tara's hands.

"Put them out on the little ledge by the window," Tara said.

That made no sense in a moving vehicle. Even after seeing this happier version of Tara, Nikki knew it wasn't a good idea for her to travel alone. It took two people to do all that was required to live in an Airstream. As much as Tara tried, she wasn't an outdoor adventure type of woman. And while Nikki now understood her mother's choice more, she didn't know why *now*. She'd been married to Devon for years without making a change. So what had happened?

Her phone vibrated. A text from Jay. The longer she was gone, the more strained things became between them. She would send him pictures of waterfalls, trails, mountains, and their meals. He would give them a thumbs-up emoji. The distance between them wasn't just in miles. He didn't want to talk about Tara, so she didn't tell him that she was seeing her mom in new ways and learning things she'd never known. Instead, Nikki would steer the conversation toward him and his day. She'd ask how his cases were going, whether he'd made time to relax. A few days ago, she'd asked if there had been any updates around the missing ring. He had quickly changed the subject.

In her journal, Nikki had a list of topics she and Jay couldn't discuss. It was getting longer after each conversation. "Mom, I'm going to go for a walk. I'll text you to see where you are in a little while."

Tara waved her off. "I'll be wandering."

She left the store. The crisp air in the small town surrounded by mountains made her feel better. It was early enough that her long-sleeved thin sweater was cozy, though she knew she'd have to roll up the sleeves by afternoon. She checked the message.

I'm here.

She glanced around. Her heart raced. He'd come for her. Each day, Nikki sent a pin of their location to Heena and Jay. Her heart soared and her hands shook as she called him. "Where is here?"

"Main Street," he said. "In front of the tattoo parlor."

She walked a block over, turned the corner, and spotted him at the end of the street. Overwhelmed, she ran toward him. He was in his weekend uniform, the Red Sox cap facing forward. She instinctively jumped into his arms and he caught her. Then she cupped his face and kissed him. "I missed you."

He nodded, put her back on the ground, and let go.

"What are you doing here? I mean, I'm glad you came." Nikki stumbled over her words. "Don't you have a baseball game today?" He was in intramural leagues for basketball, baseball, and soccer.

"I, uh, we need to talk and it's better to do it face-to-face."

She stopped breathing for a full ten seconds. He couldn't meet her eyes. She didn't understand. Some people laugh when they're afraid. Nikki got nauseous. He was here to end it. He had told her time and again that she needed to prioritize their relationship. He had a right to be upset at Nikki's inability to give him an exact date. She'd missed their concert, and instead of going with a friend, he'd stayed home. "I see."

She promised herself that she wouldn't cry in front of Jay. She wouldn't make him feel manipulated or responsible. Anger joined fear. This was all it took for him to call it off. A week away, not putting him first. Their relationship was too tenuous to survive a lifetime.

They stood in silence. Nikki refused to speak first. He would have to use his words and tell her. She would accept it, watch him walk away. She'd wait until she was alone before she let her heart break.

"How are you?" Jay asked.

I'm terrified that I will never know a love like this again.

He finally reached over and brushed her hair away from her face. "Don't take this the wrong way, but you look like you've been in the wilderness for a month."

Nikki laughed. The tension eased, but not enough. "It's been a long week." She looked at the chipped polish on her nails. "I stink, don't I?"

"Eau de campground," he said.

"I've used a lot of wet wipes in between tepid showers." This was good. Small talk.

"Hungry?"

She nodded. They walked side by side in silence. This was hard for him. Jay was rarely pensive. The urge to smooth it over, do it for him, was so strong, Nikki squeezed her nails into her palm to stop herself. She didn't want this. Her whole body rebelled at the idea of not being with him. A few minutes later, he led them into Lil Britain, a fish and chips shop. She sat at a small table with black cafeteria chairs and stared at a giant replica red telephone booth while Jay ordered.

"I got two orders for fish and chips and a root beer for you," he said, sliding across from her.

"I hate root beer."

He put a can of ginger ale and a plastic glass in front of her. "I was going to make a corny joke about forgetting your beverage preferences, but you look too tired to mess with."

"I appreciate the restraint."

Jay fidgeted with the cap of his orange soda bottle.

"How was the traffic?" She winced at her attempt to avoid the situation they faced.

"Heavy in town," he said. "Clear after Worcester."

Nikki toyed with her plastic glass, which reminded her of her high school cafeteria.

"How are things going with you? And your mom."

Now you ask? "Fine. Good. She wants to stay on the road forever."

"And you?"

She shook her head. "Of course not. I have a life back in Boston." *You.* "I just need to get her through whatever is going on with her."

"It's her choice," he said. "Not your burden."

"You still don't get it," she said.

"You're right." He shrugged.

Their food arrived, and Nikki's stomach turned as the smell of fried oil permeated the air. She took a small bite of a french fry.

"We need to talk," he said.

Her shoulders ached from holding herself so tightly. "That's why you're here."

"I don't know how to word it," Jay said, "so I'll just come out with it. My mother is suing yours."

So many things swirled around in her head. She blurted out the only thing that mattered. "You're not breaking up with me?"

"What?"

She waved it off. "Bijal auntie is suing my mom?"

"Go back," he said. "Why did you think we were breaking up? Is that what you've been thinking about this past week?"

She closed her eyes to think. "You came here, said you needed to talk. In person. I thought . . ."

"And?" He waited for her response.

"No," she said. "I don't want that. I know you're upset, so I thought you might be done. It's not what I want, just to state it on record."

He gave her a lopsided smile. "Record, huh?"

Nikki sat up. "Yes. Have it notarized or whatever makes it more official."

"It's true that I'm upset," he said. "I want you to come home. I don't like that you're making yourself responsible for your mother. But then this happened."

Nikki put her head in her hands. "Why is Bijal auntie doing this?"

"The ring," he said. "She insists that your mom has it."

"Jay, she doesn't have it," Nikki said. "At least not here. I've gone through everything in the Airstream and all my mother's things. It's not here."

He rubbed his hands over his face. "It's a mess."

"And you're helping your mom," Nikki said. "Ironic."

He pursed his lips and popped a chunk of fried fish in his mouth, chewed, then swallowed. "This is different. Your mother's existential crisis is for her to figure out, but a ring worth a quarter of a million dollars that's been in my family for hundreds of years is a bigger problem."

Nikki regretted her words. Stayed silent.

"Why did Tara auntie run?" Jay asked.

Nikki couldn't believe it. "You agree with your mom!"

"That's not an answer," he said.

"Don't lawyer this," she yelled.

"Your mom doesn't want us to get married. She has been acting out of character. She laughed it off when she was accused and hasn't explicitly said she didn't steal it." He wiped his mouth with a napkin. "And the very next morning after it disappeared she left your family and went on the lam."

"Circumstantial." Nikki didn't know whether it was or not, but it was what people said on TV. "Besides, she was frisked just like you and I were."

"That was more a TSA-like pat down. We didn't even have to remove our shoes," he argued.

"She isn't in hiding. You found us easily. And why would she take it?"

"Money," Jay said. "You yourself said she plans to live on the road. How is she going to afford it?"

It was as if Jay were a stranger. It was baffling. Her mom had gone from caterpillar to butterfly and Jay was doing the reverse. "I can't believe you would think this way about my family. Me," Nikki said, before shooting up from the table in shock.

He stood along with her. "I'm not saying it's you or that you're an accessory."

"Oh my God," she said. "Do you hear yourself?"

"Nikki," he said. "This is serious. It's not about what you and I think. It is a federal crime to carry stolen goods across the state line. You could face accessory charges."

She stared at him. "Who are you?"

"I'm trying to help," he said. "This conversation went off the rails. I want us to work together on this."

"But you've already decided my mom is guilty," Nikki said.

"Maybe I should have called instead," Jay said, punctuating his exasperation with a sigh. "You want to help your mom? Come back to Boston."

With that, Jay walked out.

CHAPTER THIRTY-FOUR

Newton, Massachusetts, 2007

The internet was Tara's favorite invention since the telescope. Mainly because it made her small, insular life vast. She had access to things in ways that had been unimaginable. There were blogs, RSS feeds, and social websites like Facebook and Twitter where you could find people from your past. On Amazon, people were able to buy more than just books. Tara didn't have an iPhone like Devon, but she had a laptop that connected her to so much more than the library.

For her, it was a gateway to a world she could explore at leisure from the comfort of her home. Using Internet Explorer, she could access websites and forums and see people's shared photos on Flickr. All this helped Tara see, not just imagine. There were so many ways to live. Before, she had known only the people she interacted with in real life. Now there were communities who talked to one another on message boards. Instead of a few, there were thousands upon thousands who had similar curiosities. There were discussions under articles where she could read their thoughts to see how they interpreted the information. It wasn't a classroom; it was open for all.

The best part, especially now that Mona knew her real life, was that Tara could be whoever she wanted to be online without anyone knowing. When Mona went back to California, Tara discovered *The Sims*, where she could design a life other than the one she lived. With the Discover University and Apartment Life packs, Tara could play at what might have been. MIT. A fellowship. NASA. She learned how to create and decorate her apartment. Though she learned that her imagination was limited, even with the help of game options. Her dreams remained small. Drilled down to only one. Independence without obligations. Which was impossible, especially when she had a sixteen-year-old and a fourteen-year-old. Oh, and a husband, his friends, and her in-laws. She also had to be a part of Devon's business circle.

When she was left on her own, in among cooking, doing all the mom- and wife-related errands, cleaning, and doing everything else that came with managing Devon's big life, Tara spent her time online. She would read whatever she could get her hands on, mainly websites about science, especially physics. It was reassuring that while she would never be able to follow in the footsteps of the physicist Chien-Shiung Wu, she hadn't lost interest in keeping up with the field.

Tara knew her ability to understand physics had faded over time, but with the internet she was able to relearn, practice, and think. She could spend hours on the lectures of Richard Feynman. She filled notebooks as if studying for imaginary tests. She could stare into space and let her mind think, ponder, stretch. That was what drew her to physics. Tara hadn't been able to make the time to sit and wonder about the universe. She was merely a dabbler. Still, there was so much to learn and read.

After an hour-long stretch on the website Quantum Diaries, Tara rolled her neck and stretched her arms over her head. She wasn't good at sitting hunched over, eyes on a screen. She wished the magazines and journals she read in the library could be brought home, that they could be updated as fast as the internet. But that meant asking Devon for money, and she couldn't stomach it. She'd learned a long time ago that he tolerated her passion but didn't think it was necessary.

Then she looked at the blinking cursor in the search box. She'd been toying with the idea for months but hadn't had the courage to type the two words that could bring her simultaneously to the time before she'd been married and to future possibilities.

Tara reached for the bottom drawer of her desk. She grabbed the notebook at the bottom of the stack, where she'd put the piece of paper Mona had given her so long ago. Ben Anand. University of Maine. Department of Oceanography.

She could do it, just to see where he was or what he might be up to. But her hands didn't reach for the keyboard. She rubbed her denim-clad thighs as nerves gathered in her stomach. Her breath became rougher. She wanted to know and not know. Schrödinger's cat. Right now, he was a memory. Pure. Perfect. Flannels and curls that flew in the wind as the sailboat cut through the deep waters of the ocean. He was who she wanted him to be. But once she looked for him, she might not be able to retain the fantasy of Ben. Once you know a person's truth, you can never make them be who they're not.

Did she want to know?

She scratched her arms with her short, unpainted nails, then hugged herself. He could be that person. Solitary in his work and life. He could be married. The mere thought of it pained her, though it was the most likely scenario. And she was not the type to long for a man who was with someone else, even if Ben, like her, was restless and unsatisfied. But what if he wasn't? Maybe he had chosen his career over marriage. Men were afforded that privilege more than women.

He could be a lauded oceanographer with papers and findings about the mysteries of the sea. She could write to him. Start a conversation by asking him what he liked to research. See if he remembered her from so long ago. She blushed as she relived that one night one more time.

Her face lit up in a smile. Her knee shook as she recalled the intensity of her attraction for him. It was as if she'd regressed back to her twenty-one-year-old self. Her face warmed as she typed in his full name along with other information she'd accumulated. Then, with a deep breath, she hit Enter. And waited.

CHAPTER THIRTY-FIVE

Your boundaries. Your choice.
—*YNLIN*

Lake Champlain, Vermont, present

The lapping water at the lake's edge did not make Nikki calm. Her mind wouldn't settle enough to appreciate the blue sky, the white puffy clouds, or the warm sunshine on her face. Since Jay had left her in Bennington, she'd gone through every emotion possible. He hadn't texted to let her know he'd gotten back to Boston safely. She hadn't sent him a "good night, sweet dreams" message. They had retreated to their corners, each with their own mom.

She had yet to tell Tara about the lawsuit. She'd spent the evening on her laptop trying to find examples of cases like this. Her fear was that if the situation wasn't defused, she and Jay wouldn't survive. Every muscle in her body ached, and not only from sleeping on a forty-year-old cot in a metal tube. She had to go back and deal with everything. She hoped Tara would come with her.

Thoughts of home, the perfect sofa, her teas, the warmth of her fuzzy blanket, they all beckoned Nikki.

"Breakfast!" Tara came out with two plates of toast with smashed boiled eggs on top. She'd seasoned them with Tajín.

Nikki grabbed one of the plastic dishes. "Thanks."

"What a gorgeous day." Tara scooched next to her on the bench. "We should see if there are any kayaks to rent."

"Have you ever been in one?" Nikki asked.

"Grumpy? I heard you toss and turn during the night." Tara bit into the toast. "Is it work?"

"No," Nikki snapped. "Sorry. It's . . . we have a problem."

"Out here, there is no such thing," Tara said.

"Back there, though, it's not going well." Nikki pointed to what she hoped was south.

"Put it away for now. We're here." Tara spread her arms out.

For all the changes Nikki had witnessed in Tara, the core remained. Her mother did not want to deal with anything that would involve direct conversations. It was disappointing. "Don't you want to know what's going on?"

Tara shook her head. "Nikki, I don't live there anymore."

Nikki couldn't help it. She laughed. "Oh yes you do."

"I have everything I need in that van." Tara indicated the Airstream.

"What about Heena? The grandkids? Dad?" Nikki said. "You can't walk away. Not without fixing the mess you left behind."

"It's the only way," Tara said. "I don't belong there."

She heard the familiar sadness return to her mother's voice. This time, Nikki needed to push through. "What happened? Why are you doing all this? Turning your back on not just your life but your family? Fine, you didn't want children. You have two. And the twins. Don't you have any feelings?"

Tara put her plate of leftover toast off to the side. "You. The day you came to my study and told me you were choosing to get married, it changed something in me. I had made peace with Heena's decision, but I believed you would be the one to fulfill my wish for independence. Then I sat through that fancy dinner watching everyone celebrate something that I believed I had devoted my life to preventing."

Each word was like a paper cut on her heart. "I'm the reason you left?"

Tara shook her head. "No. I'm not saying it right. When I was young, I knew the life I wanted. Getting married was a means. When it didn't work out, I was full of resentment. It was so heavy it affected every aspect of my life. When you told me your news, the blurry glass I had been looking through became clear. I made choices and built the life I had. I kept saying it's not what I want but I never changed my circumstances. I thought if you became what I had wanted for me, then all of these years would have been worth it. I don't know how to explain it."

"I didn't want to disappoint you," Nikki said.

"You don't understand," Tara said. "You chose to get engaged despite knowing I would disapprove. I never had that kind of courage. I knew I had to do something. W equals F times D. I had to work to overcome force and distance moved. The only way I know how is to keep going further from resistance, which for me is Boston. If I go back, I will lose this."

"That's not true," Nikki said. "You're changing."

"Not fully," Tara said. "You and Heena deserve better. I know I can't change the past. All I can do is put miles between that and whatever is in the future."

Nikki stood, arms crossed, facing the lake. "Is this it? You're never going back?"

"As of right now, no," Tara whispered. "I can't." She heard her mother's voice break.

Never ask a question if you're afraid to hear the answer. She'd heard that in a movie or TV show or maybe read it in a book. It had stuck

with her as good advice. Yet Nikki had. "I'm going to call a rideshare and find a flight or a bus to go home."
Tara said nothing.
"What's your next stop?" Nikki asked.
Tara watched as Nikki turned toward her. "Maine."

CHAPTER THIRTY-SIX

Allston, Massachusetts, 2015

Tara hefted another box labeled "Kitchen" and navigated through the narrow hallway of Nikki's new apartment. If she didn't have a sore back and her knees didn't ache from climbing up and down three flights, she might have been able to pretend this was her move. The one that she never got to do after graduating from BU. As she set the box down on the laminate countertop, a twinge of envy tugged at her heart.

She watched Nikki bustle around the small space, her face happy with excitement. This tiny three-bedroom in Allston wasn't impressive. The walls needed a coat of paint, the kitchen was dated enough that Devon had checked to make sure the appliances were in working order. The wooden floors were uneven at best. But Nikki had found two roommates online to move into this place with. They were already talking about how they would set it up and decorate. Tara wondered what it would have been like to have had this experience herself—to have lived on her own, even for a little while.

"Mom, where should I put these plants?" Nikki called from the living room, interrupting Tara's reverie.

"Somewhere near the window." Tara's mind was still half-lost in what-ifs. Nikki had a full life, she should be satisfied. Instead, she was jealous. And ashamed.

She should be proud that Nikki was surrounded by friends. Instead, Tara bemoaned the emptiness in her own life. She had lost or destroyed the two friendships she'd managed to have on her own. Mayuri was so far in the past that it was hard to recall anything except the strongest memories. She had found Mona on Facebook but hadn't reached out. What could she possibly say? Tara saw the images of her friend's life from a distance. Mona's photos were mainly of her being a mom. Her son at various milestones and moments over the years. There was the two of them on a trip to Italy, her pride as she stood next to him with a giant bow on a new car. It seemed as if her friend was thriving, that she had reclaimed her life in ways Tara couldn't imagine now for herself.

She'd been so resistant to being only a mom that she never registered their milestones as hers. Yes, she pushed them, celebrated them, but this apartment wasn't hers. She'd gone from her parents' to her husband's with the exception of college. *Sex and the City* was a foreign documentary. She'd never dated or dreamed about anyone other than Ben. Occasionally, she would look again, but there wasn't anything personal about him on the internet. Tara often hoped that he was still unmarried, thriving on his boat in the middle of the ocean, perhaps thinking of her. Which was ridiculous because she was not delusional. That he'd achieved what he'd once told her he wanted to do. She wanted that for Ben. Everyone she'd known had followed their paths, done the things they'd said they would.

Except her.

"Mom, Colleen has a lot of kitchen stuff too." Nikki came into the kitchen. "Maybe whatever doubles we have you can take back. Stephanie bought pillows, too, for the living room, so if we like hers better, you can take ours back."

Tara nodded as she stacked plates into a scratched-up wooden cabinet. She imagined an alternate reality where she hadn't given in to her parents' pressure to marry Devon. In this daydream, she and Mayuri shared an apartment like this one, but in the South End. A brownstone building with bay windows and high ceilings. They would stay up late, share bottles of wine while talking about their hopes for the future. Maybe they'd go on spontaneous road trips. It was something she had thought of doing after graduation. A cross-country trip, the northern route on the way there, southern on the return trip. Tara wanted to see all the mountains, lakes, and everything in between. She wanted to look at the stars above Big Sky, Montana, and stand at the edge of the Grand Canyon.

Tara could almost taste the s'mores as she camped along the way. In this imaginary life, Tara wasn't someone's wife or someone's mother, she was simply free and full of possibilities.

"Mom? Are you okay?" Nikki's voice pulled Tara back to the present. Her face was full of concern.

Tara blinked, realizing she'd been staring at the same plate for several minutes. "I'm fine, beta. Just . . . remembering."

Nikki tilted her head. "You've been quiet. I mean, more than usual."

For a moment, Tara considered deflecting, but something in her daughter's open expression made her pause. "I am proud of you. For doing this, building your own life."

Nikki reached over and hugged Tara. They rarely showed affection. Heena and Nikki were always affectionate with Devon. Tara usually stood off to the side, observing her family instead of being part of it.

"You'll have to come visit," Nikki said.

Tara nodded, knowing that from now on she would be seeing her daughter less and less as the years passed. She would return to the house she shared with Devon. The emptiness would grow. But she could take comfort in the fact that she'd done her job. Nikki didn't see herself as a traditional Gujarati woman or aspire to be a wife cooking for her family. As they stood there in the sunlit kitchen, surrounded by boxes and the promise of new beginnings, Tara felt a shift within herself. Maybe it wasn't too late. Maybe there were still adventures to be had, still parts of herself to discover. As they returned to unpacking, Tara felt a spark of excitement she hadn't experienced in years. This apartment might be Nikki's fresh start, but perhaps now could be a new beginning for Tara. It could be her time, a second chance.

The duffel bag was still in her closet, she'd never returned it. All she needed was to find the courage to go through with it, but she knew deep down that she never would.

CHAPTER THIRTY-SEVEN

Every moment makes you who you are.
—YNLIN

Cambridge, Massachusetts, present

The familiar scent of antiseptics greeted Nikki as she entered the waiting room of her father's dental practice. The receptionist stacked magazines for the day's use and turned on the television. Nikki nodded to Helen, a kind-faced woman who had known Nikki since childhood, then went down the hallway. Patient cubbies lined both sides of the hall. At the end were two small offices shared among the three partners. She found her father in his preferred one.

She'd gotten back to her apartment late the night before. She'd let Jay know, but he hadn't come over. Then again, she hadn't asked. She didn't know how to tell him that she hadn't even told Tara about the lawsuit. She'd meant to, but she'd realized there would be no point. Tara wasn't coming back. She didn't want to see disappointment in his eyes. First she would get through the task list she'd made during her painfully long bus ride.

"Nikita, you're back!" Devon stood behind his desk. "I missed you."

She wrapped her arms around her dad. "Hi, Dad." It was strange to see him, knowing all that Tara had shared.

He let her go. "How are things? Is your mom okay?"

Nikki sat in the visitors' chair across from him. She didn't know how to answer that. "She's working through a few things."

"By herself as usual," he said. "So many times she would just check out, stop talking to me. This is taking it too far."

"She's been unhappy, Dad."

Devon rubbed his face. "She's not the only one. Your mom isn't an easy person to live with, you know. She's moody and never says what she's thinking. It's her way, always."

"You've been together a long time," Nikki said. "I'm sure there were moments when it was hard for her as well."

Devon shook his head. "I gave her everything. The house, the car, never having to work. I did my part. All I wanted was for her to mix in more with my friends. Be more caring toward my parents, and me. And appreciate this life I've provided for our family."

Nikki didn't like this version of her father. It was too much "I," as if Tara had contributed nothing to their life. "Mom took care of the house and raised Heena and me. She cooked and cleaned for all the parties you had. She drove your parents to all of their appointments. She supported our family in every way. She did her part."

"She made it known that she didn't enjoy it," Devon said.

What Nikki had once believed to be checking off mom-wife to-dos was not menial. Her mother had built an existence around what her father took for granted. Women's work. "Dad, she wanted more. She told me about MIT."

Devon flopped back in his chair. "Again with this. Yes, it wasn't the right time early on, but once you girls were in high school, she could have tried again."

"It would have been hard for her," Nikki said. "You can understand that, right?"

Devon nodded. "I see what's happening. She turned you against me. Told you all her sad stories. Now I'm the bad one."

"I'm here for both of you. I came to see how you're doing. Have you been taking care of yourself? Are you eating regularly? I know cooking isn't one of your talents."

"Heena downloaded a food delivery app on my phone." He held it up. "It's magic."

Nikki nodded. "I'll do some shopping for you so you can make yourself a few things, like a salad. I know how much you love eating healthy."

Devon made a face. "Chewing all those leaves makes me feel like a cow."

"It's good for your cholesterol," Nikki said.

"Did she say when she's coming back?" Devon asked.

Nikki avoided the question. "Have you talked to Kirit uncle? Is there any update on the lawsuit?"

"No," he said. "I won't dignify their actions. Tara would never do such a thing."

Nikki nodded, glad he was on the right side of the whole mess. "I'm going to go talk to Bijal auntie."

"Don't," Devon said. "She shouldn't have dragged your mom into something like this without proof. I have a list of friends who would line up to proclaim Tara's innocence."

"You still care," Nikki said.

"She is my wife. Even if she doesn't want me to be her husband. How is she, really?" Devon was in his crisp white shirt and black slacks, a few more lines on his face that weren't there the last time she'd seen him. Maybe it was her imagination, but he looked tired, weighed down.

"She's different." It would be cruel to tell him that Tara was happier, lighter, more independent and adventurous. "Do you remember that time when Heena tried to pull my tooth out in here? I was seven, maybe?" As a child, she and Heena would be relegated here to play on the rare occasions that their dad brought them to the office.

Devon laughed. "Yes, you screamed so loud, Helen thought you were dying."

"It felt like it. It wasn't even loose or a baby tooth."

A weary expression crossed his face. "We were a good family, weren't we? The four of us. It wasn't perfect. Still, we have good memories."

"We will make more," Nikki said. "We might be scattered now, have separate lives, but you're still my dad, and I've forgiven Heena for the tooth thing."

"I'm glad you and your sister are close," Devon said. "I remember you two always played nice, doing your homework together and looking out for each other."

"I talked to her last night. She mentioned starting a new sculpture."

"Did she tell you where she got her inspiration?"

Nikki shook her head.

"From being questioned by the police," Devon said. "At your engagement."

"I can't with her," Nikki said.

"It hasn't been more than a week, and yet it feels like forever ago." Devon's voice was pensive. "Last week, I was looking for old photo albums. I decided to put them out in the living room for when Tara comes back so that we can go through them together and I can remind her of the good times we had."

Nikki fiddled with her hands. "I'm sorry, Dad."

He nodded. "Me too. I'm fine. I will be. But it's hard when she won't talk to me."

Nikki glanced at him. "You still love Mom."

Devon looked away, clasped his hands on his desk. "She's been my wife for more than three decades. We built a life together. I care for her. Deeply."

Nikki heard the emotion in his voice and held back her tears.

"I still remember the first time I met Tara," Devon continued. "She was beautiful and elegant. She was shy and quiet, well behaved. I believed she would be a good daughter-in-law to my parents, a good mother to our children. I'd met a few other girls, and some were too outspoken, others too homely. Tara was a good choice. I don't regret it."

"And then you fell in love."

"Not like the way you kids define it," he said. "Arranged marriage is different. You don't start with feelings. It's an agreement, a promise to build a family together, a commitment to face challenges together, grow with each other. For some, love comes from that."

"Not you?" The way he described it made her sad for both of them.

Devon shrugged.

"Did you ever want more? Like the kind of romance in movies."

"Eh, a movie is two hours, a marriage can be seventy-five years," Devon said. "There are hundreds of movies in every marriage, times when it's hard, when it's easy. You can't look at those things as a comparison."

Nikki wondered how many movies she and Jay would have or if the end was already coming. "Did Mom ever tell you why she chose to marry you?"

He spread his arms out. "Look at me. I'm a handsome man."

His exuberance seemed forced. "So it was your sense of humor."

Devon laughed. "Your mother and I never talked about it. We both said yes and then we were married." He leaned back in his chair. "Getting older is weird. Most of the time, I still see myself as that young guy. Your mother as that pretty girl. You live day by day and you forget the passing of time. I look at you. One day I'm putting a bandage on your knee, and now you're sitting across from me, all grown up. There are thousands of things I've forgotten about my life with Tara. That doesn't mean they didn't happen or exist. We played our parts. I built this, she took care of our home and family. I know there were moments when things were hard for her. But she'd always been steady. Predictable. I can count on one hand the number of times your mother surprised me. The last time was the morning after your engagement party when she ran away."

"Now you miss her."

"What's that cliché about not knowing what you have until it's gone?"

Nikki left him with a heavy heart. Her parents were so far apart in how they viewed their relationship, she didn't know if they would ever find peace.

CHAPTER THIRTY-EIGHT

Newton, Massachusetts, 2019

Tara stared at her feet as she stood at the threshold of the front door. Her black boots were laced, the cuffs of her jeans tucked into the slouchy socks. It was an ordinary Tuesday, all she had to do was walk through the door for it to become a day of note. December 10, 1903, Marie Curie is awarded the Nobel Prize. March 17, 1905, Albert Einstein published his paper on the quantum theory of light. July 26, 2018, the Very Large Telescope in Chile observes a black hole that proves gravitation redshift.

April 9, 2019, Tara Parekh leaves her life behind with a black duffel bag in hand. It wouldn't have an impact on any understanding in the universe, but it would be momentous for her. If she had the courage. It was the perfect time. She was no longer needed by anyone. Devon's practice was successful, and he had enough free time to play golf with his partners. The girls had their own lives, Heena in her marriage and Nikki on her own. Tara no longer had to live in this house with too many rooms and not enough warmth. All she had to do was take one step. Then another.

She had memorized the schedule of the bus that would take her to South Station. Then another bus to Portland, Maine. There was a budget hotel where she could get her bearings and send an email to Devon, Heena, and Nikki to let them know she had left. She didn't know how to tell them why, only that she could no longer spend her days suffocating in a life she'd never wanted. She would get a job. Except she had no résumé. Her college diploma was from thirty years earlier. She reached for the knob. She would do it. Find a way. She'd once believed she was smart enough to make an impact in the world of physics, this shouldn't be hard. Though she'd become a reader of others' accomplishments. Since she'd never actually *done* anything, there was no way for her to know if she was capable.

Her fear was double sided. Leaving into the unknown versus staying in the unbearable. Both paralyzed her. She wiggled her toes. *Move*, she willed her feet. They stayed in place. She stared at the cherrywood door. It appeared impenetrable.

She jolted as her cell phone rang. She let it go to voicemail. Tara took a deep breath for strength. It was time. There were no more excuses. She'd done her duty, put in her time. If she didn't free herself, she would grow old in this house, die without ever knowing what it meant to live.

With effort, she opened the door. The bright midmorning sun blinded her. She closed her eyes and basked in its warmth. With great effort she lifted one heavy leg onto the front step. She was doing it. Relieved, giddy, and afraid, she lifted her other leg. The phone rang again. She stayed in a small split, one foot on either side. She had to see who it was. She was a mother, her biology demanded she ensure the safety of her daughters regardless of how old they were.

Tara was aware that she wasn't good at the role she had played for decades. Still, she wasn't a monster; she did love Heena and Nikki. It was that she didn't know how to express it. She reached for the phone. It was Heena. She would just say hello and then go. She answered.

"Mom!"

Heena's voice was loud and had a tinge of panic. "What's wrong?"

"I'm on my way to see you," Heena said. "There's something I need to tell you in person."

Tara closed her eyes. A tear fell. "Are you all right?"

"I think so," Heena said. "I'm close. Be there in five or so."

Tara lifted the leg on the front stoop and brought it back in. She closed the door with her on the inside. Her heart slowed, weighed down by disappointment with herself. It would be another ordinary Tuesday where Tara did nothing of note. She had failed, and deep within herself, Tara knew that she would never succeed. Not in leaving. Not in anything.

She removed her shoes, went upstairs to hide her duffel bag in the back of her closet. By the time she came back down, Heena had already come in using the door passcode.

"Mom!"

Tara met her in the front room. Heena was easily excitable and prone to drama. Still, Tara scanned for injuries and blood. "What is going on?"

The front door opened again. Devon came in. Tara was confused.

"Heena, what's the emergency?" Devon asked.

"One minute." Heena removed her jacket and slung her scarf on the back of the sofa. "Nikki's on her way."

Tara's stomach dropped. This was going to be bad. Heena needed all of them. Tara sat on the edge of the sofa, her hands clasped on her thighs. A few minutes later, Nikki entered.

"Okay, sit down," Heena said.

"What is this?" Nikki asked. "I'm busy."

"Yeah, well, this is big," Heena said.

"Good news or bad news?" Nikki perched on the arm of the sofa. "Because you're excited but your eyes say you're scared."

"Good? Maybe? I don't know," Heena said. "That's why I wanted to tell you in person."

"Say it already." Nikki poked Heena in the arm.

"Hey, be gentle." Heena exaggerated her reaction. "I'm with child."

Tara stayed silent and seated while Devon and Nikki jumped up to hug Heena. They were yelling excited questions.

"You said it may not be good news?" Tara asked.

Heena nodded. "Right. Caleb and I weren't trying. It was always if it happened, we'd be okay with it." Heena patted her flat stomach. "We didn't expect twins."

There was silence. Then Devon hugged Heena again. "Fantastic news. Two for the price of one."

"Dad, that's not a nice thing to say," Nikki said. "And it's Heena, she can barely take care of herself. Two babies?"

"You'll all have to help." Heena sat on the opposite sofa. "Caleb is telling his parents right now. We will need everybody's help to keep two babies alive and make sure they don't turn into psychopaths."

"It's not something you become," Nikki said. "You're born one. The amygdala . . ."

Heena threw a pillow at Nikki. "Now is not the time. Mom? You're quiet."

She'd been so close. If she hadn't hesitated, she might have been on the bus right now. "I worry about your health."

"Right." Heena looked away. "You didn't want me to get married, and now I've disappointed you again by getting pregnant."

Tara wanted to agree. This wasn't what she'd wanted for either of her children. "If you're happy, then that's all that matters." She didn't know how to bury her disappointment even deeper.

"I am." Heena stood. "And just once, I'd like you to be too. I was hoping we could go have a celebratory lunch, but I'm not in the mood anymore."

"Don't be like that," Nikki said. "Wherever you want. Dad's treat."

"As always," Devon said. "Tara, let's go. Our family is expanding. Don't worry about Heena. She knows how to take care of herself."

Tara walked through the front door behind her husband and children. It was easy because it was what she knew. Once again, she'd chosen to stay stuck. And added another role. Wife. Mother. Grandmother. She was nowhere in those labels.

CHAPTER THIRTY-NINE

Let go of what you can't control.
—*YNLIN*

Newton, Massachusetts, present

Jay's family home was different from the one Nikki had grown up in. The living room had an explosion of color with silk fabrics and painted wood. There was a bench swing in one corner that looked to be imported from India. Family photos decorated walls, mantels, and tables. Her eyes were drawn to a graduation photo, likely from law school. Jay looked so boyish and happy standing between his mom and dad. She loved his smile, so genuine and easy.

"You're here. Why?" Bijal asked.

Nikki sat on the edge of the sofa across from Jay's mother. "I wanted to come see you. Hopefully we can talk. So much has happened since the engagement party. Jay told me that you're still upset."

"Is your mother back?" Bijal asked.

"She's . . . not yet." Nikki reminded herself to stay calm. Bijal had a right to be upset. She'd lost something valuable.

"Then what is there to talk about?"

"I wanted to check in on you. See how you are," Nikki said. "Jay told me how upset you've been since the engagement party."

"Unless you have the ring, this is a waste of time," Bijal said. "You want to make nice so that I will welcome you into this family, but that is not possible anymore. I've failed my ancestors. I should have known better. Jay should have gone to the mall and gotten you a small diamond. Then none of this would have happened."

"Then it might have fit on my bony fingers." Nikki tried to laugh it off. And winced because this was not the time. But she was nervous and now she was making it worse.

"You're making fun?"

Nikki shook her head. "No, I just . . . I want to help. To see what I can do to make up for your loss."

"Mom."

Nikki whipped her head around as Jay burst into the room.

"What are you doing here? In the middle of the day?" Bijal asked.

"Nikki texted me that she was coming over," Jay said.

Nikki shook her head. "I said I wanted to talk to her one-on-one."

"That's not a good idea," Jay said. "For either of you."

"Because?" Bijal asked.

Nikki echoed his mother.

"There is a pending lawsuit," Jay said. "You're on opposite sides."

"No," Nikki said. "It's between my mother and Bijal auntie."

"You're being called out. As an accessory."

Nikki stared at Bijal auntie, then at Jay, then back at his mother. "What?"

"Calm down," Bijal said. "It's not criminal, it's a civil suit. You don't have anything to worry about. Unless you are helping Tara."

Jay sighed. "Mom, you've watched too many episodes of *Suits*. This isn't how it works."

"Auntie. I'm sorry you lost . . . the ring was lost," Nikki said. "But my mother didn't take it. She doesn't have it."

"Then why won't she come back and say that directly to me?" Bijal asked.

"She's traveling." It was a weak answer. But it was impossible to explain all that was going on with Tara.

"In a camper van," Bijal said. "There is a lot of gossip. Your parents are getting divorced, apparently Tara is having a secret affair. She needs the money."

"Affair? No." The idea of it gave her heartburn. "It's not like that. Yes, my parents are having a tough time, and they might divorce. But there is no infidelity on either side. It's two people who grew apart."

"You remember that Tara and I were in high school together," Bijal said.

Nikki nodded.

"Everyone thought she was a mouse," Bijal continued. "I saw the real Tara. She thought she was smarter than us. Always had every answer. We stayed out of each other's path. I had a lot of friends. Not Tara. She had only one. Vicky. Our senior years, we had to do a family history report with an artifact. I talked about the bridal emerald. My mother wouldn't let me bring it to school, even though I promised to be careful. We got into a huge fight, but my mom won. So I got a fake ring but had a picture of the real one."

"Mom," Jay warned. "Where is this going?"

Bijal glared at him. "I had it in my locker. Before history class, I went to get it, and my ring, the report, and the picture were gone. Stolen."

"I don't understand," Nikki said.

"I was crying," Bijal said. "I would fail the assignment. Worse, what if it had been the real ring?"

"What does this have to do with my mother?"

"After school, I saw Tara at her locker, which was across from mine. On the door was the picture of the ring. I ran up to her and all three items were in her locker."

Nikki was nauseous. "It can't be true."

"She denied she took it, of course," Bijal said. "But the truth was all there. One of my friends told me that she'd seen Tara watching whenever I put the combination in. Tara hadn't been in the cafeteria for lunch that day. It started to add up. At that time, I couldn't figure out why she'd do something like that. Then I understood. Jealousy. I told the principal, who made Tara apologize to me. *That's* why I believe she has the ring."

"This is . . . I don't even know how to process it," Nikki said. "You never mentioned this? At our engagement announcement dinner you said you barely knew one another."

"And your mother ignored me," Bijal said. "I could see the guilt on Tara's face. At the party, she came up with a plan. She would play drunk and then be the victim."

"Okay, that's enough," Jay said. "This happened forty years ago. And your accusations are all assumptions."

Nikki put her hand on Jay's arm. "I'll ask my mother about it, the high school incident. Either way, I don't want you to feel like my family has caused you harm." Nikki offered the only option available. "I'll pay you back, in installments. I know it doesn't bring the actual ring back, but you will still recoup the money."

"It was covered by insurance," Jay said.

"Then why the lawsuit?" Nikki asked Jay.

"Mental anguish," Bijal said.

She was marrying into this family. She couldn't imagine bridging this chasm between them. She and Jay would have to choose sides forever.

"This is between you and Tara auntie," Jay said. "Let's go, Nikki."

She hung her head. "Jay, this is what being part of a family looks like. You fight for one another, you support, you listen, you help. Even if you don't agree, you stand by them."

"All of those things, sure," he said. "But we didn't start this fight. Something that started four decades ago isn't ours to fix. Mom, I really am sorry, but Nikki and I are out."

Just like Tara. She didn't want to deal so she ran away. But Nikki wasn't a runner or an avoider. "Is this how it's going to be with us? Whenever things get tough, you'll see yourself out?"

He looked at her, stunned. "Is that how you see me? Really? That's what you think is going on here?" She watched the pain on his face as he excused himself.

Nikki apologized to Bijal auntie, then ran after Jay. She caught him on the sidewalk. "Stop. Help me understand. For months you've been acting like it's only you and me. But we can't be responsible only for ourselves."

"You haven't been listening," Jay said. "I'm not saying alone. Nikki, you and I are in a relationship, one that's going to last the rest of our lives. That means you are my priority, and I should be yours. Every time you talk about fighting for family, it's actually your mom and dad. I know we're not married yet, but it feels like you don't see me as yours."

Nikki's face burned. "I can't believe you think that." She grabbed his hands. "You and I are first."

"Yet you didn't even talk to me before taking off with your mom." He let go.

"That's not fair." He didn't understand. He never would. "My parents are in trouble. My mom needed me. You didn't."

He rubbed his face. "I'm not the bad guy here. I know your parents need support, but we just got engaged and you threw yourself into it all not for us, but for them." Jay pointed to the house. "In between work and party planning, you ran your father's errands. Sent your mother articles. You were on the phone with your sister for hours. It was all in for you. We couldn't even get through one night to just be together. To revel in the fact that we found each other and love each other enough to commit to forever."

He was right. Not about everything, but he had a point. She didn't feel like they were engaged, and it wasn't because she hadn't worn a ring. Instead of coming together, she'd put distance between them, even before she'd taken off in the camper van. She needed to think and regroup. This was too important to brush off with an apology. "I don't want to talk about this on the sidewalk."

He ran his hand through his hair. "Fine."

"Will you come over later?"

"I can't," he said. "I need to prep for court tomorrow. Ride?"

She waved him off. "Go back to work, I'll call a rideshare."

"I'll text."

"Me too."

He stepped in and wrapped his arms around her. Nikki let herself sink into his heart, allowed herself a few seconds of comfort. Then she pulled away and told him to go.

CHAPTER FORTY

Fort Point State Park, Maine, present

The warm Maine air caressed Tara's face as she stepped out of her camper van and headed toward Penobscot Bay. The sun was slowly creeping up the horizon. It was a crisp morning, and Tara wrapped her cardigan tight around her body. She'd been wearing it ever since she'd crossed the state line from New Hampshire. Partly to keep warm, mostly for comfort. For two days she'd traveled through small towns on quaint roads, navigating to different RV parks. The season was kicking off as more people started their summer vacations. They'd rarely taken one as a family, as Devon usually had to work. But they'd done daylong leaf-peeping tours for a few years when the girls were in middle school.

As she neared the water, she watched the painted sky with its hues of pink and orange. The air was clean as it traveled through her lungs and deep into her belly. This was what she'd imagined freedom to feel like. She loved being on her own. There was freedom in figuring out what to eat when, in not having errands. Her chores were as compact as her space. The only clock was based on sunrise and sunset.

There was a mystery about where she might go, what she would do. She kept crisscrossing between western Massachusetts, New Hampshire, and Vermont. She'd gone north to south, east to west, and now to Maine. Had even dipped into eastern New York. Today, she was here. Tomorrow? She didn't know. That in and of itself was exciting. Tara was less and less afraid as the hours and days passed. She was doing it. The life she'd had was in the past. There was no one to please or obey except herself. Life didn't seem finite anymore.

In this version of herself, she was courageous. Though she hadn't changed over to reckless.

She wasn't ready. Not yet. But she was close.

The University of Maine was a few miles north. She'd circled it the previous evening, driven past the campus with its colonial redbrick buildings, nestled among forests, the bay, and the Gulf of Maine. It was as she'd imagined. She could see her version of Ben walking among trees that had yet to fully bloom. Then she'd driven away. From the first time, the only time, she'd met Ben, Tara had yearned to see him again.

For most of her life, Tara had felt as if she were the sole person on a seesaw. Some years she was at the bottom, sitting on the ground, knowing that was her only place. Or she was high atop with flailing legs, soaring with thoughts of flying off into the unknown. Whenever she'd wanted to leave, it wasn't away, but toward. And it wasn't a destination, but a person. If she listened to her heart, even after all this time, Ben was her north. Her Dhruva, in a sense. It was what he represented, a different choice.

He was ever present in the sky. There were times when she searched for him among the stars and nights when she didn't look up at all.

Tara remembered the sadness in Nikki's eyes. She was sorry for the pain she'd caused her child, but she wanted to experience this freedom. It was finally her turn. She recalled Devon sleeping, on his preferred left side of the bed, as she'd whispered her goodbye before picking up her duffel. She hadn't given herself time to hesitate, merely rushed out the door to buy an Airstream. They might miss her, but that would be temporary. Tara breathed. As with caterpillars and butterflies, transitions were difficult, required endurance and strength. She believed she was finally capable of becoming the person she'd imagined—fearless, unconstrained, and free. She didn't have daughters to tend to or in-laws to please, and she had ensured financial security for herself. At least for a little while. The rest of it would unfold if she believed she could do the hard things.

Tara walked along the sand with one eye toward the sunrise. As light began to flood the sky, the water began to wake, little ripples lapping near her feet. She'd known only one thing about herself, that she wasn't brave. At every turn, from Mayuri offering the getaway car to the number of times she'd stuffed her duffel back in the closet, she'd allowed her fear to win out, even as she rationalized about it not being the right time. And in the process, she'd done harm. Especially to Devon. Not only had he spent a big part of his life in a loveless marriage, but she'd left the undoing of it to him.

She'd never forged a close relationship with his parents. He would have to tell them along with their friends. They would sympathize with him. He'd been the more likable of the two. People reached out to him first, for anything from news to upcoming plans. He would be supported and cared for. Hopefully, they would do a better job than she'd done. She wondered if he hated her. She deserved it.

Her chest heavy, Tara crossed her arms as if to stop the ache. She swallowed her tears. It had taken thirty-five years to work up the courage to get to this spot. On her own. Returning meant failure, acceptance that this was a fleeting exercise, a whim, a break from routine. She'd read somewhere that the brain will always want the easy and resist the hard. Right now, thoughts of turning back, heading south, calmed her nerves. She could be home by evening if she started driving right this minute.

Tara shook her head, then released her arms and shook them out. She'd made it this far, and she would see it through. If she didn't take these last few steps, find Ben, see him again, her life would remain incomplete. She'd spent three and a half decades wondering. That wasn't an option for the next thirty-five years. Tara took a few deep breaths until her lungs expanded enough to clear the fear out of her mind.

This was her point of no return. She would head north. She would see Ben again.

CHAPTER FORTY-ONE

Therapy is a choice, not something done to you.
—YNLIN

Jamaica Plain, Massachusetts, present

The early-afternoon sun cast shadows across the outdoor seating area of the small café in Jamaica Plain. Nikki picked at her Greek salad, pushing a chunk of feta around with her fork, while across the table Heena twirled her chopsticks through a generous portion of vegan pad Thai. After Heena gave updates on the twins, they had eaten quietly, the silence broken only by the occasional clink of cutlery and the ambient chatter of other patrons.

"You want to tell me why we're here?" Heena said. "Or are you practicing before you take a vow of silence?"

It had been two days since she'd talked to Jay on the sidewalk. They hadn't seen each other since, only exchanged text messages. Every time she tried to think about Jay's concerns, her heart wouldn't settle. She needed her big sister. "Can you not be you for just one lunch?"

"Nope." Heena munched on a piece of baby corn.

Nikki ignored her.

"Come on," Heena said. "I'm kid-free, and it's a gorgeous day. You said you needed to talk. Ask Dear Heena for advice."

"How do you do this?" Nikki asked. "Not care that Mom took off?"

Heena shrugged. "I have my own stuff. The twins. Caleb."

That was it. "They come first."

Heena furrowed her brow. "Yes. That's how it works."

Nikki glanced over at the empty table next to them. "It's weird, isn't it? The four of us are family. We've always been that. Then one day you meet someone, decide to get married, and that person comes before the people I grew up with and shared so much of my life with."

"When you put it like that," Heena said, "I guess. But it's what happens. Our parents, grandparents. The family unit becomes the people you're with daily. Right now, my husband, my emergency contact, is taking an archery lesson. Would I much rather Dad still be the one they call? Yup. But that's not how it works."

"I don't know how to do it," Nikki said.

"Some life coach," Heena quipped.

"Ha. Ha. I'm serious," Nikki said. "I'm worried about Mom and Dad. Jay wants me to stop and focus on him. I'm seeing a side of him that I didn't know. Is he needy? Am I the one in the wrong because I'm trying to be there for Mom?"

"He's right," Heena said. "Don't give me that look. I've known you your whole life. You live to make an unhappy woman happy."

"I love her," Nikki said.

"So do I." Heena pointed her chopsticks. "That doesn't mean I'm responsible for her."

"And instead, I have to switch over to Jay." Nikki was no longer hungry.

Heena laughed. "No, dummy. Jay isn't asking you to make your whole life about him. If he did that, I would kick him out of your life. When was the last time you did something you wanted?"

"What does that have to do with anything?"

"Answer the question," Heena said.

"You sound like you're in court."

"I've been watching *The Good Wife* to practice for Bijal auntie's lawsuit."

Nikki couldn't meet her sister's eyes. "When I said yes to Jay."

"How did that feel?"

Nikki tossed a crouton at Heena. "Fine. I see your point."

"I should be writing your newsletter," Heena said. "It's not about putting yourself first, it's how to live your life, for you. That's all Jay wants. I mean, I tried with you and it didn't work. Now it's Jay's turn."

"You tapped out so long ago when it came to Mom. It all fell on me."

Heena put her fork next to her plate. "You chose to do it, I never asked. Mom and I are what we are. We love each other, but we accept our disappointment in one another. I wanted Tami Taylor from *Friday Night Lights*, and she wanted me to become the female Damien Hirst. Unlike you, I treat her like an adult. She has her own stuff she needs to fix for herself. None of us can change another person, only ourselves. And to be honest, I am happy she's doing this. Maybe it'll be good for all of us, or just her, but either way, it's necessary. Be your life coach."

"And Dad?"

"Same goes for him," Heena said. "We support him, but he has to ultimately come to terms with what's happened."

"You sound like Jay," Nikki pushed back.

Heena leaned back and crossed her arms. "Our house wasn't exactly full of love and laughter. For the most part, it was quiet. No music, no blaring TV, very few conversations. Our parents rarely had people over, even though Dad loves parties and get-togethers. I don't remember them spending any time together, just the two of them. It wasn't until Caleb and I bought our own place, had the twins, that I realized the difference between a home where there is love and one where there's an absence of it."

Nikki let the words sit in the pit of her stomach.

"What I learned," Heena continued, "is that I can create my happiness in shapes that I draw myself. I'm not a perfect mom, there isn't such a thing, but I can parent my twins differently. Mom and Dad had an arranged marriage, but I know what it feels like to fall in love, to be loved by someone like Caleb. You should try it."

Nikki picked at her pale pink nail polish. "Jay loves me. A lot. And it's wonderful." Had she ever told him that?

"Tell him, often. Every day. Even when you're angry with each other," Heena said. "This is one of those things where you must use your words, not only your actions. Don't you think he worries? Or that he's uncertain? Insecure about where he stands with you?"

"It's not like he doesn't know." Nikki tried not to sound defensive. "I open up to him. The other day, he found my migraine pills, and I told him I got severe headaches." He'd become concerned until she explained that she knew how to take care of herself.

"Cool," she said. "That's exactly the same as 'I love you.'"

"It's showing, not telling." Except, Heena was right, she hadn't considered that he would be insecure about Nikki's feelings for him. "I messed up."

Heena took Nikki's hand in hers. "Awareness is the first step. But it's not fatal. It's something you and Jay can work on. Caleb and I have lost count of how many ways we've hurt each other, by accident or on purpose. We have different approaches to parenting. We also know our fights will never lead to a permanent breakup because we love each other so fiercely that I'm it for him and he for me."

Nikki clutched her sister's hand. "I have to talk to Jay, don't I?"

Heena nodded. "Wear something sexy. Men listen better when they're distracted."

"Noted." Nikki took a bite of her salad. "There's this other problem, though. We can't ignore the lawsuit."

"Do you have the ring?"

Nikki's mouth opened. "No, of course not." Nikki told Heena about her conversation with Bijal auntie.

"Mom's a lot of things," Heena said. "But she isn't a thief."

"I agree," Nikki said. "But it's hard to prove."

"So is Bijal auntie's accusation," Heena said. "Maybe Mom's being set up."

Nikki sat back. "By who?"

"Bijal auntie," Heena said. "She's still harping on something from high school. Their high school, which they went to in the last century. Maybe she thought this would be a good opportunity for revenge."

Nikki rolled her eyes. "We're not in a Turkish soap opera."

"That would be so fun," Heena said. "I'm going to play Mom for a minute, ready? 'Two objects related to each other depend on force. Sometimes they move in the same direction, equal in magnitude. Other times one hurtles in a different direction, and the related object can either move with it or away.'"

"You don't understand physics," Nikki said. "Like, at all."

"Yeah, I butchered that," Heena said. "Let me say it a different way. Stop worrying about Mom, Bijal auntie, the ring, and everything else. You are constantly moving wherever you're needed instead of figuring out your own equilibrium."

"This is what happens when you don't take any science classes beyond biology," Nikki muttered.

"Blue eyes are dominant, right?"

Nikki shook her head. "Hopeless."

After their meal, Nikki walked along the historic Emerald Necklace Park in her neighborhood. Arnold Arboretum was her favorite. This summer the trees were lush, and the flowers were bright and abundant. She watched dogs chase squirrels while their humans tried to keep them under control.

Heena was right. Nikki had to make some choices. For herself.

CHAPTER FORTY-TWO

Orono, Maine, present

There was a flutter of excitement in Tara's chest, reminiscent of her college days when she was eager to get to her favorite classes. Each day had been different then with the randomness of running into friends in the cafeteria or sitting on the grass watching people play hacky sack. She sighed, appreciating the courage she'd amassed to stand here.

The University of Maine was different from Boston University, which stretched for a mile along the density of Commonwealth Avenue. Here there were big buildings, well-mowed lawns, and an openness. It was quieter without the horns and the constant bells of the Green Line trolley she used to hop on to go from one side of the campus to the other.

She made her way across the sprawling campus, her eyes drinking in the mix of modern and historic buildings. Finally she followed the map on her phone to the Marine Science faculty offices at Aubert Hall. It was a massive building that looked like a small hospital with a redbrick facade. On the grassy knoll, near the bicycle racks, Tara stood under the shade of a small tree and kept an eye on the entrance.

What am I doing? Doubt had seized her all morning. It had been more than three decades since she'd last seen Ben. Her image of him had blurred with time, she might not recognize him. And the likelihood of him knowing her was slim. Still, she believed her heart would recognize him if he appeared. Her stomach had been in knots for hours. She'd gone to bed with determination and hope. She'd woken up to fear and uncertainty. Worse, she couldn't think of a single thing to say.

Would a simple hello be enough? She didn't want to appear unhinged, and if she told him she'd fallen in love with him so long ago, he might guide her to the health center for observation. Still, her feet stayed planted. She would see this through. Whatever happened, she reminded herself, she was here for herself. To do the bravest thing she'd ever done. The urge to walk away was met with the same force as the need to stay. She breathed deeply again. Though she'd done that all morning and was now on the verge of hyperventilating.

Tara watched as people ambled in and out of the building. The summer term had ended a week ago, but it was a good sign that there were still students around. It was a clear day and most wore only light jackets, though the young men had already transitioned to T-shirts and shorts. Nervously she chewed on a torn cuticle, careful not to tear it. She didn't want to shake his hand with a bloody thumb.

Tara sensed him before she saw him. Her breath caught as she slowly watched him coming out of the building. It was Ben. There, not ten feet away from her. He resembled the photo on the faculty page of the website, but even without that clue, she would have known it was him. Her memories of him were clear. Of course, he was older now, with hair more salt than pepper, his face weathered with lines that she hoped had been earned by time spent on the sea. But his curls were still there, thick and unruly as they ruffled in the breeze. He walked with purpose, a leather satchel slung over one shoulder, looking like a stereotypical image of a distinguished professor.

This was it. The moment she'd both longed for and dreaded since embarking on this journey. Taking a deep breath, Tara forced herself to move. *One foot in front of the other,* she reminded herself. *You've come too far to turn back now.* She adjusted her soft, thin, melon-colored shirt at the hem. Then she tucked her hair behind her ears, to make herself appear younger and more confident.

As he came closer, Ben's gaze flickered in her direction. Tara summoned a smile, willing her voice to remain steady. "Excuse me," she called out, her heart pounding. "I'm sorry to bother you, but . . . you look familiar. Have we met before?" The old pickup line was the only thing that came to her mind. "I don't mean that as—I mean, I really do think we know each other."

Ben paused, his brow furrowing slightly as he studied her face. "I'm not sure." His voice was deeper than she remembered. "Maybe. I've traveled a lot."

"This would have been a long time ago. Decades. Did you go to Boston University?" She tried to refresh his memory.

He laughed. "No. I did go there a few times to visit some friends during undergrad. That was over thirty years ago."

Her heart raced. "Right, yes. You and I spent the night together." She winced. Somehow her brain had reverted to her twenty-one-year-old self's. "I don't mean—"

He tilted his head and stared.

"On the Esplanade," she said. "We watched the stars."

He grinned. "Oreos."

Tara laughed. "Yes. And carrots."

"I'm sorry," he said. "I remember the night but not your name."

It felt as if the tip of a knife punctured her heart. Her smile dropped but she recovered. "Of course not. It was a while ago."

"I'm Ben." He held out his hand.

She flashed back to the other time he'd introduced himself. She'd lived an entire life between then and now. "Tara." She shook his hand.

His palm was warm, dry, and calloused. His clasp was reassuring.

"This is really something," he said. "I keep thinking that line about 'all the gin joints.'"

She didn't know the reference, but Tara nodded.

"What are you doing here in our little corner of Maine?"

She'd relived that night for so long that his mannerisms were familiar. He still didn't seem to be in a hurry. The pace of his sentences hadn't changed from its slow cadence. "I was nearby and thought I'd take a look at the campus."

"That's a first," he said. "We're not exactly a tourist destination."

"I'm doing an off-the-beaten-path tour." She shifted her weight from one foot to the other.

"Wait, you were into stars if I remember," he said.

"At MIT."

"Nice. Are you thinking about teaching here? We have a decent physics program."

The life she could have lived. Tara wanted to lie, but she'd learned her lesson with Mona. "No. I never got my graduate degree," she said. "What about you? You said you were going to live on a boat in the middle of the ocean."

"You have a good memory. Yeah, I get out there sometimes," he said. "You can draw out what your life is going to be like when you're twenty but forget that maps change because the Earth is never in the same place."

"There are no stationary objects in the universe."

"Exactly," he said. "Hmm. Did we talk like this back then?"

She nodded. It was like they had a rhythm of their own. Like their conversations always started in the middle.

"We must have been so full of ourselves," he said.

It was sad, yet he was right. "Naive and idealistic."

"That's a better way to put it."

She didn't want the conversation to end. "How long have you been here? At this university, I mean."

He nodded. "Came here when I was eighteen and I knew this was where I wanted to be, a home base of sorts."

"I can see that you love it."

"I do," he said. "It helps me to know where to look when I want to see the ocean."

She pointed to her left. He put her arm down. Lifted the right one. "I've never been good at directions. Except up there." Tara gestured toward the sky.

"We all have our thing," he said. "How long are you in town?"

For as long as you want me around. "I don't have a schedule."

"Great. I have a meeting I'm heading to right now, which is going to take the rest of the afternoon. Maybe we can grab dinner?"

An actual date. With Ben Anand. Her only love. Even if one-sided. Even if imaginary. Tara could barely get the words out to accept. She almost dropped her phone when they exchanged numbers. With a wave, he took off in the direction he'd been heading before she'd stopped him.

Tara leaned against the tree. She could finally catch her breath and process what had just happened. She'd done it. She'd found Ben, spoken to him, and was going to go out with him. When he turned the corner and she was sure he couldn't see her, she jumped up and down. This was what it felt like to take a risk.

The adrenaline coursed through her as she made her way back to her Airstream. Her mind was a whirlwind of thoughts and emotions. Part of her was elated—the connection she'd felt all those years ago hadn't been imagined. He'd remembered her, even if only vaguely. As she settled into the small bench in the RV, doubt began to surface. What would happen over dinner? Would they find they had nothing in common after all these years? Would he ask about her life, her family? How much should she reveal the real reasons for being here?

Tara turned her head and caught sight of herself in the small mirror above the sink. The woman who looked back at her was both familiar and unrecognizable—the same eyes that had gazed at Ben more than three decades earlier, but now framed by lines that spoke of a life lived, choices made, paths not taken.

She thought of Devon, of Nikki and Heena. She was a grandmother. She was supposed to retire, not restart. There was an email from an attorney she had yet to open. Urgent messages from Nikki and Heena. It was selfish of her to chase a fantasy while she'd left wreckage for others to clean up. But Tara knew that if she went back, this would evaporate. She would never take this step again. She had to stay on this road. It was the only thing in her life she felt she had accomplished from start to finish.

Tara wondered if this was what mountaineers felt like. The excitement of a clear goal. The struggle of each hour, day, week. In her case years. And then arrival at the peak. Tara breathed with ease for the first time in forever. She'd done this. Reclaimed her life. She finally believed she could do anything. Reach for any dream. By herself. For herself. She would live with the guilt.

CHAPTER FORTY-THREE

Love requires acceptance.
—*YNLIN*

Boston, Massachusetts, present

Jay's neighborhood was more dense, less leafy than Jamaica Plain. In Southie, the buildings were old, and the pubs were Irish. Young professionals and college students were making inroads, but the locals were too proud to give up the fight. Jay liked his apartment on the second floor of a triple-decker. Nikki gave herself a minute before putting her key into the lock. Last night she'd sat in quiet and reflected. She'd done a lot of personal work to authentically offer advice to her subscribers. She'd thought she knew who she was, and she was proud of her ambition. She'd believed centering her family was a virtue. It had also become her blind spot.

Taking Heena's advice, she'd made a list of what *she* wanted. When her mind couldn't come up with anything, she'd admitted that she didn't know. She was a fixer, but it wasn't something she wanted to be. She overvalued what others wanted from her. With a deep breath, she let herself in. To figure out how to be, she needed to change.

Jay was on the couch, watching a game.

"Are they winning?" Nikki asked.

"Nope," he said.

Jay had been a fan of the Red Sox since birth, or so he claimed. Though he'd never been one to make the game so important that it affected his mood, she could sense his disappointment. She'd hoped he would be in a better mood. Typically she would wait, try to lighten things up before a heavy conversation so as not to . . . she stopped herself . . . *coddle* was the word that came to mind. If she and Jay were going to spend their lives together, she couldn't be afraid of his emotions. "Jay, if you're not into the game, can we talk?"

He turned off the television and sat up. She put her purse on an empty side chair and sat on the coffee table to face him. "You were right."

"Sweet," he said. "About?"

"Our argument outside of your parents' house."

He nodded. "Right."

"You don't remember?" Nikki had spent days rehashing it.

"I said I wanted time for just us," he said. "You're here saying I'm right. What more is there?"

She stood and paced. "You said a lot more than that. Like I was putting my family over you and not being there for you."

"Yeah, I did say that." Jay stretched his arm along the back of the couch.

"We have to talk about that," she said.

"Not *we*," Jay said. "You. I'm good with action."

"What does that mean?"

He patted his thigh. "Come here, I'll show you."

She couldn't help the laugh that escaped her. "This is who you are, isn't it?"

He touched his face with his hand to double-check.

"You haven't spent this time upset," she said. "You didn't expect me to come groveling or apologize."

"I was upset, babe," he said. "Then I told you. I figured you needed time. Now you're here."

He meant it. Navigating minefields had become such second nature to Nikki that she'd started seeing bombs where there were none. She'd thought Jay was like Tara, when he was just himself. He got upset and said his piece, and her coming here to spend time with him was him seeing that she was meeting him where he was, at her pace.

She sat next to him and stroked his thigh. The fabric of his shorts was warm under her hand. "You are probably the most emotionally mature person I know."

"It's the first thing people think when they see all this." He indicated his body.

She leaned into his arms, her head on his chest. She sighed when his arm came around her. He twirled a section of her hair around his hand. "Since you think so highly of me, I will tell you that I did spend time thinking about that conversation. I shouldn't have gotten so frustrated with you. I was pissed that you took off with your mom, and I should have understood. She's a lot, but she's yours. And I love that you care so much. I'm sorry I gave you a hard time."

It soothed her heart to hear him say that. "Family will always be important to me, Jay, and you and I are family too. Besides, you may not have to deal with my mother. She's not planning to come back."

Jay tilted her chin up to look at him. "How does that land for you?"

She shrugged. "I hope she can find what she's looking for. I want to be here, with you, and enjoy the fact that you proposed. And I said yes."

"Yeah, you did," he said.

They stayed like that in silence. Being in his arms helped her relax more than a thirty-minute meditation session. Then she started to make a mental list of all the things they could do this summer. The Cape. Weekend in Nantucket. Kayaking in Western Mass.

"I can hear your brain," he said. "Turn it off."

She stroked his chest. There was one thing that needed to be addressed before she could give in to the bliss of this night. "Jay?"

"Mm."

"Have you talked to your mom? Things were a little tense when we were at her house." She felt his heartbeat change its rhythm under her palm.

"No," he said.

"Why not?" It was hard because she knew he didn't want to talk about it, but she did.

"Because she won't drop it no matter what I say," he said. "My dad tried to reason with her, too, but she's got this baggage from high school that she won't let go."

"Heena thinks your mom is framing mine," Nikki said.

Jay sighed. "All I want is one night with you that has nothing to do with your parents or mine. Can we do that?"

She moved away, and she saw the disappointment in his eyes. She stood, then settled onto his lap. "How should we spend this precious time together?"

He grabbed her waist and brought her closer. Then he kissed her. Slow and gentle. She felt his muscles flex under her hands. Then he stopped. Stared into her eyes. Waited. "It's been so long, I think I forgot what comes next."

She laughed and cupped his face. "I'll remind you of what goes where."

He stopped. "I'm scared, babe."

She looked at him with curiosity.

"I've developed this irrational fear of the door buzzer."

"Huh?"

"Coitus interruptus."

She shoved him as he laughed. "Jerk."

"It's traumatic," he said. "Heal me. Make me believe we can go the distance."

Nikki got to her feet and helped him up. "You're ridiculous."

He picked her up, carried her, and tossed her on the bed. Then he lowered himself over her, settled between her legs. She played with the hair at the nape of his neck. He leaned over and nipped her collarbone. Left small kisses from one to the other.

She tugged and moved him to remove his T-shirt. She loved the feel of his skin, loved to trace the ridges, the valleys. He was both soft and strong. She moaned as he lifted her shirt, stroked his fingers along the lace of her bra, pressed more firmly on her nipple. Then she cackled as his phone vibrated with an incoming call.

He buried his face in her neck. "You have got to be kidding me."

"Answer it." She patted his back.

"Strip," he said.

"It could be important," she said. "It's still going. Grab it before it falls off the nightstand."

He reached for it. "Mood killer. It's my mom."

She twisted out from under him. "Talk to her."

"It stopped." He put it back on the table. "Where were we?"

"Call her back," she said.

"Why is this so important to you?"

"You two left things unresolved, and she's reaching out to you." Nikki sat up, her back against the fabric-covered headboard.

His jaw clenched. But he sat up and grabbed the phone. "What?" he said when it connected.

She gently punched him in the back. "Be nice."

"I'm busy right now," he said. "Yeah, I called you back. Nikki made me. The woman you insulted is more on your side than mine."

She punched him again.

"You did what?" he shouted. "Mom. Calm down. You're taking this too far."

Nikki couldn't hear his mother's side of the conversation, but she didn't need to to know this was very bad.

"We can talk about this tomorrow," he said. "Email me his info."

Jay tossed the phone, then hung his head in his hands.

"What happened?"

He flopped on his back. His head on her lap. "You had to make me call back."

She stroked his forehead. Waited until he was ready to tell her.

"I have a dilemma, my love," he said.

"Tell me." She traced his thick eyebrows.

"I want us to finish what we started." Jay rolled over and kissed her stomach.

"That doesn't sound like a problem," she said.

He shifted up and balanced himself on his elbows. "If I tell you what my mom did, you're going to be too mad for sex. But if I don't, we can." He pushed himself up, dragged her down and kissed her.

Nikki knew it was up to her. She brought him back to her, held him. For tonight, she would let this be enough.

CHAPTER FORTY-FOUR

Midcoast Maine, present

The salty breeze ruffled Tara's hair as she waited for Ben. She'd come early because she was sick of pacing back and forth in the small camper van. She'd done yoga, meditated, and gone on a short hike. All to help her stay calm. This was her second date. Well, not a date, but her stomach didn't know the difference. This time, though, instead of sitting at a Formica table, she was on a wooden picnic bench. The man she was meeting wasn't someone chosen by her parents. There were no expectations of any kind, she reminded herself.

Her pride in this moment was hers alone. For most of her life she'd seen herself as a toy, spun and pulled by others. As if she had no choice or ownership in her life. Now she knew what she was capable of. It shocked her that she was capable of this kind of courage. That it had taken almost sixty years to get here didn't make it any less monumental. Tara looked out at the ocean to her left. This was where she'd imagined him in her daydreams. The foamy water crashed over the rocky shoreline. The smell of fried oil mixed with salt from the sea permeated the air.

"You found the place." Ben took a seat across from her outside the rustic seafood shack.

She was elated that he'd shown up. There was awareness of him, an attraction because he was as handsome as she remembered, maybe more so now that the boyish face had morphed with age. "GPS makes it easy."

"Right," he said.

Silence. She had searched for conversation topics, but nothing fit. "Do you come here often?" She winced. Why did her openers sound like dated pickup lines?

"Yeah." He seemed to have not noticed. "It's only open for a few months over the summer, so I get here when I can."

"It's quaint." There were no menus, just a chalkboard on the side of a hut. "I like that there are only a few things to choose from."

"Fried clams or lobster roll. Fresh from right there." Ben pointed to the water.

"I can go order," she offered.

He gave a nod to the hefty woman behind the counter. She wore a leather apron and gloves. Her hair up in a net. "What are you thinking?"

"Lobster roll," Tara said.

Ben raised his arm and held up two fingers. The woman nodded. "We can cash out when we're done. She knows me."

She was charmed by how embedded he seemed to be in this community. "That's nice. In Boston, I go to the same deli every week, and no one recognizes me." She sat on her hands to stop herself from babbling.

"It's a quantity thing." He spoke slowly as if there was no hurry to get all the words out. "Less people here."

"You sound like a local too." His accent was a mash-up of Boston and Ireland.

"Ayuh." He exaggerated.

She laughed, a little harder than it warranted, then reined it back in as a teenager came out from the shack and placed their food on the table. Two paper boats held generous portions of lobster, the sweet meat spilling out of toasted buns. Chopped celery and scallions were peppered over the chilled rolls. "It looks amazing."

As they ate, he asked about her travels. She filled him in on their hikes, the lakes, the drive. Quaint towns and RV park camaraderie. He was easy to talk to, and she thought maybe they could just keep it like this. Easy, casual. They could stay in touch and talk occasionally. She could invite him to—then she stopped. There was nowhere. Tara's home was the Airstream, not the four-bedroom Victorian in Newton.

"You okay?"

She nodded. "Sorry, sometimes my mind wanders."

"Solving the mysteries of the universe?" He took a bite of his pickle.

She shook her head as her happiness turned to melancholy. "I never pursued physics."

He wiped his mouth with a napkin. "Interests change."

"Or destiny," she said. "I never believed in it. Or fate. That didn't fit through the lens of what's knowable. Lately, I wonder."

"Maybe it's like the horoscope," he said. "I do believe there is an invisible force that leads us, we choose how to follow."

She watched the surf crash against the rocks. "Some of us do it blindly." She could have done things differently, not bowed to fear or obligation. "Do you think it's too late?"

He frowned. "For?"

"I keep thinking about the butterfly effect and chaos theory," she said. "How a tiny change can ripple. That night on the Esplanade, if we hadn't met, what would my life have been like?"

"Probably not that different," he said. "We never saw each other again. Until now."

"Or if I'd called after you gave me your number. Maybe we would have been friends. I could have learned how to sail. Maybe the spark I felt that long-ago night would have become a flame."

"We could have gotten to know each other," he said. "Had a fling, something deeper. You would become frustrated because I wouldn't commit. You would have wanted to get married, and that has never been me. You might have cried because I would go out to sea for six months."

"You can draw the map, but no object is stationary." She repeated his words from earlier.

"Why didn't you call?"

"I was getting married," she said. "Arranged. It would have been wrong."

He nodded. "Interesting. What happened?"

She glanced out at the horizon. "Had two children, daughters who are incredibly accomplished. One has twins. I followed the path that was before me. I stopped looking at the horizon."

"One of the things I love about the ocean is its power," Ben said. "It will always win against man. Even the lives that live within it are at its mercy. But still, we try to sail the surface, dive into its depth. People can be conquered, but the ocean? Never."

She could listen to him talk all day. "You must be the professor all the students have a crush on."

He laughed. "That's not what they say in my reviews. What I mean is that we think we acquiesce to forces that are stronger than us. But like the universe, humans don't stay in one spot. Sure, you were likely swept in by the undercurrent, but in the process, you learned how to navigate."

"How do you know?"

"You're here," he said.

She didn't know if she understood his reasoning. She rested her chin on her hand. "What about regret? That is also a powerful force."

"So is acceptance," he said.

She laughed. "Touché."

"Fine," he said. "I watched *Back to the Future*, so I know how time machines work. What would you change?"

For most of her life, Tara had believed she knew the answer. She would have called Ben. She would not have married Devon. But that would mean no Nikki or Heena. No friends like Mona. "Touché again. Because altering the past means the present as we know it no longer exists."

"Butterfly effect."

She laughed.

Ben considered the question. "Since it's not possible, I don't think about regrets. At least in the timeline we currently live in."

"You don't have anything you'd do differently?"

"Oh, a lot," he said. "That's different than mourning a missed opportunity. I'd like to think I grow instead, make other mistakes."

"You're happy," she said. "Past and present are both equally good to you."

"Happiness isn't constant," he said. "It can't be. It's situational. For example, right now, in this moment, yes, I am happy. Tomorrow, when I have to work on a thorny research problem that's been plaguing me for months, I'll be frustrated."

She realized she was happy too.

Ben's eyes softened as he looked at her. "You forgot to look at the North Star. I can't remember what you call it, the Sanskrit name, but you said it guided you. I don't think it's fate or regret. Maybe you stopped looking up."

Sometimes it's a word or a sentence that shifts your entire way of thinking. She'd thought she was chasing, changing, leaving, searching. The truth was that she was aimless. "You're right. On this road trip, in the mountains, near lakes, I spent nights under the big sky and stared at Dhruva every clear night. Observed it from different locations. But I'm still lost." She'd thought once she'd found Ben, things would fall into place. She would experience contentment. She would know what came next. "I don't know where I'm going. Literally or figuratively."

"Maine's a big state," he said. "Lots of sky."

They sat for a while longer. He shared stories from the sea. She realized he wasn't the Ben of her imagination. This person was a stranger who had lived without her knowledge. He was kind and personable. He'd never know the outsize influence he'd had on her life. And that was how it should be. She wasn't a scared twenty-one-year-old longing for a romantic hero to save her. She was a woman who had made mistakes. Too many to ever correct.

After Ben left, she stayed on the bench. The sun had yet to set, but the color of the sky was changing. Light pink would darken, deepen to purple, which would fade until it was time for the stars to illuminate this corner of the Earth. She slowly made her way back to the Airstream and climbed into the driver's seat. Once again, she'd pinned her happiness on someone else. It was no way to live. This adventure was a step, not a means to an end.

CHAPTER FORTY-FIVE

> Ruined moods ruin moods. Don't make others responsible for yours.
> —*YNLIN*

Boston, Massachusetts, present

"What are you talking about?" Nikki held a cup of tea in her hands as she sat at her kitchen counter. The intimate mood of the night before had turned into a blissful walk around Jamaica Pond before they came back to her place. He'd finally told her why his mom had called once he'd finished making breakfast.

"Nikki, have you talked to your mom? Filled her in on the case?"

Nikki closed her eyes for a minute. She couldn't avoid it. "I haven't."

He ran his hands over his face.

"I've left her messages to call me," Nikki said.

Jay finished his coffee and poured another mug. "In a civil case, my mom filed the complaint. Since Tara auntie is MIA, they have to find her to give her notice of the pending lawsuit, and then your mom has to respond."

Nikki grabbed her phone. "I'll try again." She dialed, but Tara didn't answer. "But seriously, your mom is taking this too far. I mean, now it's false accusations, right? How can you sue someone without proof?"

"People do it all the time." Jay rubbed her shoulder. "Listen, there are a lot of steps in this, precedence, discovery, motions."

Nikki squirmed away from him. Her mom was about to be served, and Tara was somewhere driving around in a camper van.

"Look, it's not going to get far. This is just my mom taking her anger out on yours. I'm going to go over to my parents' this afternoon and get her to drop it," he said. "Stop worrying."

"You're not the one being sued," Nikki said.

"Neither are you."

"I have to figure this out, call my dad." Nikki scanned her phone. "I need to find a lawyer that specializes in this kind of case."

He took the phone from her and then held her hands. "Babe, it's not going to come to that."

She tugged out of them. She was angry at his mom, but Jay was the one standing in front of her. Nikki couldn't imagine her mom being questioned or being compelled to return only to be arrested. An image of Tara in jail made it hard to breathe. "This is bad. Really bad."

"I guess we're going to do this instead of eat pancakes in peace."

"Seriously? Your family is doing this to mine and you're thinking of pancakes?" She went to the fridge and poured herself a glass of water.

"I'm trying to tell you it's not going to get to that."

"How?" Nikki faced him. "My mom could go to jail."

"This is a civil case," he muttered.

His calm demeanor put her over the edge. "Not all of us are lawyers, Jay, but being served, going to court—all of it is bad."

He turned to watch her, his back against the counter. "Why don't you finish breakfast. You need to eat before you get a migraine."

Nikki ignored him as she paced to calm herself from fear and anger. She went to her desk and opened her planner. There were so many items on her to-do list. She'd worked so hard to establish her business, and now she was behind on client deliverables, billing, and new business. She slammed her planner on the desk. "There is chaos everywhere." A knife pierced through her brain, and she closed her eyes to breathe through it. She was losing it, and now was not the time for a debilitating headache. Nikki took a few steadying breaths.

Jay took her by the arm. "Easy."

She wrenched herself out of his grip. "Join me in this panic attack, won't you?" She needed him to also worry, to also be afraid.

"Nikki."

"Damn this stupid ring." Nikki rubbed her temples. She grabbed her phone to call her mom again. It went straight to voicemail. She threw it on the chair. "Her phone is off. For once, can she not be her? Can she stop being so selfish? I'm trying to help her and she's just going through her days sightseeing. It's New England! We've lived here all our lives. The trees are the same. The coast is rocky, the ocean is cold."

"You're losing it, babe. Take a breath." He stood next to her. Rubbed her back.

She didn't want his comfort. "Go home, Jay."

"I'm not leaving you like this," he said.

"None of this would have happened if you hadn't blurted out, 'Will you marry me?'" She regretted the words as soon as she said them. Then she saw his eyes shutter and knew it was unfair.

"Low blow," he said.

She went to the couch and lay on her side. She was sorry but didn't have the energy to apologize. She heard footsteps and waited to hear the front door shut. Instead, he came back to her.

"I thought we sorted this out," he said. "But here you are, right back in it. Pushing me away and prioritizing your mom. Who, by the way, doesn't seem to care as much as you do. You're the one suffering, and I can't watch you do this to yourself again. Sit up. Take your pills." He helped her up, then handed her the medication and water.

"I didn't mean to," Nikki whispered.

"The thing is, you don't see your mom as capable," he said. "You think she's weak because she's passive. As long as you see her like that, you'll never break free."

She lay down, not sure if her tears were from the pain in her head or the pain in her heart. He covered her with a blanket, kissed her forehead, and let himself out. How had she gone right back to being Tara's savior? She closed her eyes and waited for the pain to pass.

CHAPTER FORTY-SIX

From Maine to Vermont, present

Tara headed south. Her mind and heart were sore. Learning lessons, facing accountability, weren't for the faint of heart. She'd naively thought she could have a future without the past. Her delusion shamed her.

All that she'd done to her family gnawed at her heart. She'd been unfair to Devon, to her daughters, and to everyone else who had the misfortune to be in her messy orbit. The cost to the way she'd lived her life was immeasurable. She'd wished, wanted, and waited. When she'd driven toward Maine, alone, she'd been so proud. She'd told herself she'd done it, accomplished her life's mission. She'd believed the past thirty-five years had been empty because she hadn't wanted to look at the moments of abundance. Heena excitedly hanging up pictures she'd drawn. The times Nikki had presented her report card with the soundtrack to *Star Wars*.

Devon. She couldn't think about him. Not yet.

She'd turned her back on the very people who saw her as theirs in her belief that she wanted to be alone. The Airstream, once a symbol of freedom and new beginnings, had become a cage of its own. Tara sat up, shifted in her seat, adjusted the belt that pressed against her. The scenery was no longer dramatic or dreamy. She was on a two-lane highway with signs for fast-food restaurants, coffee shops, and places to fill the gas tank. The mundane facts of life.

That now included lawyers. The texts she ignored from those she had run away from continued to pour in. The number had crept up. She'd convinced herself that the notification pings were unnecessary annoyances. Now she realized that even as she'd turned her back on her daughters, on Devon, they hadn't let her go. She wiped her runny nose with the back of her hand. It was useless to cry about it.

While stopped at a gas station, Tara grabbed her phone and opened her social media app. It said a lot about the way Tara had lived her life that she had barely anyone to call. She quickly typed a private message and without reconsidering pushed send. She clutched her phone. It would be justified if there was no response. Tara wasn't owed anything. Still, she waited. It wasn't as if Tara had anywhere to go except back to Boston. And that would mean accepting failure.

She jumped when her phone rang. Saw an unknown number but still answered.

"Hello?"

She heard the voice that had been absent in her life for far too long.

"Tara?" Mona's voice was still the same. "I was surprised to get your message about reconnecting after all this time."

"I'm sorry," Tara said. "I know it's sudden, and maybe you don't want to hear from me."

"You sound funny," Mona said. "Are you okay?"

That was the thing with people who were kind. They showed concern first, regardless of the past. "I am. I think so. Maybe. No."

"Tara, what is going on? Do you need help?"

Her voice caught in her throat. "I need a friend. I sometimes check your page and saw that you moved back east. There were so many times I wanted to reach out, but I didn't think you'd want to hear from me."

There was silence on the other end. Tara wouldn't blame Mona for hanging up.

"Where are you?" Mona asked.

"Maine."

"I'm in Bennington, Vermont," Mona said. "Why don't you come see me?"

Tara was so grateful. She knew she didn't deserve to be welcomed back into Mona's life, yet her friend hadn't hesitated. "I can be there this evening."

They decided on a restaurant in town and a time. Relieved, Tara pulled out of the gas station and plugged the directions into her phone. Her heart raced. This was different from her search for Ben. He'd been a fantasy that helped her get through the drudgery of her life. But Mona—and their friendship—was real.

A few hours later, Tara waited at Pangea, an upscale farm-to-table type of place. She fidgeted with the cutlery on the white tablecloth and kept looking at the door. Maybe Mona wouldn't come. Tara wouldn't blame her.

When Mona entered, Tara exhaled. Mona came toward the table with a smile. She was recognizable but different. Her once-long hair was now in a short bob. It was still lush and black.

"You haven't aged at all," Tara said.

"Botox." Mona sat across from her.

Tara touched her cheeks. "I must look old."

"We are," Mona said. "I just try to match the way I look to how old I think I am."

Tara smiled. "You're still the same."

"I hope not," Mona said. "When I lived in Boston, I was a worried, insecure, emotionally stunted woman."

"You just described me." Tara thanked the server for pouring water. "Not then—well, not completely. But now."

"We all have our epiphanies at our own pace," Mona said.

Once they placed their order, they chatted about Mona's adjustment to small-town life. Mona shared stories of the neighborhood battles over leaf blowing and holiday decorations. Tara listened and was genuinely in awe of how happy Mona seemed. There was no heaviness, just sincere joy.

"I didn't know I would become a Vermonter." Mona sipped her wine. "Not that I can claim that, because I'm still considered a Californian even though I have a chicken coop in my backyard. They all ran away after a few weeks, but the coop is still there."

Tara laughed. "Did you chase them?"

"God, no. I waved them off. Chickens are evil. I'd rather focus on my work. I'm an instructional designer for a tech company. I work from home, belong to a book club, attend town hall meetings, and putter. I love doing little things here and there and then sitting on my butt with the TV on."

"You're happy," Tara said.

"I am." Mona nodded. "I'm still a romantic too. None of my relationships have lasted after my divorce, but I have fun. I'm still hoping to meet a lumberjack in flannel."

"You will," Tara said.

"Now tell me why, after all this time, you wanted to come see me."

"I don't know where to start." Tara leaned back as the server placed her plate of salmon and couscous in front of her. "A few weeks ago, I bought an Airstream and left. I've been on the road ever since."

Mona stared at her without blinking. "What?"

"I left my husband. And my daughters." Shame burned her cheeks.

"Wow," Mona said. "That is unexpected."

Tara smiled. "No one has ever called me that. I've never been someone who would do something like this."

"Well, you are," Mona said. "Because you did."

"I guess." Tara toyed with her fork. "I want to be like you. Carefree. Happy. I thought leaving would magically change everything. It did.

It made me realize that I'm the one to blame for the way my life turned out."

"You were young when you got married," Mona offered.

"But then I wasn't," Tara said. "I blamed everyone for my circumstances, decade after decade. Staying didn't work. Neither did leaving. I don't have friends of my own. You were my last one, and you know how that went."

"I've never seen someone beat themselves up this much," Mona said.

"I deserve it."

Mona shook her head. "You need a good night's sleep in a real bed, not in a camper. Come and stay with me for the night. In the morning, we can talk about getting you out of this misery."

Tara was surprised at Mona's generosity. "Thank you."

They finished their meal while sharing stories of their children. Tara showed Mona pictures of the twins and photos of Heena's art. She sent Mona a link to subscribe to Nikki's newsletter. It was as if they were back at that bookstore. This time Tara was herself and talked about her actual life. And it felt wonderful.

CHAPTER FORTY-SEVEN

Start from where you are. Learn from where you've been.
—YNLIN

Newton, Massachusetts, present

The rich aroma of spices and broth filled the air as Nikki and Heena sat across from each other at a small table in Little Big Diner, Newton Centre's popular ramen spot. Nikki absently stirred her spicy miso ramen, watching the steam rise in lazy curls, while Heena expertly maneuvered her chopsticks through a bowl of shoyu ramen.

"You look terrible," Heena said, breaking the silence that had settled between them.

"Thanks." Nikki pushed a stray noodle around her bowl. "It's a new skin care routine, a mask made of salty tears."

"I'm not sure it's going to catch on," Heena said. "Then again, you're the business wiz."

Nikki ignored her. "Have you heard from Mom?"

"Was it my turn to watch her?"

Nikki sighed. "I've been calling and texting. I've sent emails. I'm about to hire a skywriter to reach her."

"I say we do nothing." Heena slurped noodles.

"Jay told you," Nikki said.

"About the lawsuit? Yeah. Mom created this problem; we should let her deal with it," Heena said.

While still on the road in the Airstream, Nikki had filled Heena in about why Tara had run away and the way their father had gone back on his word. "Why are you still indifferent? You told me you understood what happened between Mom and Dad, that it wasn't all her fault."

"I did. I do," Heena said. "I never said it was all her fault. I said it was for them to figure out. Dad wasn't a great husband, and Mom wasn't a good wife. But this is all on them."

"She's not a thief." She was frustrated at her sister's indifference.

"And she should come back and say it from her whole chest," Heena said.

Nikki sat back and crossed her arms. "If you were in trouble, wouldn't you want the twins to come to your defense?"

Heena thought for a moment. "I would like to think that I wouldn't run away and leave my kids to handle it for me."

The rational part of Nikki understood her sister, but she couldn't help wanting to take care of her mom. Some strings were hard to cut.

"Let's talk about you," Heena said. "How are you and Jay doing? I mean being on opposite sides of the figurative courtroom. It's like you're in one of those movies. Two lovers caught in a family feud. OMG, you're a cliché."

"Do you like having these conversations with yourself?" Nikki asked. "To answer your actual question, we're fine. I mean, you know Jay. He doesn't blow things out of proportion. He's so even-keeled."

"That makes it hard to fight," Heena said.

"Exactly." Nikki pointed her spoon at her sister. "And I feel bad when we do because he's nice to me and I feel like I'm being mean to him."

"That jerk," Heena said. "How dare he?"

Nikki leaned back in her chair. "You're making fun."

"A little. But here's the thing. Stop. Worrying. About. His. Feelings." Nikki clapped after each word. "If you need to scream at him, do it. He's your fiancé. He'll become your husband. You get to take your mood out on him. He gets to react."

"Wow." Nikki sat back.

"You know what your problem is?"

"You're going to tell me," Nikki said.

"It's this coaching stuff." Heena wiped her mouth with a napkin. "You read all this research, self-help books, and come up with these ideas of how things should be. It's messing with you."

"I offer a guide." Nikki didn't want Heena to dismiss all she'd worked to build. "I'm not saying it has to be exact."

"Yeah, and people get a few tips a week. If it fits them, it'll help," Heena said.

Nikki sat up. "Exactly."

"Then they go about their day. But you start reading more, researching. More advice from more people. Then it swirls." Heena circled her finger around her head.

"Maybe." Nikki crossed her arms.

"Instead of how it should be, figure out how to just, you know, be. I can't believe you got better grades than me," Heena said. "How are you smart and dumb at the same time?"

Nikki finished her iced tea. "I don't want to talk about this anymore. We have bigger problems. Whatever happened to that ring?"

Heena laughed. "I took it."

"I wish," Nikki said. "I'd turn you in myself. But maybe Dad? He was there too."

Heena disagreed. "Now you're just throwing out names. What about Jay's father?"

"Maybe," Nikki said. "I thought Dad was a little suspicious, trying to get us all to leave."

"We were exhausted," Heena said. "It probably fell out of her bag and either got thrown out, or someone picked it up and they're now retired in Turks and Caicos."

"I don't know." Nikki was at a loss.

"I'm going to say something," Heena said. "You won't like it. But everything points to Mom. She's been unlike herself, she'd been drinking. The next day, she leaves town. I've watched a lot of true crime on ID TV. I mean, the woman bought an Airstream."

"Using a credit card," Nikki said.

"For the interim," Heena said. "But maybe she was worried about how to support herself afterward. Money or love are the two most common reasons for crime. Didn't you say that she was trying to get you to leave her after you joined her on the road? And she stopped responding to all of us. Nothing. Not even to let us know she's alive."

Nikki rubbed her temples. "What would happen if what you say is true?"

"Depends on Bijal auntie," Heena said. "Worst case? Mom is arrested and convicted."

Nikki sagged in her chair. "Do you even believe we're having this conversation? We're a typical suburban Indian American family. Mom in jail?"

"I don't think orange is Mom's color."

Nikki closed her eyes and prayed for patience. She needed this to be over. This time, though, she wouldn't do it by herself. Everyone needed to be there.

CHAPTER FORTY-EIGHT

Bennington, Vermont, present

The midmorning sun cast long shadows across the small sitting room in Mona's charming home. It was the last one at the end of a short street. The room faced the back. Through the window, Tara could see into a wooded area.

"Your house is lovely," Tara said. "It feels like Concord, very New England with the wood and lace."

"I'm going for Jane Austen meets *Little House on the Prairie*." Mona handed her a mug. "Every year I say I need to update the kitchen or get the windows insulated, but I don't know, it's comfortable and has character."

"And it's yours." Tara savored her coffee. She'd slept well and deeply and hadn't felt this rested in a long time.

"Yeah," Mona said. "I never thought I could own a home by myself. Who would change the batteries in the smoke detector, mow the lawn, shovel snow? Me. I do all of that now."

"It's funny." Tara cradled her mug. "My mother worked, throughout my childhood, in factories and retail. And she would cook, clean, make sure the house was well kept. Yet she raised me to need a husband. That I couldn't navigate life on my own."

"Mine too," Mona said. "That's all they knew. I think we're lucky."

Tara looked at her friend. Mona had changed from the well-put-together, fashionable woman with the perfect manicure to someone who seemed comfortable without makeup and in casual clothes. "I think the opposite. I wasn't taught to dream, to become someone of renown on my own. We were raised to be wives."

Mona sat on the pale-pink velvet sofa. "True. The cooking, cleaning, and all that. I wanted to get married, have a child and a husband. I hoped for what my mother wished for me. After my divorce, well, I started seeing it differently. This place, it's not anything like the big house in Newton or the condo we moved into after we got married in Oakland. The wood is warped, the floors are uneven, but it's mine. I found a career, not just a job. I learned how to do what had been 'husband' things. I am grateful that I was able to know both versions of myself, the wife and the self-made woman. Our children won't have that."

Tara hadn't crossed that Rubicon. "They'll have their own stuff, thanks to us."

Mona laughed. "Yup. My son has a stepmother and stepsiblings. He's had a lot of relationships, but he's fine when they don't work out."

"I'm not a good grandmother," Tara said. "Heena's mother-in-law planned the baby shower. I never babysat. Devon bought them gifts, added my name to them. It's like everything after the night I spent on the Esplanade happened to someone else. It was me who walked seven times around the fire with Devon, I know that. At the same time, it wasn't."

Mona stayed quiet.

Tara gave her friend a small smile. "I could have done more. Adapted, like you have."

Mona moved to sit next to Tara on the settee. "You can change course. It's not hopeless."

"I tried," Tara said. "I um . . . I found Ben."

Mona's face lit up. "Wow. *The* guy. The Matt Damon look-alike. That's amazing."

"Yesterday, he and I ate lobster rolls. For decades I thought he would be my savior. Seeing him again, talking, I realized he was just a person I once met. He'd gone on with his life, knows who he is and isn't. I was so ashamed. I hadn't moved on from who I was when I met him."

"You think that, but it's not all bad, right?"

Tara rubbed her hands on her thighs. "I loved an imaginary person for the whole of my married life."

"That wasn't love," Mona said. "You were escaping in a happy memory to cope. Now you're aware and you can move past this. Find a way to forgive yourself."

Tara gave a laugh. "I don't know if I'm capable of such a thing. Not just me. I still blame my parents for making me get married. I haven't been able to accept Devon going back on his promise that I would be able to go back to school. I lived with all that bitterness. I can't let myself off the hook."

"I didn't say that." Mona touched Tara's shoulder. "I learned that you don't forgive with words, but with action. You have to put in the work, every day, for as long as it takes. Then when you feel at peace, you can let go. Saying sorry is easy. Earning forgiveness is hard. And it should be."

"Is that how you got over your divorce?" Tara asked.

Mona stared into her mug. "My marriage was different. Love at first sight. We were inseparable in college. Our first few years of marriage were bliss. He'd always been a golden child. Honor roll, champion athlete, and successful in every aspect of his life. Then he lost his job. Men and women are different, you know. We can handle hard things. It's our burden, societally and biologically. This was the first time Rahul didn't win. It changed him. We moved away from our family and friends. He wouldn't accept any work that he didn't deem worthy. I supported him as much as I could. You know what I had to forgive myself for? That I held on. He was the one to end our marriage. I stayed longer than I should have. I kept thinking I was being a good wife, maybe. But I was a bad mother for keeping my son in that environment. I wasn't kind to myself by staying."

"How long did it take?"

"A while," Mona said. "I started with doing what was right for my son. I overcompensated, made mistakes. I realized all he wanted was for me to be happy. So I did things that brought me joy. Like this house. When you and I met, I would never have believed I could live in a place that didn't have heated floors or a wine fridge."

Tara smiled. "I'm in awe of you."

"Go ahead." Mona stretched out her arms. "Bask in my glory."

Tara put her mug on the coffee table. "I never wore a wedding ring. Or my mangal sutra because it would make me somebody I never wanted to be."

"And now?" Mona asked. "Do you miss your husband?"

Tara shook her head. "I don't."

"That's a start," Mona said. "Now you know what you have to do."

"Finish it," Tara said.

Mona uncurled her legs, placed her mug next to Tara's, and reached over to give Tara a hug.

Tara reached her arms around Mona. She was ready. It was time for her to face the consequences of her actions.

CHAPTER FORTY-NINE

There is no greater value than self-worth.
—*YNLIN*

Boston, Massachusetts, present

Nikki waited for Jay by pacing around her apartment, then looked in the oven. He loved zucchini bread, and while she hadn't made it herself, it was from their favorite bakery.

She glanced at the clock on the wall. 6:18. Traffic must be bad. It was a rainy day, which meant the T was likely delayed. She hoped he had remembered to wear his rain jacket in the morning. He didn't believe in umbrellas. She smiled. Even his quirks were mild. Knowing him, Nikki went to get a towel out of the linen closet for when he came in, likely soaked. He would try to hug her, and she didn't want her blue spaghetti strap maxi dress to get wet.

After turning off the oven, she went to her desk to review her plan, then checked the phone in case her mom decided to reenter life. Nothing. Nikki heard footsteps as they climbed two flights. Then his key in the lock. As expected, he was more than damp. His white shirt stuck to his skin. She pointed to the towel. He shook his head and advanced toward her.

"Jay. Stop." She walked backward to avoid him.

He rushed her. Grabbed her in his arms and tucked his wet head into her neck. She laughed and gave in. He gave her a sloppy kiss before letting her go. He handed her the towel first before wiping himself off. "I'm going to change."

She watched him as he went into the bedroom. She'd forgotten how hot Jay was. She gloated. He was hers. Nikki took the zucchini bread from the oven and placed it on the counter next to the salad and the charcuterie board she'd laid out for dinner.

"I see you cooked?" He winked.

"Be nice or no zucchini bread for you," she said.

He hugged her from behind, his gray T-shirt soft against the backs of her shoulders. "This is perfect. Thank you." He kissed the side of her neck.

"Do you want something to drink?" she asked.

"Am I going to need one?"

She pulled out of his arms. "What do you mean?"

"I love you, babe," he said. "And I know you. You're up to something."

"You think you're so smart," Nikki said.

"I am."

Her heart flipped over again. She grabbed highball glasses, added two cubes of ice to each before pouring whiskey. "How was your day?"

He clinked his glass against hers as he sat next to her at the counter. "Good. A twelve-year-old was rightly found not guilty."

"I'm proud of you," she said.

He leaned over and kissed her before popping a cracker with cheese. They ate in silence, and Nikki was hesitant to talk about a topic that would ruin this moment. He'd had a good day, and they were having a nice meal.

"Jay," Nikki started. "I want to talk about the lawsuit. It's escalating. My dad hired an attorney and is planning a countersuit for defamation of character."

Jay looked at her, wide-eyed. Then shook his head. "The law isn't a game. And it's a waste when there's no substance to either case."

"Then let's work together," Nikki pleaded. "Instead of letting them handle it, which they're not doing a good job of, we can help."

He wiped his hands with a paper towel.

"I'm not trying to ruin our evening," Nikki continued. "I want to know why you're so hesitant to get involved. You're a subject matter expert."

He stood to refill his glass with whiskey. "Because it could end us."

She heard more than frustration in his voice. Fear. "Not if we don't let it."

He ran his hand over his damp hair. "I grew up with a lot of drama. My father is the oldest on his side, my mother on hers. There were constant fights among their siblings. The smallest things became yearslong rifts. My mother wasn't invited to her sister's daughter's husband's parents anniversary party and she was so offended that she cut her sister and my cousins off. When I ignored her and hung out with them because I didn't care, my mom cried and wailed at my lack of support. My dad feeds her irrational behavior because he loves being in the middle of all that."

She hadn't known. Nikki had thought he was the adored son and got along well with his parents. "You don't have to deal with them alone. I can help."

He shook his head. "Since the night of the engagement party, my mom has been on my case to end our relationship. Now, with everything that's happened, my dad agrees with her. According to them, your family isn't suitable anymore."

"I had no idea." The sarcasm was thick in her voice.

"It doesn't have anything to do with us," he said. "It's between them."

She looked at him. "They're our parents. We're not going to stop being a part of their lives or them in ours. And me taking off with my mom made it worse." It had been more than not discussing it with Jay. He had been dealing with his family while she was running after Tara.

"DEFCON 1," Jay said. "Family is so important to you. You've been trying to win over my parents, and it's hard to watch because I don't think they'll ever accept you. You won't be okay with that. And then what? You tell me over and again in so many ways that you and I aren't an island unto ourselves. But I don't see it unfolding any other way."

She stood and wrapped her arms around him. "I'm so sorry." Her heart ached for him. "Jay, it's important to you too. I remember how happy you were the first time the twins called you uncle. You were giddy for weeks. You put their picture on your phone screen."

"They're adorable," he said.

"And you see them as your niece and nephew," she said. "Caleb is more than a friend, he's become your brother."

"You can have Heena," Jay said.

"You would do anything for her," Nikki replied.

He kissed the top of her head and let her go. "What's the plan?"

It would be harder to execute based on what she'd learned, but Nikki knew they had to try. "A gathering of the clan." She fumbled a Scottish accent.

He furrowed his brow. "*Outlander?*"

She clicked her tongue. "*Game of Thrones.*"

"You've never seen it, have you?"

She shrugged. "We need to get everyone together and discuss it. Make your mom feel heard and acknowledge how upset she is, and have my dad apologize and offer to withdraw the suit."

"And your mom?"

Nikki shook her head and clenched her hands into fists. "I've sent her the time and place and told her to be there. I wasn't nice about it either."

"You've already scheduled it, huh?"

She shrugged again. "Tomorrow at two p.m. Your parents' house. I want your mom to have home court advantage."

"It's not going to go over well," he said.

"I don't know what else to do."

"I don't think I've ever heard you say that sentence," Jay said. "You have plans A through M at all times."

She laughed. "I ran out of the alphabet with all these failed attempts."

He put his glass on the counter. "Okay."

She sat up. "Yes?"

"I'll help," he said.

She threw herself into his arms.

"If it doesn't work," he said, "beach wedding in Belize and the parents can fend for themselves. Deal?"

She nodded, her face tucked in his chest. "Deal."

He tipped her chin up and brushed his lips against hers. She sank into him. After a few minutes he pulled back. "Wait." He reached for his phone, then asked for hers.

"What are you doing?"

"Turning them off." Then he made sure the door was locked.

She laughed.

"No interruptions tonight." He lifted her up, threw her over his shoulder, and headed into the bedroom.

Nikki gave in to his demands, and for the first time in months, she let her worries go. She could handle anything by herself, but with Jay next to her, it felt good to know she didn't have to.

CHAPTER FIFTY

Bennington, Vermont, present

After their conversation, Tara took a luxurious shower in Mona's bathroom before packing her bag. Then she headed down the creaky stairs to find Mona in the kitchen. Her friend was cracking eggs.

"Early lunch?" Mona asked.

"I need to get on the road."

Mona turned with the bowl and whisk in hand. "Good."

Tara nodded. "You've been great. Thank you for letting me stay here last night. I'm rested and my mind is clear. I feel strong, which is new for me."

"At least have a sandwich," Mona said. "Then you won't have to stop. Three hours is a long time."

"As long as you push me out right after." Tara was afraid she would change her mind. Going back to Boston was scarier than leaving it.

"I'll use my leg, shove you out," Mona said.

In the quiet ease that came with renewed friendship, they made their meal. Cheese, sliced turkey, lettuce, tomato, and mayo. After Mona added potato chips to their plates, the two sat at the small kitchen table.

"I'm glad I called you," Tara said. "Time here has done more for me than being on the road, the maniacal need to find Ben, the silent treatment toward my family."

"I'm glad," Mona said. "You're welcome. Whenever you want."

"It's going to be difficult," Tara said. "I can face it. I must. You showed me that it's possible to find happiness. I will have to earn the right, and I'm willing to try."

"You're going to do great," Mona said. "I believe in you."

Tara blushed. It felt good to know that someone had faith in her. "I did a lot of things, created chaos, hurt the people who love me. Who I love. I need to repair everything I broke."

"They will forgive you," Mona said. "Especially your daughters."

"You haven't met them," Tara said. "Heena will make it more difficult than Nikki."

"Do you want me to come with you?"

It would be so easy to say yes. "This is mine to do." It was time for her to stand up, stop leaning on the past, fight for herself, and act. "I had this best friend, in college. Mayuri. I'm finally making her proud."

"As the founder of the two-person women's club, I give you this imaginary badge of courage." Mona mimed granting Tara an award.

Tara mimed receiving it and pinning it on her T-shirt. "I am honored."

"Ready?" Mona asked when they finished eating.

She was. They walked through the short hallway. Tara gathered her bag and purse, then left the quaint house with window boxes full of flowers. She gave Mona one more wave as she headed to the Airstream parked near the woods. Once inside, she stowed the bags and belted herself into the driver's seat. With a twist of the keys, the vehicle came to life. She knew where she was headed.

CHAPTER FIFTY-ONE

Family members are all actors in a terrible play. Appreciate them for who they are, not the roles they play.
—*YNLIN*

Newton, Massachusetts, present

Nikki couldn't control her shaking knee. Jay's parents, her father, Heena, and Nikki were seated in Bijal auntie's living room. Heena was on an indoor Indian bench swing made of solid wood with an intricately carved back. Jay had once told her that his mom had it shipped from Jaipur, where it was handcrafted. Nikki would never dare to sit on it, but Heena didn't have any qualms. Instead, she and Jay sat on the long sofa. Chai had been poured, with mugs on the coffee table. They hadn't exchanged pleasantries, and the air was thick with tension.

"We should wait until the lawyer gets here before we say anything to each other." Bijal was the first to speak. "Our conversation should be on the record."

"This is a family gathering, Mom," Jay said. "There's no need."

Bijal pointed. "They are not related to us. I'm tired of being ambushed."

"That's not what this is," Nikki said. "We thought you'd be more comfortable at home."

"I will be once I get my ring back." Bijal sat in a wingback chair that looked like her throne. "Where is your mother?"

"I'm not sure," Nikki said. "My dad and my sister are here, though. We wanted to show you that we care about your loss and app—"

"I want her found," Bijal said.

"So do we. I am worried," Devon added. "She could have had an accident, out there on her own. She's not the type to handle even a flat tire."

Nikki silently pleaded with her father to not add more drama to the situation. "If that were the case, we would have heard."

"And she would be served, immediately," Kirit added.

Nikki winced. "Bijal auntie. No one in my family has the ring. I am sure of it. However, we do owe you an apology. Not only for us, but also for my mom. We're all so sorry to have caused you worry and pain."

"Yes," Bijal said. "That ring is incredibly valuable."

"The ring was insured," Jay said.

"We're your parents, Jay," Kirit countered. "You will show us respect. You have done nothing to ease your mother's anguish."

Nikki put her hand on top of Jay's as they sat side by side on the sofa, her dad on the other side of her.

Devon interjected. "It isn't in Tara's nature to steal."

"Nature?" Bijal said. "You don't know your wife at all. Is that why she left you?"

"Hey." Heena raised her voice. "That's not necessary."

Bijal turned her head away from everyone.

"We're getting off topic," Nikki said.

"Maybe the ring is still here, in this house," Devon said.

"Are you accusing me of lying?" Bijal added.

"I won't stand for this." Kirit rose from his seat in the other wingback chair. "This is my house. You aren't allowed to insult us."

Nikki looked at her sister, who mimed her craving for popcorn.

"Stop," Nikki said loudly. "What are we doing?" She was panting out of anger and fear. Unfortunately, the person she was most angry with hadn't shown up. "Can we sit and talk like reasonable people?"

They all regained their composure, and Kirit resumed his seat. Nikki stood and paced. Her plan was turning into dust. She glanced at Jay. She'd dragged him here thinking it would get resolved, but it was getting worse.

Jay took her hand and urged her to sit.

Nikki complied. "Though insurance will cover the value, I also know that the ring was priceless because it was a family heirloom. I was thinking I could purchase a new ring—an emerald, to keep the tradition alive."

"No, she won't," Jay said. "I'll buy an engagement ring for Nikki. That's all."

"You still plan to marry her?" Kirit said. "This family is not worthy enough to join ours."

"I won't accept it," Bijal added.

"Wow," Heena chimed in. "This is like a Bollywood movie. A bad one."

Nikki glared at her sister.

"Heena has a point," Jay said, then turned to his parents. "It's not your say. Nikki and I are getting married. We're going to be a family to each other. You can be a part of that or not."

"Jay." Nikki tried to calm him down.

"No," Jay said. "It's time for this to end. You have no proof. You're causing drama with hearsay and assumptions. Enough already."

Bijal started to cry. "My own son. I didn't raise you to speak to me like this."

Nikki closed her eyes and prayed to be somewhere else. She gave Jay a silent apology. She'd hoped their chaotic parents might become more rational, more adult. But no, they still clung to beliefs and their own versions of what might be.

The doorbell rang and Jay stood up. "No one say anything to anyone." Then he went to answer the door.

"I'm going to use the restroom." Devon left in the opposite direction.

A few minutes later, Jay came in. Nikki expected to see Bijal auntie's lawyer, but it was Tara. Relief and anger weighed her down, left her unable to react. She merely stared. Her mother looked relaxed; her skin had a glow as if she'd spent a few weeks in the sun.

"Tara auntie, welcome." Jay led her to a vacant armchair.

Like Nikki, Heena didn't say a word in greeting. Her face showed her disappointment in their mother.

"Thank you." Tara perched at the edge of the seat.

"Finally," Bijal said. "Where is my ring?"

"I don't have it," Tara said. "I never did."

"You lied to me the last time you stole from me." Bijal pointed at Tara.

"What are you talking about?" Tara looked around, confused.

"High school," Bijal said. "My report and the fake ring. They were in your locker."

Tara laughed. "Really? I told you the truth then, just like now. Someone put that stuff in my locker. Your friends were always teasing me, playing jokes on me, tugging my ponytail in the hallway in between classes."

"Did you know about that, Mom? That Tara auntie was being bullied by your friends?"

Nikki looked at her mother. Saw the truth in Tara's eyes. Her mom hadn't stolen anything, then or now.

"It was silly fun," Bijal said.

"Right," Jay said. "Drop this. Now. This drama needs to end."

The room went silent as everyone stared at Bijal, waiting to see what she would say next.

"Jay is right. This has gone too far." Devon held out his hand. "Here is the ring."

Nikki saw the red box. Bijal snatched it from him. Opened it and the ring slid into Bijal's palm. She cried in her husband's arms.

Nikki couldn't look at either of her parents. Or Jay. She was stunned. Her dad? All this time. He'd said nothing.

"Uncle?" Jay asked.

"I was going to leave it somewhere for you to find," Devon said. "But I couldn't do that. I was the one who took it. Not from your purse. It wasn't intentional or planned. It sort of happened. One of your relatives nudged you. She was wearing a black sari, an older woman. I saw it fall out. But the woman didn't notice. When you walked away, I picked it up. I was going to return it, but . . ."

"Holy moly," Heena said. "I want to curse but I have kids."

"But the police searched everyone," Nikki said.

"I hid it before I was patted down, then grabbed it," Devon said.

Nikki was too stunned to form a thought.

"Why?" Jay asked. "You saw what was happening. Why would you do it?"

"I wasn't thinking. I had a few drinks, and I was upset," Devon whispered. "She was going to leave me, and I thought, it was stupid, but when she was accused, I thought she deserved it. I let the anger get to me. Then Tara left and I didn't know how to make anything right. There were so many times I wanted to come here and return it, confess to you. Then the police and lawyers got involved and I didn't know how to handle it. I don't want the girls to pay for my actions."

"Just Mom," Nikki said. "You were okay with her being blamed."

"Marriage is complicated, beta." Devon touched Nikki's shoulder. "I had a lot of anger and resentment that was built up. I may not have been the best husband, but I thought I had done my best. And she acted like it was so simple to just throw away thirty-five years."

Nikki moved out of his grasp. She was ashamed and embarrassed. She'd denied that her family had anything to do with it, and her father had let her. She didn't recognize him either. She glanced at Tara and then Devon. Neither were the mom and dad she'd known her whole life. She'd never thought they were a great love story, but they'd been solid. They had been good parents. Tears rose and she looked over at Heena. Her sister came and grabbed Nikki's hand. Squeezed.

Jay stood. "Okay, the ring is back. Mom, it's yours. There will be no lawsuits of any kind."

"But what about mental anguish? Devon caused it," Kirit said.

He shook his head. "This is over. You four don't ever have to get along, but as a lawyer, you don't have a case. You'll waste money. There are no winners here. Once you've had time to digest what happened here, think about how you want our two families to come together. Because we will be getting married. Come to the wedding or don't. We're done here."

Nikki took the hand Jay offered and let him lead her out. She heard Heena's clapping as they left his parents' house. She smiled. This was what it meant to cut the cord. She couldn't fix them, they would have to do it themselves. She reached up and brought Jay in for a kiss. She would be his priority, and he would be hers.

CHAPTER FIFTY-TWO

Newton, Massachusetts, present

It was strange to be back in the house she'd felt trapped in for decades. Tara looked at the photos on the wall. Nikki's graduation. Heena's wedding. The twins' first birthday. Not all her memories were tortured. Maybe none were. She was at the kitchen table. Devon had offered to make chai. Apparently he'd been practicing.

She thanked him as he placed a steaming mug in front of her. The cardamom was strong and sweet. She smiled. It was his preferred recipe. This had been her kitchen. "I never liked cooking. I think your tea is better than mine."

"You had some good dishes," he said.

They'd only ever been good at small talk, surface conversations. Yet he'd taken the ring. To make Tara suffer. But she couldn't be mad at him without looking at her actions. "I'm sorry for the way I treated you."

She could see the surprise on his face.

"Why did you leave?" Devon asked. "Why did you come back?"

She appreciated his willingness to have a direct conversation. She wasn't used to it, but she would face whatever he said to her. "It's hard to explain."

"I'd like to know."

She nodded. "I couldn't forgive you for breaking your promise. It changed the course of my life. Every year that passed, my dreams, my ambitions, became further out of reach."

He nodded. "I'm sorry. I didn't know how important it was to you."

"You didn't care." It felt good to finally say how she felt. "We barely knew each other and then we were married. All I could do was trust you. I learned otherwise. You were so busy trying to be the man. I felt like I was being dragged along as you lived your life."

"I used to go in your closet occasionally to see if the black bag was still there," he said. "I knew you wanted to leave. That bag became a fixation for me. Ever since we moved into this house, I waited for the day you would leave. I resented you. Decades of silence, indifference, occasional affection, yet you stayed."

"You wish I'd left sooner."

He shook his head. "No. I wanted you to change. Maybe even like me."

Tara understood. "For years, I felt invisible in this marriage. All I knew was how to keep to myself. It's how I handled growing up with my parents. We each lived our own lives. I didn't have any siblings, so I thought, *I'll just exist*, the way I always had. My parents were okay with it. I believed you were too."

"My parents weren't big on talking about feelings," he said. "We were chatty, but we never dug into anything that involved emotions."

"We were young," Tara continued.

"I was older," he said. "And I'd met a few girls before you, but I didn't have any experience in having a relationship."

"It still bothers me that your life continued as planned," Tara said. "But I know I can't blame you for it anymore. I could have followed through once the girls were old enough. I was too scared. It was easier to make you responsible for me not pursuing what I wanted."

"My life panned out." Devon cradled his mug. "I didn't have ambition like you. Well, I cared about making money. I liked going to work, coming home, having kids, spending time with friends. That was enough. Then, once Heena and Nikki were into their teenage years, their focus was on crushes and boys, that was the first time I wondered what love would be like, not only for them but us. I realized we didn't have that between us."

The truth was finally spoken. "It's okay. I wasn't someone you could love."

He smiled. "I thought, *think*, you're beautiful, but that's not enough, is it?"

She reached over, and for the first time, with sincerity, Tara put her hand on his arm. "You deserve someone who is vibrant and can match your energy. A person who enjoys taking care of you and this home. A woman who gets along with your friends and their wives. It's okay."

Tara felt the last bit of weight she'd been carrying leave her.

"What about you? What's your type?"

She laughed. She'd accepted that it wasn't Ben. "I'm not sure."

"Will you ever be able to forgive me?" he asked.

"I'm starting to do the work," she said. "For me and for our family."

"Family," he repeated. "Where do we go from here?"

"Well, I live in a house on wheels," she said.

"You can stay here," he said. "There's plenty of space."

"Or I can find an apartment," she said. "I'm going apply to graduate programs in physics. There are a lot of universities and colleges in this state."

He grinned. "I'll give you a strong recommendation."

"I'll pay you back," Tara said. "For the Airstream."

"It's fine," he said. "We can sort it out as part of the divorce."

She was relieved that he'd accepted it. It was the right thing to do. For both of them.

"Do you think we can be friends?" he asked.

"You're the expert on friendships," she replied. "Maybe you could teach me."

"We can start with Red Sox games," Devon teased.

Tara felt lighter than ever before. This was freedom. Not because of people or because of a place but because of hard-won contentment. "Does that mean you'll go to physics lectures with me?"

He winced. "Maybe we can start with grabbing a meal once in a while."

She laughed. "Heena and Nikki are angry with me," she admitted. "I don't know if they'll be as understanding."

"It's been pretty hard," Devon said. "Especially after you stopped answering their messages and calls."

"It was cruel of me," Tara said. "I thought I needed to not have any contact with my old life."

"I noticed."

"I don't know how to apologize to them," she said. "What kind of mother am I to act this way?"

"Hey, I stole an emerald," he said. "Neither one of our children won the parental lottery. Be honest with them. They'll make us both grovel first."

Tara hoped he was right.

CHAPTER FIFTY-THREE

A simple hug can turn your day around.
—*YNLIN*

Boston, Massachusetts, present

Nikki drifted in and out of sleep as she lay on her side. Her mom was back, her father had stolen the ring, and she'd decided to disengage from both of them. Heena and Caleb had come over the night before, and the four of them had gone over all that had happened. Nikki had apologized to Jay even though he didn't think it was necessary and said something about actions and intent. Heena and Nikki told the guys that they were not going to talk to their parents for a few days. This time Nikki had been the one to send Tara's calls to voicemail.

She waved something off her forehead and encountered a hand. Slowly she blinked her eyes open.

"Afternoon nap?" Jay sat at the coffee table and brushed hair away from her face. "You're a mystery, babe."

She sat up. "I thought you and Caleb were golfing."

"We did the front nine, had a few beers, and now I'm home."

She stared at him. "What time is it? How long did I sleep?" She checked her watch.

"Headache?" He stroked her forehead.

She took his hand in hers. "It's not a migraine. I was tired."

"Good." He brought her hands to his lips.

She didn't understand why he was behaving like this. "What are you up to?"

"You owe me," he said.

She sat up. "For?"

"What did I say about the gathering of the clan?"

"That it wasn't from *Game of Thrones*?" She wasn't going to give him the satisfaction of being right.

"Actually, it turned into that," he said. "Now you must pay the price."

She gave an exaggerated sigh. Then she held her wrists out for him to cuff her.

"Good girl." He wrapped his hands around them. "What did you do wrong?"

Even though this was a game, she answered honestly. "So many things. I don't even know where to start. I could have let my mom go alone. I should have suspected my dad and pushed him to confess."

"Wrong answer." He cut her off with a kiss.

"I was a bad girl."

He pulled her close. "That's the Nikki I know and love." He leaned over and kissed her. Once, twice, then deepened the kiss. She wrapped her arms around him, tugged at him until he joined her on the couch. When he tugged her shirt over her head, she stopped thinking. He was warm and smooth when she stroked his back. She loved the way she fit on his lap. In this moment, there was nothing to resolve. It was simply the two of them, skin to skin. Lips against lips. They found their rhythm and poured themselves into one another.

Afterward, she covered them with a blanket and rested her head on his chest. This was her forever. He would be her first and last thought every day. Unfortunately, the phone buzzed. He glanced over at the coffee table.

"Your mom," he said.

"I don't care." She snuggled closer.

"What happened to the woman who needed to resolve every problem right away?"

"She met a man who believed everything in good time," Nikki replied.

He kissed the top of her head. "Sometimes your way is better. I know it bothers you."

"I'm so mad," Nikki said. "She ghosted us. That's not okay. Especially when she knew what was going on here. But that's my mom. She never thinks she's the problem."

"Mine is no picnic," he said. "But they're what we have."

"I can't believe you," she said. "You kept saying I was too involved, to let her be. Now you're telling me to talk to her?"

"Hey, I can grow too," he said. "I know this bothers you, and I don't like it. You're holding everything you need to say to her. Once you do, you can choose whether or not to keep your distance."

Nikki intertwined her fingers with Jay's. "Do the police rent out interrogation rooms?"

"No," he said.

He was right. She didn't want to carry these feelings. She wanted to move on so she and Jay could get on with their lives. Summer was in full swing and she wanted them to make the most of it, because winters were long. She untangled herself from him. "We should go to the Berkshires. I hike now. Or a weekend in Nantucket. I don't want to miss too much of this season. I have too many sleeveless dresses that need to be worn. Let me get my planner." She climbed over the coffee table and put her T-shirt and shorts back on. "Open your phone. We can sync calendars."

He rolled his neck. "Not now, babe. Let's order dinner instead."

"We can do that too," she said. "I'm prioritizing us. As a couple."

She came back to the couch. He grabbed her waist and tucked her into his side. "You're overthinking."

"I don't want to take us for granted."

He twined his fingers with hers. "I'll remind you if you do."

She crossed her arms. She wanted to show him effort.

"Our relationship is going to be up and down." He brought their hands up, brushed his lips over her knuckle. "We'll talk. We'll fight. We will figure it out. There is no secret formula. We'll make up the answers as we go."

CHAPTER FIFTY-FOUR

Boston, Massachusetts, present

It had taken a week for Heena and Nikki to agree to meet with Tara. Tara had accepted it and continued to reach out. She wanted to show them that she didn't want to be checked out of their life or hers. She saw them across from her. They had met for lunch near Heena's house in Roslindale. The Boston neighborhood fit her older daughter, with residents who tended to be earth loving.

They were grown. She had watched it happen with purpose. Now, she could simply appreciate the people they'd become. "Thank you for meeting me."

"Unlike you, we reply to messages." Heena stacked and unstacked the jam packets on their table. "After a week or so. But you know how life is."

She accepted the sarcasm, was ready to take anything they gave her. All she wanted them to know was that she was going to work on being a better mother and grandmother. She understood it was up to her to lead the conversation. If she wanted their forgiveness, she couldn't revert to her old ways and stay silent until someone else took up the burden.

She knew it was going to be tough. She'd made multiple outreaches, and they'd responded with cold aloofness. That they'd agreed to meet was a welcome sign. "How are the twins?"

"Older," Heena said.

"I hope I can come see them," Tara said. "Nikki, how are things with Jay?" She had reminded herself not to focus on Nikki's work. Tara wanted to show her daughter that she not only accepted Nikki's choice to get married but was fully on board.

"Good, considering." Nikki avoided looking at Tara.

"I called him to apologize," Tara said. "As did your father."

Nikki nodded. "He mentioned it."

"Your father and I also worked things out between us." Tara would keep trying even if this was all they did during this meeting.

"Are you getting back together?" Nikki finally met Tara's eyes.

"No," she said. "I mean that we're in a good place right now."

"Congratulations." Heena's tone was dry.

"I'm sorry," Tara said. "That is what I want to say to you. I know I hurt both of you. I have my reasons, but I'll save them for another day."

Heena turned to Nikki. "If you order the steak, I'll get the shrimp scampi, and we can do half and half."

Tara had known it wasn't going to be easy. "I behaved badly with both of you. And left you to clean up the mess I made. Especially you, Nikki."

"And a side of spinach," Heena added. "We have to get our veggies in."

Tara looked at Nikki. "Won't you say something? Whatever it is, I'll listen."

"Nothing comes to mind," Nikki said.

"Good talk," Heena added. "Our server is coming and I'm hungry."

Once the server came and they put in their orders, they sat in awkward silence.

"I know you're trying to protect your sister, Heena," Tara added. "Let her speak her mind. I deserve whatever you both need to say to me. I promise to not defend the indefensible."

"We're both angry, Mom. And believe it or not, Heena was the one who supported you being on the run." She gestured to Heena. "She's been there for me all my life. More than you ever have."

The words were lashes against her heart. "I agree. You're a good sister, Heena."

"You said you had your reasons," Nikki said.

"We don't want to hear them," Heena chimed in. "You can check out again. We're good."

"You have a hard shell." Tara smiled at her older daughter. "But you were always more sensitive than Nikita. Your feelings get hurt easily and it's hard for you to move on. We're similar in that regard."

"I'm not anything like you," Heena said.

"You wouldn't behave as I did." Tara helped her daughter understand. "You would never not be a part of your children's lives."

"Well, they can barely handle sleeping in their own beds," Heena said. "But yeah."

Tara turned to Nikki. "I've always envied your ability to take care of everyone around you, including me. It wasn't fair. I wasn't as I should have been while you were growing up."

"Where are you staying?" Nikki asked.

"At the house," she said. "Until I find an affordable apartment. I'm also going to apply to graduate programs."

Nikki nodded.

"Your life is great," Heena said. "Thanks for telling us."

The server returned with their meals and Tara's stomach grumbled, not from hunger but from the hurt she saw in her daughters. Their anger, their snark, it was a coating. What she'd done wasn't something that could heal over a hearty meal.

"For most of my life," Tara said, "I did what I was supposed to. I wasn't a rebel. When I got married, I thought I would build a house, create a home. Instead, I made a sandcastle. Every day I waited for a wave to crash over it, tear it down to return to its original form. Every day, water lapped and eroded the edges. I made you grow up in something fragile. I'm truly sorry."

They were quiet. She saw tears in Heena's eyes. Nikki took a sip of water.

"And now?" Heena asked.

"Graphene. One of the strongest materials on earth," Tara said. "I'll have to learn, but it won't be your responsibility to teach me. I will be in your life in whatever capacity you need."

"What's going to happen to the Airstream?" Nikki asked.

"I'm selling it," Tara said. "You were right. There's no place to park it around here."

"Did you get what you needed from it?" Nikki continued.

"Yes," Tara said. "And more. Remember when the shower suddenly turned on while you were in the bathroom?"

Nikki didn't laugh.

Tara accepted that it was too soon to go through those memories.

"Are you happy?" Nikki asked.

Tara nodded. "Yes. I will continue to revisit the memories we made as a family. I appreciate them. We had good times. Mostly, though, I am proud of the people you've become. The way you've shaped your lives, despite what I wanted for you. You have friends, love, children. You are more than your professions. I hope to learn from you as I figure out this version of me."

Neither replied. Nikki lifted her wineglass. Heena did the same. Then Tara raised hers. They clinked.

"Caleb is giving the twins a spelling test right now," Heena said.

"They are four," Nikki argued.

"It's mostly three-letter words," Heena said.

Nikki took a shrimp from Heena's plate. "This is good."

Heena took a piece of steak from Nikki. "Don't eat all of it."

Tara watched them as they tucked into their food. It was going to be a work in progress. For now, it was enough that they sat with her and listened. The rest she would have to let unfold.

CHAPTER FIFTY-FIVE

Opt for real life over fairy tales.
—*YNLIN*

Boston, Massachusetts, present

The bustling energy of downtown Boston swirled around Nikki as she sat on a warm stone bench outside the city courthouse. Her eyes scanned the crowd, searching for Jay's familiar face. In her lap a paper bag held his favorite banh mi, along with a green papaya salad for her.

It was a hot day, so she'd worn her blue silk dress. It was too formal for lunchtime, but this wasn't an ordinary meal. She'd bought a thin shawl to keep on her lap so she wouldn't flash anyone. Her phone vibrated with an incoming text.

Heena: What's your status?

Nikki replied to tell her she was still waiting. Then she tucked her cell back in her big purse that did not match her outfit. She scanned the crowd until she spotted Jay.

"Hey." Jay gave her a quick kiss, then settled beside her on the bench.

"Hi." Nikki offered him the sandwich. "I brought your favorite."

"Sweet. I'm starving. I don't have you on my schedule, and you didn't mention it during our weekly review three days ago."

"Funny," she said.

He grinned, then bit into his sandwich.

She let him eat in peace for a moment, the cacophony of city life providing a backdrop to her thoughts. Finally Nikki took a deep breath and turned to face him.

"What's going on, babe?"

"We're having lunch." She shifted, and the stone chafed the backs of her thighs.

"Don't think I didn't notice the dress." He stared at the people in front of them. "Are you going to sneak me into the nearest bathroom stall? The federal building has a lot of security."

"You're hilarious today," she said.

"I'm in a good mood. I got a kid out of trouble and back with his family, my girl brought me lunch, and it's nice out." He took another bite.

"Only you would say ninety degrees is nice." He preferred heat to cold.

"I'm used to wearing suits all the time, so I don't mind." He finished his food and scrunched the wrapper and put it back in the paper bag. "You didn't eat."

"I'm not hungry." Her nerves were going haywire. It was strange. She wasn't afraid, but she couldn't relax.

He grabbed her hand. "You're shaking."

"I'm uh . . . everything is good." She said it more to herself than to him. "With us? You and me. We're good."

He looked at her with curiosity.

"I didn't mean for it to sound like a question." Enough. She had to do this. Then it would be over, and she wouldn't feel like she was waiting for a thousand arrows to strike her. Nikki took a deep breath to brace herself for what came next. She took the box from her purse in a way that he wouldn't notice, then stood. "No, stay seated." She kept her hand on his shoulder.

"Something wrong with your shoe?" He looked down at her feet.

Slowly Nikki knelt, but because of her fitted dress she couldn't do it the traditional way, so both her bare knees scraped the ground.

"Um, babe, we're in public," he said. "Though I'm okay with getting arrested."

"Can you be serious for one minute please?" Nikki stared into his eyes. "Jay, I am completely, madly in love with you. You are kind, funny (sometimes), laid back in a way that usually drives me up the wall. I know your love language. You make me want to be a better person. Will you be my emergency contact? I mean, will you marry me? With this ring."

He sat in silence. Her nerves reached her brain, and the entire planet went quiet. She could see his surprise. "Say it again."

His voice broke through. He hadn't heard her. "Will you—"

"No, the part about completely, madly . . ."

She relaxed. "I love you."

"Once a day," he said. "I want us to give each other those words, every day."

"You have a lot of rules." He had yet to answer her. She waited.

"Yes." He stood. Tugged her up. "How could there be any other reply, especially when you're wearing that dress." Then he wrapped his arms around her and spun. He kissed her for a long time.

A person walking by made a snarky comment about getting a room, and Nikki let him go. She opened the box to reveal a gold signet ring with the letter J etched on the surface. "It's vintage. I had a few antique dealers help me find it."

He popped it on his ring finger. Then raised his hand and yelled, "I said yes!"

A few people nearby clapped. Nikki tugged him back to the bench.

"Calm down," she said.

He wrapped an arm around her and kissed her again.

"This puts a lot of pressure on me to get you a diamond," Jay said.

"I think I'm more of an emerald girl," Nikki teased.

"Don't even," he said. "We'll go together. You can pick out anything. Just remember, money is an object."

She kissed him again.

"Could you imagine if I had said no?" Jay stared at his ring.

"You're going to enjoy telling this story, aren't you?"

"For sure," he said. "And I'm going to embellish. A lot. The way I'll tell it, you'll be crying, pleading—"

Nikki punched him lightly.

"And you did it in front of what is known to be the ugliest building in the city of Boston," Jay said. "Who taught you romance?"

"Heena wanted me to cook for you, light candles," she said.

"This is better. I won't get food poisoning."

She leaned on his shoulder. "However you want to tell it, I'll agree with every word."

She looked forward to a lifetime of experiences with him. And she would try not to plan every moment.

ACKNOWLEDGMENTS

This was a tough book for a lot of reasons, but mainly because I really wanted to do this story justice. There are so many people who held my figurative hand and helped me solve gnarly problems, including incredible authors who have now become invaluable friends. Thank you, Karen Winn, KJ Dell'Antonia, Mansi Shah, Nisha Sharma, and Mona Shroff.

I am privileged to have incredible friends who listened to me go on and on about how writing this novel was hard, and yet they still took my calls and replied to my texts. Thank you, Cassie Blausey, Stephanie Crane, Patrick Gallagher, Leandro Baretto, Colleen Battista, and Laura Holton.

To my family, who has no choice but to love me. Thank you to my parents, Arvind and Pushpa; my sisters Deena and Amy; my cousins Shan and Priya; and so many more. This book was written during a particularly difficult time, when we lost the man this book is dedicated to. We still mourn, but we are healing.

To my team. I am forever grateful to have you in my corner. This book would be a hot mess without your guidance, your talent, and some much-needed tough love. Thank you to Sarah Younger, Megha Parekh, Jenna Land Free, Kimberly Glyder, and the art, production, and editing group at Lake Union, including S. B. Kleinman and Nicole Thomas.

Finally, to the two people who lifted me up. Their unwavering belief and support with this book was extraordinary. Arianne George and Raela Ripaldi, I don't want to know what 2024 would have been like without the two of you.

ABOUT THE AUTHOR

Photo © 2021 Andy Dean

Namrata Patel is the bestselling author of *The Curious Secrets of Yesterday*, *Scent of a Garden*, and *The Candid Life of Meena Dave*. Her writing examines diaspora and dual-cultural identity among Indian Americans, multigenerational tensions tied to assimilation, and historical awareness of Indian American achievements. She has led writing and publishing workshops for several organizations, sat on panels discussing craft and theme, and participated in various mentoring programs. Additionally, she has taught courses at Emerson College and Boston College. Namrata has lived in India, New Jersey, Spokane, London, and New York City and currently calls Boston home. For more information, visit www.nampatel.com.